ALSO BY J.A. LEAKE

The Girl Who Got Away

with Jack McSporran

(coming Winter 2021)

For my preschool mama friends, especially Jennifer—I wouldn't have survived the preschool years without you!

THE PRESENT

The ambulance arrives, illuminating stricken faces with red light as they load her carefully into the back.

Silence descends as everyone at the party holds onto one another for comfort, carefully-manicured nails digging into lean muscular arms.

The moment the ambulance roars away, sirens piercing the night, they turn on each other again.

It was your *fault!*

You're such a bitch.

I can't believe you were in the bathroom with him in the middle of a kids' party! Who knew I was married to such a slut?

Let's not forget who's truly at fault here: the mother.

As they tear into vulnerabilities and faults with one another, I stand in their midst and seek comfort from no one. My mind splinters and cracks, threatening to swallow me whole. How could it be that only twenty minutes earlier,

I'd been congratulating myself on a job well done? Reveling in the beauty of the chaos swirling around me. Watching the others snap at each other like wolves.

And then…the unthinkable had happened.

You've gone too far, the voice that had been absent these past few months suddenly whispers in my ear.

I cover my face with my hands.

What have I done?

NINE MONTHS BEFORE THE PARTY

MARIA

On the first day of the school year, Maria Ronzonelli parked her small Honda at the end of a row of gleaming high-end SUVs and glanced at her phone again. She wore a grimace on her face like she was about to have her leg amputated. Her first instinct was to immediately delete the email even though she knew it didn't change anything. She couldn't believe the same damn problems had followed them from New York to South Carolina.

"Is this my new school, Mommy?"

With effort, Maria replaced the grimace with a fake smile. She turned to her four-year-old daughter, Ariana, who was looking out the window, dark eyes bright.

"Mm-hm. What do you think?" Maria had to admit that the red brick building surrounded by magnolia trees and elaborate landscaping was picture perfect.

"My friends will love my new backpack."

Maria smiled down at her. "They definitely will."

It was that easy for her, Maria knew. She'd go in, a bright smile on her face, show off her pink kitty backpack, and end the day with the whole class in love with her. Making friends was second-nature to Ariana, and Maria was glad she hadn't inherited her reticence. Even though she wasn't the one about to start a new school, Maria's stomach fluttered uncomfortably.

The email warning of a low balance creeped into her mind again, and she gripped her phone tighter.

"Aren't you going to get me out?" Ariana demanded.

"Of course!" Maria said with fake excitement. She was glad Ariana wasn't old enough to notice.

I can't think about this right now, she told herself. *It's not fair to Ariana.*

With a deep breath, Maria shut off the car and came around to the back to let Ariana out of her car seat. Once freed, Ariana hopped from foot to foot, her two shiny braids bouncing along with the movement.

"Come on, Mommy!"

"Just a sec," Maria called, retrieving Ariana's backpack that she'd left behind. She tried not to notice how dented their car was compared to the spotless ones on either side, and she was thankful Ariana was completely unaware of the difference between her mom's old sedan and all the other cars in the parking lot.

As usual, Ariana was too keyed up to wait and darted to the sidewalk, nearly careening into another little girl with a fringe of thick bangs.

"Hi! I'm Ariana."

The little girl hurried back to her mom, who was

4

dressed in the effortlessly elegant way of the very rich, with heels, tailored jeans, and a loose floral blouse. Her makeup was flawless, and Maria—who usually didn't care about rolling out of the house pretty much as-is—felt suddenly dumpy in her tank top and shorts. Maria knew she should have taken more care choosing her clothes this morning, but she'd barely managed to get Ariana dressed in time. Maria had spent all night worrying about Ariana's first day, and then she'd passed out some time around six, only to have to wake up again in an hour. At this point, the bags under her eyes had bags.

"This is Sophie," the little girl's mom said with a smile. "She's being shy." Sophie buried her face into her mom's legs. "I'm Sarah Anne," she said, putting out her hand for Maria to shake, "and I'm fortunately not shy."

Maria laughed, but cut it off abruptly when it came out too loud. Was it too loud? It sounded like a donkey's bray. "Maria."

"It's so nice to meet you both! Are you new here? I don't remember seeing you last year in K3."

"We just moved to Greenville this summer from New York."

"New York! Well, that's a big change," Sarah Anne said with a smile. Her teeth were perfectly straight and dazzlingly white. Maria knew her own teeth weren't that white—she had an addiction to strong coffee and an aversion to dentists since she was convinced they were all crooks. She was also positive she had never once thought about the color of her teeth until this moment.

"My husband just started working at Mercedes."

"Oh! My husband works there, too. He's in charge of engineering."

Maria had been told most of the Mercedes employees sent their kids to this preschool, but it still felt like fate was smiling down at her if the first person she ran into had a husband who worked there, too.

"Come on, Mommy!" Ariana repeated, tugging on Maria's hand.

Sophie glanced up at Ariana before hiding her face again.

"Okay, I'm coming," Maria said to Ariana before shooting Sarah Anne an apologetic look. "She's excited about her first day."

"Sophie is, too," she said, falling into step beside Maria as they walked along the sidewalk. Beside them was a vibrantly-green lawn shaded by enormous magnolia trees. Still pressed to her mom's side, Sophie looked anything but excited. "Which teachers did y'all get?"

"Katie and Jenny."

"We did too! Oh, you're going to love them. My little boy had them when he was in K4 last year. Now he's off to kindergarten." She sighed. "Do you have any other children?"

"No, only Ariana."

"So are you done? Having children?"

Maria's eyebrows rose while her brain struggled to think of a response. She wasn't prepared for this level of intrusiveness with someone she'd only just met. "I'm not sure."

Sarah Anne just laughed. "Well, I had my two, so I'm done! I think Mark—my husband—would throw a huge fit if I wanted another." She covered Sophie's ears. "They weren't the easiest babies, bless their hearts."

"Ariana was a really easy baby, but I had to go back to

work only a couple months after she was born, so then we didn't really have time to think about trying for more."

"That must have been so hard to go back to work right away."

"It was. I missed her."

Sarah Anne shot her a sympathetic look that made it obvious she couldn't relate. "Are you working anywhere now?"

"No," Maria lied. She had a part-time job cleaning houses during Ariana's preschool hours, but she couldn't bring herself to tell Sarah Anne that. It wasn't that she was embarrassed of her job—it was a great way to supplement James's income—but more importantly, Maria was incapable of not working. She'd had a job since she was twelve helping at her family's small Italian restaurant in Long Island, and she knew that if she tried to be a stay-at-home mom, all she'd hear every day would be her mother's voice (usually as soon as the sun rose): *Get up, Maria! The restaurant isn't going to run itself!*

Maria had a feeling that if Sarah Anne worked, it definitely wasn't as a maid. She didn't want to see that look enter her eyes—the one that would say she felt sorry for Maria. Maria didn't need anyone's pity. It was true she didn't go to college, but she worked hard and read nonstop.

"Do you work anywhere?" Maria asked.

"No, I used to work in interior design, but I only take on one or two clients a year now," Sarah Anne said. "I'm just so busy with Sophie and Jackson."

The sidewalk widened, and they came upon more parents and kids running around with excitement. They reminded Maria of lab puppies, falling all over themselves, punctuating the scuffling of tiny feet with shrieks of joy. She smiled.

"Sarah Anne! Hi," a voice called, and Sarah Anne turned toward another mom in a breezy sun dress. She had delicate features and was almost intimidatingly pretty. When she smiled, though, it lit up her whole face and made her look approachable.

"Lauren! Come meet my new friend."

Friend? Could it really be that easy? Maria felt almost light-headed with relief. Now if she could just avoid acting like a mental patient, she could maybe nail this whole networking thing. As much as she loved Ariana, she wasn't sending her here for her education. It was to make friends. More specifically, for Maria to make friends with influential parents. And according to just about everyone she talked to, Magnolia Academy had the most influential parents in the entire upstate. Parents who could skyrocket James's career from factory management to corporate in a heartbeat.

"Hi there," Lauren said as they shook hands. "I'm Emily's mama. It's nice to meet you."

"Nice to meet you, too," Maria said. "I'm Ariana's mom." She indicated with a nod to the dark-haired little girl, who was still by her side, but was watching the other kids with eager interest.

A girl appeared next to Lauren then, a miniature version of her mom. She was one of those kids that you could see would get to skip out on their awkward middle school years. One of the lucky ones who would always be beautiful.

"Sophie, come play," she demanded, tugging Sophie away from her mom's legs.

"Take Ariana, too," Lauren said, and Emily immediately complied, holding out a small hand to Ariana.

And then the three of them were chasing after each other and laughing, like they'd grown up together. Maria watched them for a moment, and warmth spread through her. Maybe they could all fit in here.

"That is just too cute," Lauren said. "I hope they're all in the same class."

"They are," Sarah Anne said. "I already checked."

"Oh that's great! Look how sweet they're playing together already."

"That reminds me," Sarah Anne said with a bright smile, "we're supposed to go to a playdate at Sissy's right after school. You'll have to come and bring Ariana, Maria."

Playdates...that was something Maria had never been able to do for Ariana in New York. She'd been working too much to ever arrange anything with the other moms, and they'd been just as busy. Apparently here, moms had all the time in the world.

"That's a great idea," Lauren said.

"Is Sissy your friend? I'm not sure I should...she doesn't know us, and—"

Sarah Anne waved her off. "Oh, she won't mind! Her house is big enough for the entire preschool to come play. And yes, she's our friend. Our husbands work together."

Maria worried the strap of her crossbody bag. "Are you sure she won't mind?"

"Not at all! As soon as I see her, I'll tell her you're tagging along."

Maria glanced at Ariana, who was playing a game of tag with Emily and Sophie, her face lit up with happiness. "All right, yes. I'm sure Ariana would love that."

"She absolutely will! And it'll give you another chance to get out of the house. I'm sure you're still decorating and setting up, right? Maria just moved here from New York," she added to Lauren.

Maria barely suppressed a sarcastic snort. Yes, decorating. She thought of their sparsely furnished house, so much bigger than their one-bedroom apartment on Long Island. It had an ancient couch, their bed and dresser, a bed for Ariana, and a table with mismatching chairs. James had only just received his first paycheck from Mercedes, and the money had been quickly swallowed up by bills and debt. They barely had enough for groceries this pay period.

Maria thought of the cost of Magnolia Academy, and something close to nausea washed over her. She pulled the strap of her bag tighter. Ariana deserved to go here just like all the other Mercedes kids, dammit. It wasn't her fault her parents were morons with mountains of debt.

"Wow, welcome to Greenville! You'll have to check out Palmetto Interiors," Lauren said.

"Oh *yes*," Sarah Anne said, grabbing hold of Maria's arm, "they have the most gorgeous things. It's the place I always recommend to my clients when they're decorating their houses."

Lauren nodded. "Sarah Anne has amazing taste. She helped me with my house."

"I sure did, and I can help you with yours, too."

Maria tried not to look horrified by the idea. She loved their new house—it beat their tiny, dark apartment on Long Island any day—but she knew that one look around would immediately show these women that Maria wouldn't be shopping at an expensive furniture boutique any time soon.

"I'll have to look it up later," Maria said with a smile she hoped was bright enough to feign interest.

"You just let me know," Sarah Anne said, and Maria was relieved when she changed the subject to how Lauren's mom was doing after her recent surgery.

While they talked about people she didn't know, Maria took in some of the other parents waiting for the preschool to open. There was a group of moms in tank tops and yoga pants, their hair in matching tight ponytails. Words like "burpees" and "twenty reps" were tossed around, and Maria shuddered. She wasn't opposed to exercise in the form of getting outside and doing something, but the gym just reminded her of adult PE. And she'd spent every week in high school coming up with ways to get out of PE. In retrospect, she should have used some of that brain power to study harder, but she couldn't say that missing out on kickball had been a total waste.

Other parents were on their phones, checking emails or just scrolling—she couldn't tell from her vantage point. Some were dressed like they might be headed into a high-paying job after this, in pencil skirts and suits. But those parents were few and far between.

The young principal came out then, interrupting Maria's survey of the different parent types at the preschool.

"Welcome, everyone," she called from the doorway. "I'm so happy to see your smiling faces this year! Your babies' teachers can't wait to see them, so come on in."

Maria, Sarah Anne, and Lauren retrieved their girls from where they were playing nearby, and then they were caught in a tide of children and parents that separated them all as they were swept into the school. The distinct smell of industrial cleaner and crayons greeted Maria as she walked alongside Ariana. Even in the crush of people, a statuesque blonde mom with designer sunglasses perched on top of her head caught Maria's eye. She had been calling out cheerful greetings to everyone she saw, and Maria thought that somehow everyone at this school must be incredibly friendly. Their gazes met in the crowded hall, and Maria smiled. The woman's gaze dropped from Maria's wild, untamed hair to her scuffed flip-flops. Her head turned away, just the slightest curl to her upper lip detectable.

What's her problem? Maria thought, though she couldn't help the heat rising from her neck to her cheeks. As she dropped off Ariana with a hug and a kiss, she tried not to think about it. Surrounded by other smiling kids and parents, it was easy to convince herself she'd just imagined the other woman's slight.

When Maria returned to her car, though, she saw the same intimidatingly beautiful woman again, parked close to her. She decided she would say hello and introduce herself since her therapist had always said the best way to deal with negative thoughts was to confront them. This woman would probably turn out to be like everyone else at the school—really nice and approachable.

Before the woman could get into her shiny, black SUV, Maria raised her hand in greeting and smiled. "Hi, I'm Maria."

The woman acted like she didn't hear her at all and pulled open her door, so Maria swallowed hard and tried again. She moved closer to the woman's car so she'd know she was talking to her.

"Hi," she said, louder this time and with a wave.

The woman finally turned to her, dark sunglasses hiding her eyes. "Yes?"

"Oh, um, I just wanted to say hi and introduce myself since I just moved here. I'm Maria."

This time, the woman's gaze slid from Maria to the beat-up car at her back. "Nice to meet you, Maria," she said, but her tone was like that of a young child being forced to be polite. "If you'll excuse me, though, I don't have time for chit-chat today."

Maria's face grew hot again. She had an urge to hide in her car, but instead, she smiled as if she hadn't been dismissed like some two-bit salesman. "I'll see you around then."

The woman gave her a tight smile and nodded before getting into her SUV. The car door closed with a sound that wasn't quite a slam—but it was close.

It wasn't until she'd driven off that Maria realized she hadn't even told Maria her name. Obviously, Maria hadn't imagined the woman's attitude.

It was clear she was a huge bitch, and Maria would just have to avoid her.

3

SARAH ANNE

Sarah Anne said goodbye to Lauren and Maria one last time—they'd been goodbye-ing for the past ten minutes in the parking lot as per usual—before heading to her own shiny black Mercedes SUV. There was a literal bounce to her step. Chatting with other moms always gave her a natural high; she spent so much of her time at home with her kids that being around other adults always made her feel like she was talking a mile a minute, but she just couldn't help herself. Meeting Maria had been a highlight, though she was pretty sure the girl had to be experiencing some serious culture shock.

Sarah Anne had been to New York City just once in her life, and she'd found it to be loud, chaotic, and frantically-paced. She'd tried to order a burger at a fast food restaurant and nearly had a panic attack from all the people barking at her to hurry up and order already. Maria hadn't been like that at all. Sarah Anne understood (sort of) that New York was more than just the city, but she couldn't help picturing everyone in the state as one of those loud, frantic people she'd encountered before. Maria had an accent, but she wasn't loud or in-your-face. It could be because she'd just met her, but Sarah Anne felt like she was mysterious, and Sarah Anne loved a good mystery.

"Sarah Anne, hi," a deep voice said from two cars over.

Sarah Anne paused in opening her door. "Hampton! How are y'all?"

"Doing well," he said in that Charleston drawl. He walked over to her, dressed in a tight t-shirt and jeans. Not working today, then. Even though he was a pediatrician, he was one of the few dads who had preschool drop-off and pick-up duty. The practice he worked for was big enough that the doctors had pretty flexible hours.

"I didn't see you in there or I would have said hi."

He smiled, fine lines appearing at the corner of his eyes. He was a little older—in his mid-thirties—but to Sarah Anne, he looked the same as he had when he was in med school. He was fun to talk to and a great dad. Best of all, he gave free medical advice. His wife, though…she was what Sarah Anne's mama liked to call uppity. And in a school full of people with a lot of money, that was saying something. Erica was a successful lawyer, though, and she made it obvious that any of the moms who chose to stay at home were inferior. Sarah Anne didn't have a problem with judging people; hell, she did it every day. Sarah Anne *did* have a problem with Erica making it obvious how she felt. Erica should hide her prejudiced thoughts like the rest of them. That's what gossip was for.

Okay, it was possible Sarah Anne should not have had that cup of coffee. She'd already drunk two espressos before even getting to school, and now she felt like her thoughts were racing along faster than a hummingbird on crack. She wrestled her mind into paying attention to what Hampton was saying.

"I was there, but I got waylaid by Jenn," he said. "You know how she is."

"You shouldn't have told her you were a doctor, and you *definitely* shouldn't have told her you were a pediatrician."

"Yeah, that was a mistake," he said with a laugh. "So how was your summer? You look like you've been at the beach."

She glanced down at her arm, made golden by the sun. "We spent last month in Hilton Head. You know how Mark loves his golf."

"Y'all have a house there, right?"

She nodded. "My sister and her kids stayed, too, and then Mark and Lawrence—Carrie's husband—came on the weekends. Did you do anything over the summer?"

His expression turned wry. "Just got a divorce."

Her flitting thoughts screeched to a stop. "A divorce? Oh, Hampton. I'm so sorry."

"We actually separated last year, but we kept it all quiet from the school. No one noticed because Erica never came here anyway," he said with a trace of lingering bitterness.

"That must have been so hard. How are your babies? How are *you*?"

"They're taking it okay. They're so used to me being the one who's always around—you know, Erica sometimes works sixty hours a week—not much has changed. I'm…I don't know. I'm functioning. I moved out, so…that's been an adjustment."

"Understatement, right? I just can't believe it. I didn't

know Erica well, but it's always sad to hear about a marriage ending in divorce."

"It is," he said with a nod, "especially when it's your own."

"I can't even imagine," she said. "What can I do? Are you eating? Do you need me to bring food?"

He laughed. "No one died! I can still cook."

She rolled her eyes. "You know how it works around here. Anything bad happens, and you get a casserole. Those are the rules."

"How about we just arrange for the kids to get together this year? That's what I really need—a way to keep them entertained."

"Sure. Still have my number?"

"I don't think it's changed in a decade."

She smiled. "No, it hasn't."

"I'll text you."

"All right then, be sweet," she said, feigning a casual tone as she turned back to her car with a wave.

She watched him walk to his truck surreptitiously behind her big sunglasses. Hampton had always been incredibly attractive with a body she knew for a fact was muscular in all the right ways. He had that preppy Southern boy look with carelessly-styled blonde hair and a perpetual summer tan. When she was sure he couldn't see her anymore, she fanned her face. Memories threatened at the edges of her mind, so she pulled out her phone to distract herself. She needed to text Sissy to let her know Maria and her daughter would be joining them.

The text sent, she pushed her car's ignition button. A soft knock came at her driver's side window, making her jump.

Hampton stood there, a disarming grin on his face. Heart thumping in her chest, she rolled the window down.

"Hey, you know I was thinking…I'm headed to Café Steam now if you wanted to keep me company. Catch up on things."

There was a heat to his gaze that was impossible to ignore, and Sarah Anne knew this wasn't just a simple invitation between friends.

Tell him you have errands to run, the rational side of her said.

"I'd love to," she said instead.

"Great," he said with a wide smile. "I'll see you there in a minute then."

She nodded, watching him walk away as heat flooded her body. The memories broke free then, and this time, she didn't try and hold them back. The last time they'd gone to get coffee together, Hampton had been single.

They'd run into each other in Charleston—he on a rare break from medical school, and she on a girl's weekend away. They'd both been on the rebound, and they'd ended up all over each other like horny teenagers. She'd told her girlfriends that she had a stomach bug and had to go home. They'd rented a hotel room and spent the entire weekend there having sex and lazily exploring the city.

She remembered that he was *very* good with his hands.

But it was just a brief hookup years ago when they were still twenty-somethings. It meant nothing. They married other people.

Of course, now Hampton was very much *not* married.

Shut up, Sarah Anne, she told herself firmly.

This was just an innocent coffee. Or tea, since any more coffee for her would likely fly her ass to the moon.

But as she added a fresh coat of lip gloss and fluffed her hair, she knew she was lying to herself.

She knew what her answer would be if he asked something else of her...something that was nowhere near as innocent as coffee.

4

MARIA

Maria's palms were clammy on the steering wheel after picking up Ariana from school. As if the first email about their low bank balance this morning wasn't bad enough, the second email made Maria feel like a trapped animal. It had arrived as she'd been up to her elbows scrubbing toilets. She was late on the payment for the second time, and this was the credit card that carried the biggest balance: over $10,000. She knew she was close to the nightmare scenario of collections calling non-stop.

She hated that their debt had followed them from New York. Sweat broke out along her hairline as she imagined how quickly it could get out of control.

And she knew what she'd be tempted to do if it did.

"Mommy! Are you listening?" Ariana demanded from the back seat.

"Yeah, baby," Maria said. "You had a great first day."

"Yeah! And now we're going to a playdate! Are we still behind Sophie?"

"Looks like it," Maria said as she made sure not to follow too closely behind Sarah Anne's gleaming SUV.

Maria turned the air on even higher, trying desperately to dry her wayward curls. She'd only just had time after cleaning a new client's house to go home, shower, put on something decent, and pick up Ariana. Her stomach still clenched uncomfortably at the thought of showing up at this unknown person's house, but Sarah Anne promised she'd texted her friend Sissy ahead of time.

Maria slowed her car when she noticed Sarah Anne put on her indicator, and then they turned into a private, gated neighborhood.

Sarah Anne entered a code into a keypad and waved at Maria to follow her. Maria gawked at the houses as they drove by, knowing that even here in the South where money went further, they cost millions.

They pulled into a circular driveway in front of an enormous white house flanked by towering oak trees, magnolias, and beautifully trimmed hedges. Thick green ivy grew on either side of the house, giving it an old, dignified look.

This is why we moved here, Maria thought. Maybe they wouldn't ever be able to live in a house this nice, but they could know people who did. Wealth by association.

"Mommy, hurry! Get me out of my seat."

Maria freed Ariana from her car seat just as Sophie burst out of Sarah Anne's car, and the two of them raced up the brick walkway to the door. Sophie jumped up to reach the doorbell before Sarah Anne and Maria could join her on the porch.

Footsteps rang out beyond the door as someone approached, and Maria wiped her palms on her jeans. A beautiful woman opened the door, blonde and statuesque, with perfect features and tasteful makeup.

It took Maria a moment to recognize Sissy, but then her heart plummeted. It was the woman from the preschool hallway and the parking lot—the one who had been so rude. Maria's smile faltered and her stomach clenched. How unlucky could she be?

"Sissy, this is Maria," Sarah Anne said, and Sissy stuck out a manicured hand. It was cold to the touch, but at least she was smiling back.

"Nice to meet you," Sissy said, like Maria hadn't already introduced herself in the parking lot. "Come on in."

She stepped aside so they could enter, and then a miniature version of her was grabbing hold of Sophie's hand and dragging her toward the spiral staircase. For a moment, it looked like they'd run off and leave Ariana, but Sophie seemed to remember her before they got to the steps.

She turned back to Maria's daughter and said, "Come on, Ariana! The playroom is up here."

The girls didn't wait for permission, though, as all three galloped up the stairs as fast as their legs would carry them.

"We can sit in here," Sissy said, leading Sarah Anne and Maria past towering white columns, a grand piano, and other rooms with luxurious-looking things. She brought them to a bright and airy living room, dominated by a marble fireplace. The furniture was ambitiously white, as though kids never came in there, and the paisley throw pillows were thick and plush.

Sarah Anne plopped herself down on the beautiful sofa

like she belonged there, and Maria forced herself to do the same.

"Tea?" Sissy asked, indicating with her hand a silver tray on the cocktail table.

"Absolutely," Sarah Anne said, "I'm burning up."

Sissy handed her a crystal glass filled with iced tea, lemon, and mint. She lifted another glass inquiringly at Maria.

"Sure. Thanks."

"Lauren should be here in just a few minutes," Sarah Anne said, glancing at her phone. "I think she had to make a quick stop before coming by."

"That's fine," Sissy said, as regally as a queen.

"I found out today that Maria's husband works at Mercedes, too," Sarah Anne said. "It's the reason they moved down from New York."

This raised Sissy's eyebrows. "Really? What department?"

"He's the new maintenance manager," Maria said, and she couldn't hide the burst of pride she felt just saying that. James had come a long way from working on cars in a rundown garage in Long Island.

"Maintenance," Sissy said like it was a word she'd never heard before. "Like in the factory?"

Maria bristled at her tone but tried to hide it. "Yes."

"I don't know much about that, I'm afraid. J.D. works in corporate, but Mercedes is a really great company to work for."

"It seems like it," Maria said. "This is James's dream come true."

Sissy smiled, but it didn't seem to reach her eyes. "I'm sure."

"What does your husband do there?" Maria asked.

"He's the VP," Sissy said, and it took Maria a moment to realize she meant the vice president...as in, the person who made serious money and was essentially in charge of the Greenville Mercedes location.

"Wow," Maria said, which was a word that didn't properly encompass all the thoughts running through her head right now. If anyone was influential enough to give James a leg up in the company, it was Sissy's husband.

Unfortunately, Sissy was still looking at Maria like she was barely restraining her lip from curling in the same sneer she gave her at the preschool.

"Sissy's kinda like the VP at our school, too," Sarah Anne said with a teasing grin. "She's one of the founding board members, and she throws this amazing pool party at the end of the year."

Sissy smiled and waved away her compliment. "It's just a fun get-together for the preschool families."

"Well, certain families," Sarah Anne said with a laugh.

Unsure what to say, Maria took a sip of her tea and nearly spit it out. It was almost sickeningly sweet. She glanced up to find Sissy watching her knowingly.

"Not used to the sugar yet?" Sissy asked.

Maria shot her a sheepish look. "No, I've never had tea this sweet before."

Sissy scoffed. "Then you're going to have a hard time fitting in here."

Maria's eyes widened at the small dig, and Sarah Anne swooped in with a nervous laugh. "And here I was thinking this tea was a little sparse on the sugar! We Southerners just like our sugar syrup with a hint of tea, I guess."

Maria laughed at her attempt to joke, but it fell a little

flat. She couldn't help wondering if Sissy was usually this much of a jerk, or was it just Maria who set her off?

They were saved from further awkwardness, though, by the doorbell ringing.

"That must be Lauren," Sarah Anne said as Sissy rose gracefully from the sofa to answer the door.

"Do you know where the bathroom is?" Maria asked when Sissy left the room. She just needed a moment to compose herself. The news about the credit card and Sissy's attitude was making Maria's blood heat. She knew herself well enough that she'd end up saying something she deeply regretted if she had to endure more catty comments.

"Oh sure, honey. It's right down the hall to the left," Sarah Anne said. "Hey, and do you want me to grab a sparkling water or something for you? Sissy was just teasing about the tea, I'm sure."

"I'm fine, but thanks," Maria said with a smile that she didn't have to fake with Sarah Anne.

The bathroom was right where Sarah Anne said it was, and it was just as intimidatingly elegant as the rest of the house. It had a marble countertop, mahogany wood cabinets, and watercolor paintings that looked…expensive. Maria washed her hands with soap from a fancy bottle and took a sort of mean pleasure in wiping them all over the monogrammed guest towels. She hoped Sissy suffered from OCD.

Before she left the bathroom, she glanced down at the cabinet doors. Without even thinking about whether she should or not, she opened them. Inside were more supplies: fluffy towels, cleaning products, and soap. There were extra bottles of the liquid soap she'd used, but there were also bars of soap wrapped in pretty packaging.

She picked one up. It had a floral design with a hummingbird on it, and as she brought it to her nose, she smelled freesia and vanilla.

An intense desire came over her then. She wanted this soap. It had a French name, and she knew without a doubt it was pricey—something she'd normally never buy for herself.

She met her gaze in the mirror. There was a wild, desperate look in her eyes.

Don't do this, she thought to herself. *Not again.*

But then she thought of Sissy's sneer and mean comment, and before she knew it, she had slipped it into her bag.

It wasn't like the rich assholes couldn't afford to replace it.

5

SISSY

U sually Sissy tolerated Sarah Anne. Sure she never shut up, but that could be charming at times. Her bubbly personality and endless conversation saved Sissy from a lot of effort on her own part while socializing. But she was having trouble forgiving her for bringing that horrible New Yorker to this playdate.

When she'd arrived in that beaten-up Honda, Sissy was immediately taken back to being a teenager. Her friend Tammy had a car like that, though it was a much older model. A flash of them driving in it filled her mind: big hair, slutty outfits, and a potent mix of weed and cigarette smoke perfuming the small space.

She thought of Maria's reaction to her house, the wide eyes, the gaping mouth, and it had reminded her of herself as a teen—at least, an older, more pathetic version. There had been a time when she was awestruck by houses like this one, and she'd rather that part of her stay buried.

Meanwhile, Lauren and Sarah Anne were fully engaged in a conversation that was boring Sissy to tears about how much sleep their children were currently getting each night.

"I'm just going to get us some snacks," Sissy said, escaping into her kitchen through the side door.

She grabbed a platter of cheese and crackers already prepared in her refrigerator, as well as another plate of vegetable crudites. In no hurry to return to their stimulating intellectual conversation, she made sure to take her time.

After a few minutes spent helping herself to a few carrot sticks and checking her phone for emails, she returned to the swinging kitchen door that led back to the living room. With her hand on the door, she paused when she heard their voices had lowered suspiciously.

"I don't know what's wrong with me," Sarah Anne told Lauren, and Sissy rolled her eyes. She didn't give two shits about Sarah Anne's emotional state. "It's like as soon as I heard that he got a divorce, all I could think about was the time we'd dated years ago."

Gossip, though, was something Sissy couldn't resist. She hovered closer.

"But isn't he Sophie's doctor?" Lauren asked.

Sissy's eyebrows shot up. This was getting better and better. So Sarah Anne was talking about Hampton—he was the doctor for just about every kid at the preschool.

"We haven't done anything, not really," Sarah Anne said in a voice that was annoyingly desperate. "Just texted. And met for coffee."

"That doesn't sound that bad," Lauren said.

"And kissed."

Sissy could hear Lauren's intake of breath from her hiding spot.

"Sarah Anne! You have to stop this now before it gets out of control."

"I know. I know. I just don't know how…I can't stop thinking about him."

Sissy shook her head. As far as she knew, Sarah Anne had the life every woman around here aspired toward. Two kids, big house, fancy car, and a husband who seemed to actually like her.

"As long as you don't sleep with him, I think you can just back away from all of this."

There was silence, and Sissy imagined Sarah Anne looking guilty as hell.

"You *slept* with him?" Lauren hissed.

At that moment, a piercing cry came from another part of the house, followed by the thunderous sound of numerous feet racing down the stairs. Sissy pushed open the door into the living room only to see Maria entering from the other direction. There was something about her expression that made Sissy think maybe she wasn't the only one who had been eavesdropping.

As Sissy and Maria joined the others on the sofa, the tension in the room rose several notches. Sarah Anne couldn't meet Sissy's eyes, and Lauren's expression was guarded.

All the little girls came into the living room with wide eyes as a dark-haired little girl raced to Maria.

She practically threw herself into Maria's lap, crying like her arm was broken. "Ariana!" Maria said, looking embarrassed by her daughter's display of emotion.

"Aw," Lauren said, eyebrows drawn, "what's the matter?"

"What happened? Why are you crying?" Maria asked quietly. Ariana just shook her head and continued sobbing.

"Sophie," Sarah Anne said in a warning tone of voice. "What happened?"

Sophie's eyes darted to her daughter Mary Elizabeth because Sissy knew she had something to do with whatever had happened. For little girls, though, it could be anything from one of them taking the other's toy to actually hurting the other. They cried just as hard for a minor injustice as for pain.

"She was mean to me," Ariana finally got out.

"Who was, honey?" Sarah Anne demanded, shooting another warning glance at Sophie.

Lauren's daughter was the only one who looked truly innocent, standing behind the others, wringing her little hands.

Maria patted her daughter's shoulder with an awkward smile at all of them. "She's fine. She just got her feelings hurt, I think. You're fine, though, right?"

Ariana's wails seemed to tell a different story.

Lauren still wore a pitying expression. "I really don't think she's fine."

Sissy took a sip of her tea and willed her eyes not to roll into the back of her head.

"She can be a little dramatic," Maria said apologetically.

"I don't blame her for crying if someone was mean," Lauren said pointedly.

Sissy suppressed a sigh. It was clear she'd have to do something.

"Mary Elizabeth, what happened?"

Mary Elizabeth got that obstinate look on her face that meant she definitely did something to Ariana.

Sissy turned to the crying girl. "Was Mary Elizabeth mean to you?"

She nodded once before burying her face in Maria's stomach.

Sissy turned back to Mary Elizabeth with a look her mama would be proud of. "Mary Elizabeth, you apologize right now." When Mary Elizabeth refused to say anything, Sissy crossed her arms over her chest. "Say sorry or I'm taking away a favorite toy. Now."

"I'm sorry," Mary Elizabeth said in a grudging apology.

"See? She said sorry," Maria said. "Now go play."

"Play nicely, and if you say something mean again, then I'm taking away your American Girl doll," Sissy warned. Only Lauren's little girl took the threat seriously and nodded with wide eyes.

"Oh, an American Girl. Sophie has one, too," Sarah Anne said, her voice annoyingly cheerful. "Mary Elizabeth, why don't you show the other girls your doll? I'm sure they'd love to see her."

Sophie, being a much sweeter child than Sissy's own Mary Elizabeth, immediately walked toward the still-tearful Ariana and took her hand.

"Come on, Ariana," Sophie said.

The girls left as quickly as they appeared, and Lauren shook her head. "Poor thing. Girls can be so mean," she said with a glance at Sissy and a sip of her tea. "You know, I read an article recently about parents not being sympathetic enough to their children, and it affects their self-esteem. When a mom is all dismissive of a child being upset, for example, it makes the child feel like no one cares."

Maria bit her lip and looked down at her phone. There was no mistaking that critique of her parenting skills. Sissy was almost impressed.

"Oh, well," Sarah Anne said, "you know how kids are, though. They get in arguments so easily. I'm sure Mary Elizabeth didn't mean it, and Ariana seemed to get over it quickly."

Sissy shrugged. "Mary Elizabeth is a one-friend type of girl. She doesn't always play well in groups."

"Emily loves to play with other little girls. She's going to make the best big sister," Lauren said with a sadly hopeful smile.

"She really will," Sarah Anne said. "How have things been going? Has Wesley been keeping his baby-making appointments?"

Lauren sighed. "No, in fact, he just missed the last time I ovulated because he had a hunting trip."

"Does he hunt a lot?" Maria asked.

"Too much," Lauren said, rolling her eyes. "He's gone every weekend during hunting season. We really want another baby, but I've had some…difficulties."

Sissy imagined it was pretty difficult to have another baby when her husband was going on hunting trips instead of having sex.

"I'm sorry to hear that," Maria said.

"It sounds like a man who doesn't want another baby at all," Sissy said with a casual sip of her drink. All three women turned shocked glances her way. "In my experience, men don't let much come in the way of free sex."

Lauren looked like she'd been slapped, but Sissy didn't feel a twinge of guilt. Sometimes it hurt to hear the truth. Lauren was better off hearing it now than to continue pining for something she couldn't have.

"I don't know," Sarah Anne said with a laugh that was clearly supposed to lighten the mood, "I know a lot of men who are pretty attached to their rifles."

Maria snorted a laugh, and Sissy smiled, but Lauren continued to glare at Sissy.

"After the last baby that I lost," Lauren said, still looking at Sissy, "I told myself I'd do anything to be pregnant again as soon as I could."

Sissy could tell Lauren's comment about miscarriage was meant to shame her, or at least provide some shock value. Did Lauren think she was the only one who had suffered a miscarriage before? Sissy had too, but she didn't let it take over her life.

"My cousin was like that, too," Maria said with a nod. "The doctor told her she had to wait at least three months after her miscarriage to get pregnant again, and it was three months to the day when she got a positive test."

"You have one healthy child," Sissy said, ignoring Maria. "That's more than a lot of women have."

"That's a good point, Sissy," Lauren said in a warning tone of voice, "though I seem to remember that you have two kids of your own."

"Yes, I do," Sissy said without further comment. If Lauren thought she was going to force an apology out of her, she had another thing coming.

Lauren hid a nasty smile behind a sip of tea. "I suppose you're an expert since you have one whole kid more than me."

"Okay, clearly we all need to have a snack," Sarah Anne said as she reached for the cheese and vegetables Sissy had set out on the cocktail table. "I know when I start sniping at everyone around me, it means I'm hungry as a starving raccoon. This looks delicious, Sissy."

"Good idea," Maria said, because she'd agree with Sarah Anne even if she said they should all relax and drink some arsenic.

They helped themselves, and Sarah Anne tried valiantly to steer the conversation back onto friendly ground.

"We need to make a group text to set up another play-date," Sarah Anne said. "I'll host next time."

Lauren groaned. "Not a group text. I get overwhelmed by the endless messages."

For once, Sissy agreed with her.

Sarah Anne shot Lauren a look. "What do you care? You never respond anyway."

"I do, too! When I remember."

"Which is usually days later."

Lauren shrugged. "I'm busy."

"Girl. We're all busy."

They had a brief stare-down before dissolving into laughter. "Oh, that reminds me," Sarah Anne said to Lauren, "when's the next swim lesson?"

They launched into a discussion, then, of the swim instructors, lesson times, length of lesson times, and other mind-numbingly boring things. Maria tried to join in, though it was clear her daughter wasn't enrolled in any extracurricular activities.

Sissy found herself repeatedly checking the time on her phone, not bothering to hide what she was doing from the others.

Twenty minutes later, it was Lauren who was the first to say she had to go. Emily had a dance lesson. Sissy was so relieved everyone would start leaving now that she was almost cheerful.

After Lauren and Emily had left and Maria went to find a toy Ariana had lost upstairs, Sarah Anne offered to help Sissy bring the plates of cheese, vegetables, and tea glasses back into the kitchen.

"I'm so glad you invited us," Sarah Anne said as she laid down a plate of cheese carefully on Sissy's sparkling white marble countertop. "Sophie loves playing with Mary Elizabeth."

Sissy nodded. "They're sweet together, which is saying something for Mary Elizabeth."

Sarah Anne gave a little laugh. "I know. Poor little Ariana. We'll have more play dates, and they'll all get along fine eventually."

Sissy snorted. "I don't know if I can handle another group date. You know I'm not the most maternal woman in the world, but even I felt badly for how Maria just pushed Ariana away. Poor girl was crying her eyes out."

"Oh, I think she was just embarrassed. She's a good mama."

"She's a shameless social climber who uses her daughter as a pawn, but sure, she's a great mama," Sissy said, and Sarah Anne smacked her arm.

"Stop. You be nice now."

"The truth isn't always nice, Sarah Anne. You know that."

Sarah Anne rolled her eyes. "Well, if you know me so well, then you also know I like to sugarcoat things. And like my mama always says, 'If you can't say anything nice, then don't say anything at all.'"

Sissy grinned. "Then I'd never speak!"

Sarah Anne laughed. "You're terrible." When she started loading the glasses into the dishwasher, Sissy waved her off.

"I'll do that later. I know you have to go pick up Jackson."

"I've got time!" Sarah Anne said cheerfully while continuing to load the dishwasher. Sissy tried to relax and not control the way she was adding them to the top rack, although it wasn't the way she would have done it. "I wanted to tell you, though, that I've been thinking about throwing a party this year. For Mercedes employees, but also for preschool parents. What do you think?"

"Are you trying to upstage my end-of-the-year party?" Sissy asked with a smirk.

Sarah Anne turned away from the dishwasher with wide eyes. "No, of course not! I haven't decided exactly when to have it yet, but it won't be in May. Don't worry."

"Well, you'll have to let me know when you decide to have it," Sissy said, struggling to say something nice about it. The truth was, she knew that Sarah Anne had always been jealous of her party in May because Sarah Anne tended not to like things that weren't centered around her.

"You know I will," Sarah Anne said with an oblivious smile.

They left the kitchen together and nearly plowed right into Maria. She wouldn't meet Sissy's eyes, which made Sissy wonder if Maria had been eavesdropping again. Served her right if she heard the not-so-nice comments

Sissy made. "I was just coming to tell you goodbye and thank you."

Sissy smiled tightly. "You're welcome. Thank you for coming."

Another few minutes of gathering up their girls and their things, and then at last, Sissy's house was peaceful again.

Sissy let out a huge sigh of relief. She knew she hadn't been on her best behavior, but honestly, those bitches deserved every second of it.

6

THE PRESENT

It started out as a way to teach them a lesson. To show them that the way they lived their lives was wrong. They took their perfect families for granted. They did horribly selfish things that put their family and children at risk.

It was too easy to scare them. Too easy to manipulate them into revealing who they really were at the party.

But I was so wrapped up in serving justice that I didn't realize what was happening until it was too late.

I shake uncontrollably despite the humid heat. Tears prick my eyes, and I wrap my arms around myself.

I'm sick. I need help. I should be in the ambulance, too, bound for a psychiatric hospital.

I know this, even as I want to scream at them all that they're to blame for this, too.

Selfishly caught up in their own dramas, no one had been watching the pool. And now...

Now she might be dead.

7

SARAH ANNE

Two weeks after preschool started, Sarah Anne was trying very hard to be good. When she was with her family, she made it her policy never to think about Hampton. But in spite of her best efforts, her husband brought up Hampton after dinner and made her heart pound like it was trying to beat out a rhythm of her guilt.

It had been after Sophie and Jackson had finally gone to bed. Sarah Anne had just poured herself a glass of white wine and joined Mark on their back porch. The outdoor extension of their living room never failed to lift her spirits.

She paused to look around in satisfaction at the beautifully-decorated space; their white outdoor furniture was piled with colorful pillows in coral and turquoise. Although Sarah Anne couldn't help but notice with a resigned frown that Mark had predictably dumped most of them on the floor. Their outdoor kitchen was gleaming while sheer curtains billowed gently in the breeze.

Mark had contributed the flat screen TV hanging on the stone wall, and Sarah Anne tolerated it because it was a lot more fun to watch TV outside than in. He'd changed into shorts and his usual golf shirt, his handsome face intent on the news as he drank his own glass of wine. After seven years of marriage, he had a few wrinkles, but to Sarah Anne's everlasting annoyance, they were the type that only made him look more attractive. His sandy brown hair had resisted all grays, though, and he was still slim and muscular. He liked to go running early in the morning, while Sarah Anne kept sleeping.

The weather was cool for a September evening, and she tucked her legs beneath her on the couch as she joined him.

"What do you want to watch?" he asked.

"Nothing," she said with a sigh. "I'm too tired to focus. I wore myself out running my mouth today."

He grinned. "It's what you do best."

She snorted and nudged him in the arm. "You should feel lucky. Now I just get to sit here and listen instead of talking at you. How was your day?"

"The usual. Looked at car specs, made phone calls, did other boring engineering stuff."

She rolled her eyes. "I don't think it's boring at all."

"Sure, that's why your eyes glaze over whenever I start talking about it."

She laughed and kissed her favorite spot on his jawline. "That's not true."

"I thought you'd want to finish your wine."

She glanced up at him innocently. "I do."

"You're not going to get the chance if you keep kissing me there."

She kissed him again, but when he reached for her, she took another sip of her wine. "You're right. I do want to finish my wine."

He groaned good-naturedly. "Tease."

She laughed and cuddled closer to him. They'd have sex later though; she wasn't heartless. And honestly, she loved sex. She suspected that she and Mark were unusual among their friends, especially after reading a statistic that said married couples only had sex about once a week. There were times when she and Mark made love every other *day*.

Thoughts of another man tried to force their way into her mind, but Sarah Anne pushed them away.

"I left work early today, though. Had a tee time at two o'clock with Brian—he works with Hampton, you know?"

Sarah Anne forced herself to take a casual sip of wine. "Oh really? How did that go?"

"He won, but just barely. Anyway, he said Hampton's been going through a divorce. Did you hear about that?"

Her heart rate increased. "I heard some rumors, but…" Sarah Anne had forgotten that Hampton and Mark used to play golf together. It had been a while—Hampton never had free time, it seemed, with his ex-wife around. But the last thing Sarah Anne wanted was for Mark to remember his old friend Hampton and start golfing together again.

"Yeah, apparently the divorce was final over the summer. She's the one who moved out. I thought that took some balls to kick a woman like Erica out."

Sarah Anne didn't have to fake her reaction to that statement. She snorted into her wine. "There's no way he did. I'm sure she chose to abandon her family."

"You're probably right," he said with a shake of his

head. "She's always been mean as a snake. Colder than Sissy Harrison, even."

"I'd rather spend time with Sissy any day."

"It's just so sad for those kids."

"It is," she agreed, feeling suddenly close to tears. She imagined her own babies, how it would tear them apart, making them think their mommy and daddy didn't love them anymore. The kids always blamed themselves.

But she knew, deep down, she had another reason to be upset. Erica might have been the one to divorce her children's father, but it was Sarah Anne who was putting those poor kids' happiness at risk. Worse, she was endangering her own children's happy lives, too.

"Honey," he said, noticing her eyes welling up, "you're not crying, are you? It's not happening to our kids. You're not leaving me, right?"

She laughed tearfully, almost hysterically. She could tell by his teasing tone of voice that he'd made that comment innocently, completely unaware how close he was to the truth. "Don't be ridiculous. You know I'd never leave you or our babies."

"You have too big a heart, Sarah Anne. It's sad for them, but I don't think Erica was ever mother material. Hampton never should have married her."

"Well, now you can say that! I'm sure he didn't realize that when he was dating her."

"She went to Carolina. He should have known," he deadpanned.

It was a running joke with him that anyone who went to USC was inferior to those who went to Clemson University (his alma mater going back several generations), but she wasn't in the mood.

"Oh, stop," she said, batting at him. "Let's just go to bed."

"Now you're talking," he said with a sexy gleam in his eye.

And, God help her, she'd gone to bed with her husband and let him use his hands and mouth to make her forget just how horrible a wife and mother she was.

After, as she lay beside her softly-snoring husband, she just kept asking herself why. Why was she getting involved with Hampton again?

Her mind was quick to answer with the things Hampton said to her:

You were sexy as hell in Charleston, and you're even sexier now.

I can't stop thinking about you.

All you have to do is look at me, and I get hard.

It wasn't that Mark didn't compliment her—he did. But not all the time, and not really about steamy things like Hampton did. It was just the way marriage worked. Things became comfortable and predictable. With Hampton, though, everything felt new and exciting, and he didn't let a day go by without texting her and telling her multiple times how she made him feel.

Not that it was an affair! It definitely wasn't. That was putting too strong a label on it, and this was casual. Casual talks, casual fun…

Casual sex.

Heat traveled up her neck, and she discreetly looked over at Mark as if he might suddenly sense what she was thinking and wake up.

Honestly, what was the harm in letting her imagination run wild?

There was always tomorrow. Tomorrow, she'd be good.

The next morning, after dropping her babies off at school, Sarah Anne sat in her car in the parking lot of busy parents hurrying to get their preschoolers to their classrooms before running off to shop, or work out, or do a myriad of other innocent things. Lauren's car was there. So was Sissy's, but Sarah Anne was parked on the other side of the lot from them. She usually liked to chat with the other moms after drop-off. Today, though, she didn't want to linger.

Earlier that morning, she'd heard a text come in, and she knew there would be a message from Hampton. She hadn't let herself look at it, though. She had to pretend to be a good mother. A good mother wouldn't text the man she was running around with in front of her kids.

Now that she was alone, she grabbed her phone and pulled up the text message she knew was waiting for her.

Hey beautiful. Meet me at Café Steam after drop-off.

The message could almost be an innocent text between friends if it weren't for the whole "beautiful" thing. But hell if it didn't make Sarah Anne grin like a fool.

She put her car in reverse and sped out of the parking lot like a crazy person, her thoughts already on a morning of coffee and flirting and—let's face it, she was already cheating, might as well eat what she wanted—a cinnamon roll.

After coffee, Hampton walked her to her car. Before she could open the door, he put his arm around her. She could smell his clean soapy-scent, so unlike her own husband's with his spicy aftershave.

He leaned in like he wanted to kiss her, and she knew they shouldn't—not in public like this—but her eyes were already half-closing. It just felt so good to be *wanted.* His magnetism pulled her in, and she let out a little breathy sigh as their mouths met.

"Come back to my place?" he asked.

Sarah Anne's shoulders tensed. If she agreed, this would be the third time they had sex, and something about that number disturbed her. She imagined the conversation with Mark if she ever got caught:

How many times did you have sex? Once? Twice?

Her face would say it all because it always did.

THREE TIMES?

She had an excuse ready for Hampton on the tip of her tongue. She had a doctor's appointment to go to in only an hour. Not true, but he wouldn't know the difference.

"I'll meet you there," she said instead.

He kissed her again, running his fingers through her silky hair. "See you in a minute."

She watched him go to his own car before climbing into hers. "Lord have mercy," she muttered to herself. She should tell him never mind.

She should tell him they couldn't keep doing this.

Instead, she touched her fingers to her lips. The blood pooled low as desire ate her up.

She put the car in drive and headed for Hampton's new townhouse.

———

The anonymous text message came when she was one turn away from Hampton's house.

She heard the pleasant little chime, and thinking it was Hampton, snatched her phone up with a smile on her face.

When she saw the text, she had to pull over to make sure she saw what she thought she did.

It was a picture of the two of them, taken just minutes ago in the parking lot of Café Steam. He had her pressed up against her car, and her arms were around his neck as he kissed her. From the angle of the photo, it was obvious it was them.

As though she'd been struck by lightning, every speck of desire dried up, leaving her shaking. She knew all the color had drained from her face. And in a daze, she forced herself to continue on to Hampton's house.

Hampton was waiting for her beside his car, but Sarah Anne couldn't even stop and appreciate how sexy he looked.

When she pulled into his driveway and got out, his welcoming smile disappeared when he saw her face.

"Hey, what's the matter?"

She panted for breath as she fumbled for her phone to show him. "I got this text just now. From an anonymous number."

His brows were furrowed as he took her phone into his big hands. "What kind of text?"

But she didn't have to answer him. The picture was pulled up, and his expression quickly changed from confusion to alarm.

"Who sent you this?" he demanded.

Sarah Anne threw her hands up. "I have no idea! But it was clearly someone who was watching us at the coffee shop."

"I don't like this at all," he said, glancing over her shoulder. "We better get inside."

Sarah Anne stood with one hand on her car's door handle. "I don't know, Hampton. I don't know about this. I mean, what if this picture gets out? What if Mark sees it?"

"It didn't have a message to go with it, so it's not black-mailing you," he said, looking down at her phone again.

"It's still a threat—it's a picture of us kissing!"

He tilted his head as he looked at the picture. "Yes, but it's a little hard to tell that's you. Your hair is covering part of your face."

She leaned forward to look again. "It's enough that I can tell it's me, though."

He reached out and rubbed her shoulder. "Look, let's just go inside to talk about this, okay? If there really is someone taking pictures of us, then we shouldn't stand in the driveway and give them an opportunity."

She glanced at her car. "I think maybe I should just go home."

"Don't let whoever sent this to you ruin our day. I couldn't stop thinking about seeing you again all last night, you know. It completely wrecked my sleep. I already can't get enough of you."

If there was one thing Sarah Anne couldn't resist, it was flattery. She thrived on it; craved it, even. Ever since she was a little girl, beauty and attention had equaled love in her eyes. It was why she'd been a dancer and a cheerleader. It was why she went out with any boy who complimented her.

"You just saw me at the coffee shop," she said with what she knew was a flirty little grin.

He stepped closer to her, filling her with his smell and warmth. "Yeah, but I didn't get to see *all* of you."

She let out a shuddery breath. "Why do you have to say things like that?"

"Like what? Ones you can't resist?" He took her hand and gave it a little tug. "Look, we don't have to do anything but talk."

She could feel herself wavering, and she glanced over her shoulder at the empty street behind her. He did have a point that they shouldn't talk about this out here where anyone could see them. Inside was safer.

"Okay, fine, but we'll just go inside and talk," she added with a stern look.

He nodded. "Sure. Yes. We'll talk all you want."

8

LAUREN

L auren checked her ovulation monitor and compared it to the calendar on her phone's fertility app. According to it, she'd be ovulating again in just a few days. She let out a shaky but determined breath. The last miscarriage had been devastating because she'd had all the symptoms of pregnancy and still lost the baby. Those brief few months imagining a new baby had been enough to make her want to try again. It was another little girl; she'd been sure of it. She had imagined a little sister for Emily to grow up with so that she wouldn't have to be alone like Lauren had been. She'd even gone so far as to prepare the nursery by getting Emily's newborn clothes out of the attic where they'd been carefully stored. She'd held each piece of layette in her hands and remembered what it was like to have a baby that small.

And in just a day, that had all disappeared.

She sent a text to her husband at work:

It's baby-making time this weekend (with an emoji of a baby and hearts)

The three dots indicating a response popped up, and she waited.

Can't. Fishing tournament, remember?

A familiar spark ignited in her stomach, and she frowned at her phone. No, she didn't remember, which meant he didn't put it on the calendar in the kitchen. She rapidly typed another text.

If we miss it this time, then it'll be a whole month until we can try again. She had to restrain herself from adding a pissed-off emoji.

The dots came and went, and came and went, and she knew he was responding and then deleting what he said. She wondered what his first reaction was. What he was needing to censor.

We'll talk later. I'm at work.

Lauren muttered something ugly under her breath and tossed her phone onto the spotless white duvet. She told herself she shouldn't, but her feet still carried her from her bright and airy bedroom into the room beside hers. It was meant to be a study, but they'd converted it last summer when Lauren had first found out she was expecting another baby.

After the two miscarriages, the nursery seemed like a sad shrine to something she would never have again. They'd decorated it in gray and white chevron, accented with teal, and the small room was both cozy and beautiful. The crib was massive and the focal point, the white dresser well-stocked with newborn essentials, and the bookcase was filled with brand new copies of the baby books she'd loved to read to Emily.

She went over to the gray glider and sat down. Her phone dinged from the other room, indicating she had an email, but she didn't bother to get up. It was almost definitely a student needing her help. She taught three college English courses at an online university, and even though the semester had just started, she was already behind on her grading.

Get up, she told herself, but her body felt heavy.

When she'd been with Sarah Anne and Maria, their talk had chased away the black clouds that constantly hovered over Lauren. That reminded her of Sissy's thoughtless comment at the playdate a few weeks ago. Her words had crawled under her skin and festered.

Something dark and ugly reared its head inside Lauren, and she felt the now-familiar rise of anger. How dare Sissy, with her two children, think she could tell Lauren whether or not she should feel happy.

Happiness, Lauren thought cynically. She didn't think she'd feel that ever again.

Now that she was alone without even the distraction of an annoying conversation, the thought of getting up and doing something productive was a heavy weight on her chest. She struggled to access the motivation she'd once had. The fact that she'd managed to get Emily up and dressed today, not to mention off to school, had seemed like some kind of miracle. Any energy she'd mustered this morning left her the moment she arrived back home, and now her body ignored her mind's urging that she should at least get out of the chair. She closed her eyes and rocked gently.

Once, everyone she knew had been in awe of her organization skills and self-control, which was the only reason she could easily juggle being a full-time mother and teacher. She had to admit she loved making everyone think she was some sort of superwoman, but that was before her life had fallen apart.

As she thought about Wesley's response to her text, and that feeling of drowning only strengthened, making her breaths come faster, she knew it was more than the miscarriages.

In the end, she did make herself get up, only to move downstairs to the TV. She watched show after show for the next four hours without moving, completely ignoring all the work she should be doing.

Her phone buzzed, alerting her to a text, and she glanced down at it.

It was from Wesley. *I'm not going to be home for dinner. Got invited to go for a beer with the boss. Don't wait up.*

Lauren squeezed the phone so hard she heard it creak in protest.

She was beginning to question why she even stayed married to a husband she sometimes dreamed would have a convenient hunting accident.

———

Lauren parked her car at Emily's preschool with just a few minutes to spare. Her alarm reminding her to pick up Emily had gone off, but she'd ignored it for ten minutes before finally convincing herself to get off the couch. She hadn't had time to fix her makeup, and though she hadn't actively cried, tears had made their way down her cheeks without her knowing. She did the best she could to fix the smudges with the tissues she always kept in the car and hid the rest behind dark Ray Bans.

When she finally opened her car door, Sarah Anne was there waiting for her. "Hey, Sarah Anne," Lauren said, forcing herself to smile. She didn't know if she could handle Sarah-Anne-level intensity at the moment.

Sarah Anne reached out and grabbed Lauren's arm. She leaned in close and said, "I need to talk to you."

Lauren couldn't tell from her tone if it was a real emergency or a Sarah-Anne emergency. Two totally different things. "Are you okay?"

"I don't even know. Can we sit in your car for a second?"

Lauren glanced at her phone. "We need to pick up the girls in just a minute, though."

Sarah Anne waved her off. "Yes, but you know we end up waiting in line for ten minutes anyway. They'll be fine."

She didn't wait for Lauren to respond—just went to the passenger door and opened it. Lauren sighed and opened the driver door.

When they were both closed up in Lauren's car, Sarah Anne handed Lauren her phone.

"I got this text this morning."

Lauren glanced down at the rose gold phone. A text had been pulled up, and it consisted of a photo that made Lauren wince when she got a good look at it. It was Sarah Anne, her hair tousled by the breeze and lit beautifully by the sun, but that angelic look was marred by her mouth firmly locked onto Hampton's. His hands were shoved into her hair, and her eyes were closed in obvious pleasure.

"Oh, Sarah Anne," Lauren said with a groan.

"I know," Sarah Anne said, covering her face in her hands.

"And it just says 'private number'?"

"Yes. I can't tell who sent it, but they clearly meant to threaten me."

"But why? What do they want?"

Sarah Anne shook her head. "I don't know. That's the only text I received, but it was right after Hampton and I... right after we had coffee together," she said, a flush blooming across her face. "So whoever sent this was watching us. They were at least at the same coffee shop."

Lauren grimaced. "That's really creepy, Sarah Anne. Do you have any idea who it could be?"

"No, and this is going to sound totally egotistical of me, but it's not like I know a lot of people who hate me. For the most part, I get along with everyone. So I can't think of a single person who would want to send me a threatening text."

"It could be someone who barely knows you," Lauren said. "Think of how easy it is to find out all the details of someone's life online now."

Sarah Anne blanched. "I did post a pic of my coffee on Instagram while we were there."

"But you didn't have the location tag on, right?"

Sarah Anne looked sheepish.

Lauren groaned. "I *told* you having your location tags turned on is a horrible idea! People can stalk you so easily that way! It's especially dangerous for moms with little kids."

"I know, I know. You were right! I always meant to turn it off, but I got distracted, and...I never did it."

"Seriously, Sarah Anne, you may as well have had a tracking beacon turned on."

"Okay, not helping!"

"So what are you going to do?"

"Well, I'm going to open the privacy settings on my phone, and—"

Lauren gave her a look. "I *meant*: what are you going to do about this thing with Hampton?"

Sarah Anne avoided her eyes.

"You're not serious. You can't continue this! One picture is bad enough. What would you do if Mark found out, and it was still going on?"

"You're right—I know you're right," Sarah Anne said, shakily putting her phone back in her leather bag. "But I've held you up long enough. Let's go get our girls."

Lauren nodded, unsure what else to say. *I'm sorry you're having an affair and got caught* didn't seem to be especially comforting, so she decided not to say anything else at all.

There were still parents in line when they reached the girls' classroom, and after they'd gathered their backpacks and lunchboxes, they went outside again. Maria and Hampton had just picked up their kids and were walking back toward the cars.

Lauren found herself hoping Sarah Anne wouldn't call out to him—she didn't want to endure the awkwardness of the situation after seeing that picture of them kissing—but it was like Sarah Anne just couldn't help herself.

"Hey, y'all!" she called out cheerfully.

Maria turned and waved when she saw them. Hampton stopped, too. The kids, including Hampton's little girl, Ava, continued onto the little soccer field by the parking lot to play.

"Hi, Sarah Anne," Hampton said with a relaxed smile, as though they were just casually meeting for the first time today. "Lauren," he added with a nod and another smile, but Lauren could barely look at him.

"Maria, I'm not sure if y'all have met yet," Sarah Anne said, and when Maria shook her head, she continued. "This is Hampton Marchbanks. He's the pediatrician we all take our kids to, so if you haven't found one yet—"

"I haven't actually," Maria said with a relieved-looking smile. "It's really great to meet you."

"Pleasure is mine," he said with a warm smile. "The practice I work for is called Oakview Pediatrics."

Maria pulled out her phone and typed that in.

"They really are great," Lauren added almost grudgingly. She'd forgotten that this awkward affair of theirs affected her in a way, too. Oakview Pediatrics was the doctor's office Lauren took Emily to. "Their office hours are the best in town, and the doctors go above and beyond. When Emily was a baby, she had this little rash around her belly button, and the doctor actually texted me later that night to see if the cream helped."

Hampton nodded. "We try to show our patients we care. Not like those other unethical offices around town."

Maria's eyes widened. "Shit. Are you serious?"

"Nah, I'm just teasing you."

Sarah Anne gave Hampton a flirty little smack on the arm that made Lauren look away as if she'd caught them kissing. There was something about the way they were standing close to each other that made her feel like she was seeing something she shouldn't. And considering what she *had* just seen, there was a reason for her discomfort.

"That's one way to get more business," Sarah Anne said with a laugh.

Seeing them flirt so brazenly, Lauren had a visceral reaction: a spike of anger that made her breath hitch. It happened sometimes, ever since the first miscarriage. She'd see another pregnant woman, her stomach growing round, and Lauren would feel this sudden hatred. She hated the other woman's non-broken womb. She hated the woman's husband who clearly had sex with her when she was ovulating.

And here Sarah Anne was, two children of her own, a husband who loved her, and she was flirting with this preschool dad like none of it mattered. Like Sarah Anne didn't already have the perfect life.

But Lauren pushed those feelings down deep. She could never hate Sarah Anne.

The more she watched her with Hampton, though, the more she realized that Sarah Anne wasn't going to give up this thing with him. Not any time soon.

9

SISSY

Two weeks after school started, her daughter safe at home with the nanny, Sissy drove alone in her car. When she was well past the ritzy area of town and officially on back roads with no shoulders and a pothole every ten feet, she manually tuned her preset classical station to country. The tight muscles in her back relaxed as she rolled down the windows. A Garth Brooks song was on, taking her back to the first concert she'd ever gone to. It didn't just feel like a long time ago—it felt like she was a completely different person then.

The wind brought the smell of freshly-cut hay, and a slight smile curved her lips.

But when "Fancy" by Reba McEntire came on, she quickly changed the station from the button on her steering wheel. It hit too close to home. Though unlike Fancy in the song, it hadn't been Sissy's mama who had arranged for her to find a man to get out of town.

No, that was all Sissy's doing.

Just past a dilapidated barn and lazily grazing cows, she slowed her Mercedes. It wasn't long before she arrived at a white, weather-beaten sign that read: Misty Acres. Clouds of dust kicked up next to her as she turned onto the gravel road, and she slowed the car to a crawl, wincing at every ping that flew up.

She passed the well-tended double-wides that were clustered closer to the entrance of the neighborhood and continued toward the single-wides hidden behind sheds, RVs, and rusted vehicles.

A cloud of dust engulfed her as she stepped out of the car, heels slipping in the gravel. From somewhere near the front of the house, a rooster crowed. When he caught sight of Sissy, he charged toward her.

She bent down and scooped him up, cradling him in her arms like a puppy. "Did you miss me, Foghorn?" she cooed. As she stroked his rubbery comb, his eyes closed in a chicken version of blissful relaxation.

She carried him with her as she approached the drab, gray mobile home. The wooden steps leading to the door were freshly constructed, though, and pots overflowing with colorful flowers and bright green herbs lined the house on either side.

She knocked once before opening the door, the familiar smells of cigarette smoke and Febreze greeting her. "Mama?"

"In here," a hoarse voice called.

Sissy found her in her favorite blue recliner, an ashtray balanced precariously on the arm, and a sweater she was knitting in her lap. A cigarette dangled from her lips.

"You're dropping ash on your knitting," Sissy said.

Loretta gave her a sharp look over the top of her glasses. "I know you ain't come all this way just to talk down to your mama."

A piece of ash chose that exact moment to fall onto her piece of knitting, and Sissy's mama brushed it away impatiently.

"No, I came because your landlord called."

Loretta grumbled something under her breath. "And? What's he want?"

"He tried to complain about Foghorn, but I told him he never said you couldn't have roosters."

"That's right. He said I could have chickens. He never said nothing about whether they should be cocks or hens."

Sissy nodded, giving the comatose Foghorn another pat. "And then he said rent will be going up again."

Loretta took a deep drag on her cigarette. "How much this time?"

"Fifty dollars."

She put down her knitting. "Don't think I don't know what this is really about, Sissy Jean."

Sissy tried to appear unaffected by the use of her full name, but it still made her stomach twist to hear it. "Which is?"

"You're hoping I won't want to pay the rent and will take you up on your hare-brained offer."

Sissy let out her breath in a huff. Her mama always managed to make her feel all of sixteen. "Mama, it's a good idea. I have the money to buy you a house that you'll never have to pay rent on. You won't have to deal with Johnny the landlord ever again. It can even be close to my neighborhood. You can see Mary Elizabeth and William every day if you want to."

"But not *in* your neighborhood, right? That would be too close," her mother added with a smirk.

Sissy rolled her eyes. "You've always said you hate my neighborhood because of the HOA."

"And you don't think any neighborhood around yours will have one? What about my chickens? I won't be able to keep them."

"Then we'll find you a house in the country, with land for the chickens."

Loretta gave her a long look. "You just don't want anyone to find out I live here."

Sissy snorted. "Of course I don't!"

"Everyone has skeletons in their closet, Sissy. You think coming from the country is worse than the things those uppity friends of yours have done? If they had any sense, they'd be even more amazed you can fit in so good. A lot like that rooster there trying to fit in with swans."

Sissy wasn't sure if her mama was trying to pay her a compliment or insult her. "I just want to do right by you, Mama."

"Well, I don't need your help." She picked up her knitting again.

Sissy knew the argument was at a standstill at this point, but she would have kept on trying if her phone's alarm didn't go off.

"Mm-hm. Being paged back to that fancy life already. It's all right, honey. Foghorn and I appreciate your visit."

That sarcastic tone took Sissy right back to being a teenager, and she had to keep from rolling her eyes. "I'd stay longer just to prove you wrong, but I really do have to take Mary Elizabeth to dance."

"Go on, then."

Sissy stepped forward and kissed her mama on the cheek, the smell of cigarette smoke filling her nose. "Bye for now."

"Bring my grandbabies with you next time, and I might be more willing to chat."

Sissy smiled. "All right, I will. Love you, Mama."

"Love you, Sissy."

Sissy let Foghorn go outside, and then she walked toward the landlord's rusty mobile home. This was her real mission for coming out here: to pay Loretta's rent and shut him up about the chickens. She pulled open the flimsy storm door and knocked on the dingy wooden one.

"Yeah, I'm coming," a gruff voice said from within, and then Johnny stood in the doorway. He was skinny and gnarled, with jeans that hung off his boney body and an ancient t-shirt. Lank hair hung in his eyes, and he blew a trail of cigarette smoke practically in her face. "What do you want?"

Sissy wrinkled her nose. "I'm here to pay my mama's rent for this month and next." She took out the check, but as he reached for it, she didn't let go. "But I want you to give it a rest about the chickens. You've never had rules about them before, and this mobile home park is located in a rural district. There's no reason she can't have them."

He took a drag of his cigarette. "This is my land, though, so what I say goes."

Sissy shrugged. "Fine, then I'm taking your one good paying tenant somewhere else."

She could see the wheels turning in his head. He knew she was right, but he was a stubborn old man with a power complex. "You keep paying rent in advance like this, and we got a deal."

Sissy had planned for as much—she knew he'd want to feel like he was in control of the situation. "Yes, that's fine." He tried to pull the check from her hand, but she still held fast. "Let's have it in writing, though. I took the liberty of having something drawn up."

She whipped out the crisp piece of paper and handed it over. His gaze scanned it quickly. "Hey, this already says you'd pay rent in advance. How'd you know?"

"Just a good guess. Sign here, please."

With the cigarette dangling precariously from the side of his mouth, he took her proffered pen and scrawled his name on the line. "There. I made my mark, so hand over the check."

She did so with a nod. "Nice doing business with you as always, Johnny."

He just grunted and turned back to his door in a cloud of smoke.

As Sissy walked back to her car, her mama's words echoed in her mind. She knew Loretta thought Sissy was embarrassed about where she came from, but that just wasn't true. Sissy was proud of how far she'd come. At the same time, Loretta was right that Sissy would give anything for the uppity people in her life not to know the truth about her background. Not because it was shameful. No, she knew that if people found out, the image she'd worked so hard to cultivate—that of cold perfection—would melt away. Perfection was a slippery thing.

Especially when this wasn't the only secret Sissy kept.

———

J.D. came home that night smelling only of the air freshener his secretary had installed in his office, and some of the tightness in Sissy's chest disappeared. Maybe it would be a good night.

"Daddy!" Mary Elizabeth and William called out, running to him with open arms.

"Hi, baby," J.D. said, scooping Mary Elizabeth up in a tight hug. He patted William's shoulder. "How are you, buddy?"

They both launched into how their days at school were, and J.D. listened with a smile on his face. He was more patient than Sissy. He didn't even mind that their voices were clamoring over one another's.

After a moment, he stepped toward Sissy and gave her a kiss on the cheek. "How was your day?"

"Great," she said with a practiced smile. "Mary Elizabeth and I went to dance, and she learned a new move for her upcoming recital."

"That's my girl," J.D. said as Mary Elizabeth did a little pirouette. "Has dinner been fixed yet?"

"No, I still have to heat up what Ben left us—it's a pasta dish of some kind." Ben was their chef who came in once a week and prepared meals. Sissy could cook but not the fancy meals J.D. preferred.

"Good, because I was thinking we'd go out for dinner—just you and me."

Her eyebrows rose, but inside, her stomach tightened unpleasantly. "What's the occasion?"

"It's just been a while since we got to go out together alone. I even texted Yvette on the way home to see if she could come watch Mary Elizabeth and William."

"And she's available?" When he nodded, Sissy forced a smile. "That's great. Where were you thinking of going?"

"Lawry's?" he suggested.

Sissy knew what that meant: a little bit of steak and a lot of bourbon. "Sure, but I'll have to run upstairs and change."

He gave her a kiss on the cheek before plopping down on the sofa with the kids, the picture of a perfect father as they both snuggled up close to him. His dark hair had silver peppering it now, and even though he wasn't slim and muscular like he was when they first met, he still had the magnetism that made him charming and attractive. Wherever he went, he drew people to him.

Maybe it won't be so bad tonight, Sissy lied to herself as she turned and headed for the stairs.

She looked over the row of dresses hanging in her closet. Though she knew she was in for a night, she felt herself relaxing in here—just a bit. This closet was bigger than her room had been growing up, and she kept it meticulously cleaned and organized. The dresses were arranged by color, and she walked toward the navy blue and black ones. She needed the armor of somber colors. She couldn't stomach bright and cheerful pastels at the moment.

After slipping into a navy blue linen dress, she added a statement necklace with real diamonds and sky-high heels. The heels echoed as she moved into her marble bathroom. She sat down at her vanity to touch up her makeup. The soft lighting there masked some of her frown lines, but she knew they would only deepen over time. Her face didn't spend a lot of time wearing a different expression, after all.

She twisted her hair into a pretty chignon at the base of her neck, and she took a moment to admire how well the blonde contrasted with the navy of her dress. She'd been graced with old-Hollywood looks, with a swan neck, long legs, and curvy body. Her hair was naturally blonde, and her lips were naturally red. But it was her breasts that had gotten her the furthest in life. Even after two kids, they were still perfectly round and high on her chest. She wouldn't need a bra if they weren't so large.

Downstairs, the doorbell rang. The nanny had arrived, and at least Sissy knew her kids would have a good time tonight. Yvette would play games with them, read to them, and put them into bed with far more enthusiasm than Sissy could have mustered.

Her husband's deep voice called out a greeting, and then the kids' excited chatter made it hard to hear anything else. Soon, though, J.D. came into their bedroom.

"You look beautiful," he said with a handsome smile. "Ready to go?"

She wasn't, but she smiled and nodded anyway. Maybe she was wrong and the night would go fine.

As they walked out to their car together, arm-in-arm, she could almost believe her own lie.

———

The restaurant was warm and inviting, and Sissy wished she could enjoy the relaxing atmosphere more as they were led to a table that overlooked the river downtown.

J.D. pulled out her chair before sitting down across from her. They each picked up their menus, but Sissy's stomach was in a knot.

"May I bring you something to drink?" the waiter asked, and Sissy's gaze darted to J.D.

"Bourbon on the rocks, please," he said.

"I'll have a glass of merlot," Sissy said tightly.

"House?" the waiter asked, and she nodded. No use ordering something fancier when she'd likely just sip at it half-heartedly.

"Should we get an appetizer?" J.D. asked when the waiter left.

"You know I can always eat fried green tomatoes," Sissy said, though her appetite was non-existent at this point. She just wanted him to have a full stomach.

"These are served with crab and shrimp—that sounds good," he said with a nod. "What about your entree?"

"I'll just have the filet mignon and a salad."

He glanced up from his menu. "You're not hungry?"

"Steak fills me up. I won't be able to eat much more with it than a salad."

The waiter returned with their drinks, and then they gave him their orders.

Sissy watched J.D. take his first sip and told herself that maybe if she distracted him, he'd stick with just one. He did that occasionally, though it had been a long time.

At first, J.D. was everything she could want in a gentleman. He listened attentively, gray-blue eyes watching her face as she talked. He asked about the kids and her latest board meeting first before sharing about his week. But that was before he'd finished his first drink.

"Can I get you another, sir?" the waiter asked, and Sissy wanted to stab him in the leg.

"Yes, thank you," J.D. said.

Thanks a lot, Sissy thought to the waiter as he smiled and walked away, no doubt thinking of his tip at the end of the meal.

"Should we take another trip to the Caribbean when it gets cold again?" Sissy asked, gamely trying to keep him distracted with his favorite topic. "Or should we go skiing?"

"Whatever you'd like to do," he said with a warm smile and another sip of his drink.

He actually was easier to get along with when they went on a trip since the kids were almost always around. He managed to not drink himself into oblivion in front of them, which was his one saving grace in Sissy's eyes.

"I'd rather lie on the beach, but I bet the kids will want to go skiing again. Remember how quickly Mary Elizabeth mastered the bunny slopes? She skis better than I do already."

He laughed. "She's naturally athletic. Poor William will have to focus on his math skills. I don't think he'll be MVP of any team."

"Probably not."

The waiter came with their food, and after setting it down before them, asked if J.D. would like another refill on his bourbon. This time, Sissy couldn't help shooting the waiter an icy glare. He didn't notice and just continued watching J.D. with a stupid smile on his face.

"Yes, I'll have another," J.D. said.

Sissy tried to enjoy her food. The steak was perfectly cooked and was as tender as butter in her mouth, but she could barely stomach it.

As he tossed back his drink, J.D. ate his ribeye so fast he couldn't have possibly tasted it. All too soon, his charming smile had disappeared along with their conversation.

"Your car looked dirty. I bet you went and saw your white trash mama today," he said with a leering grin.

Here's Mr. Hyde, Sissy thought. Three bourbons in, and his normally congenial personality had been completely replaced. "Mm," she said, noncommittally. This was her first line of defense—to ignore him.

His expression darkened. "Hey, did you hear me? Your car looks like trash now."

"I'll get it cleaned tomorrow," she said evenly. He could escalate, but she had to always remain calm and collected.

"Bet you're glad you don't have to live in a trailer anymore," he said, pointing at her with his drink. Some of it sloshed onto his hand, and he licked it off.

"That was seven years ago, so I don't think of it much anymore." A lie, but she didn't want to continue this line of conversation. Dredging up her past was the worst he could do, and he knew it.

"You should be kissing my ass and blowing me every night, but there you are, with that cold look on your face."

"Lower your voice," Sissy hissed.

"Why? You don't want people to hear me begging you for blow jobs?" he demanded, his voice loud enough now that she saw several couples look their way. "It's pretty fucking sad to have to ask my wife for that, especially when I treat you like a queen."

She snorted so vehemently wine burned in her nose.

"You're just white trash wearing fancy clothes, but that doesn't change who you are, Sissy: trash."

Her eyes narrowed to slits. "Yeah? Well, you married me."

His alcohol-addled mind couldn't process her comment fast enough to come up with a retort, so he just slammed his drink back down on the table like a child throwing a tantrum.

The waiter came again, and this time, before his greedy ass could offer her drunk husband yet another expensive drink, she demanded he bring the check.

While they waited for the valet to bring their car around, Sissy leaned close enough to smell the alcohol coming off him in waves. "I'm driving us home."

"The hell you are," he snarled.

"I want to get back to our kids alive," Sissy said.

When the valet returned and brought them the keys, she stepped forward before J.D. could and took the key fob.

The valet held the passenger door open, and J.D. glared at Sissy before getting in. She knew she'd pay for it in the car, but it was a small price to pay to not have him drive.

Later, they would have sex that she didn't want. He would hold her down, possibly rip her dress, while reeking of bourbon. He'd finish in less than two minutes. She would wait until he fell asleep snoring before getting up to shower. She'd take her time in the bathroom, and then she'd sleep at the farthest side of their king-sized bed.

It wasn't the happiest marriage, but Sissy had long ago traded happiness to escape the trailer park.

Money and security beat happiness every day.

MARIA

A bead of sweat rolled unpleasantly down the side of Maria's face as she dragged her cleaning supplies into the Maid for You headquarters. She didn't know if she'd ever get used to this humidity. Even in the air-conditioned houses she cleaned, she poured sweat. Though that could be because she was pushing herself to finish fast enough to get home and change before she had to pick up Ariana in the afternoon.

She replaced all the supplies in the storage room, and then grabbed the pouch that held all the cash and checks she'd collected.

"Diane?" she called, knocking once before entering the owner's office.

She didn't see Diane anywhere, but there was a lockbox for all the checks and money. Maria walked over to it and slipped the two checks in. She had two hundred dollars in cash that needed to be fed into the slot. At first, she was proud of herself for not even noticing all that money she was putting into the box.

When she came to the last twenty dollar bill, though, she hesitated. Would Diane even notice a missing twenty bucks? She did a quick calculation in her head and knew even that relatively small amount could make a huge difference on their credit card payments. It was almost like giving herself a tip for her work. Hell, at only twenty bucks an hour and four hours of work, Maria *deserved* a tip!

Her hand holding the twenty dollars was clammy. Memories flashed through her mind: the arrest in New York City when she was eighteen. The brief stint in jail.

The color orange.

She shook her head. How could she risk it?

But then she thought of Sissy's enormous house. All the shiny cars the other moms drove. The credit card debt that was hovering over their heads like a roof about to cave in.

Before she even knew what she was doing, she pocketed the twenty dollars.

Now that she was clean and sweat-free, Maria hurried to join the line to pick up Ariana from preschool. She saw Sissy up ahead of her but didn't bother to call out. She'd learned her lesson from the playdate. When Sissy called her a shameless social climber to Sarah Anne, Maria had been standing just outside the kitchen. For a million-dollar home, it seemed to have thin walls. She hadn't even been trying to eavesdrop. That remark had ripped her apart, and she'd spent the rest of the night alternating between feeling angry enough to imagine confronting Sissy about it the next day and just feeling incredibly sorry for herself.

For once in her life, she was thankful she'd stolen something. Every time she used the soap she'd swiped from Sissy's pristine bathroom, it made her grin meanly. *Take that, you rich bitch,* she thought. Rich bitch even had a nice ring to it, but you know, Maria had always been poetic.

Up ahead of her in line, Sarah Anne was talking with that pediatrician, her eyes bright. Maria couldn't help but notice how many times she touched his arm. She thought of what she'd overheard at the playdate and shook her head. Of all the people she'd met so far, she wouldn't have thought Sarah Anne was capable of cheating with a dad from the preschool. Then again, you never knew what was happening in the secret parts of someone's life.

A little tap on her shoulder alerted her to someone behind her, and she turned to see Lauren. "Oh, hi," Maria said. While the playdate had made her see Sarah Anne in a new light, it also made her feel like she was in a secret society with Lauren. It was the Sisterhood of Women Sissy Looks Down On. It didn't seem to be a very exclusive club.

Ahead of them in line, Hampton and Sarah Anne had already retrieved their kids. Totally caught up in their own lives, they walked out the door, deep in flirty conversation.

Maria could tell by Lauren's gaze that she'd seen it, too, but she didn't seem to react. "I was going to let Emily play on the playground after school. Did you and Ariana want to join us?"

"Sure," Maria said with a genuine smile.

But when it was finally her turn to pick up Ariana, she knew immediately that something was wrong. Ariana usually screamed, "Mommy!" and ran straight for her legs, but today she seemed subdued.

"She had a hard day," Jenny, the preschool teacher, said. She gazed down at Ariana with a sympathetic look.

"What happened?" Maria asked, and she couldn't help but notice that Lauren was listening behind her.

"One of the other little girls tends to pick on Ariana, but we're working on it," Jenny hurried to assure Maria.

"Who is it?" Maria asked, but she already knew. After all, she had a problem with the mother picking on *her*.

"Mary Elizabeth," Jenny said in a voice barely above a whisper. "Little girls can be a bit more cliquish than boys, even in preschool. We're trying to help her see that Ariana can be friends with Sophie and Emily, too."

"Well, thank you for letting me know," Maria said, gathering Ariana close to her and bending down to her daughter's level. "How about we go play on the playground with Emily?"

This seemed to bring some life back into Ariana's eyes, and she looked over at Emily with a smile. "Sure!"

Lauren followed them out after the girls gathered up their backpacks. "You really need to demand a parent-teacher conference over this," she said as they walked down the sidewalk toward the playground. The girls had already raced ahead, laughing, their backpacks bouncing on their backs.

Maria couldn't hold back a laugh. "A parent-teacher conference? In preschool?"

"Yes! Bullying starts early. You need to make sure they're on top of this."

"Jenny said they were handling it. Do you think she didn't mean it?"

They caught up to where the girls were waiting for them, and Lauren opened the gate. When they were out of earshot, she turned back to Maria. "She meant it today, but asking for a conference just shows her that you're going to stay on top of the situation, too."

Maria chewed her lip. Honestly, if it was any other mom's kid, she wouldn't hesitate to follow Lauren's advice. But it wasn't. It was Sissy's kid. "Have you had trouble with Mary Elizabeth being mean to Emily, too?"

"No, but Emily is so quiet, she just lets Mary Elizabeth and Sophie decide what they'll play and never puts up a fuss. Maybe it's different with Ariana."

"She definitely has her own opinion," Maria said, watching her little girl, who even now was telling Emily that they were going to play tag. "This is all new for her, though. She didn't go to preschool in New York or have a bully pick on her. She just played with her cousins."

"Cousins can bully you, too," Lauren said, slipping on a dark pair of Ray-Bans.

Maria smiled. "That's true. Especially Italian ones."

"Oh, are you Italian?" Lauren asked. "I thought from your last name…"

"Gomez? Yeah, you probably thought I was Latino, right? And we are, or at least, Ariana is half. But I'm 100 percent Italian. My maiden name is Romano—like the cheese," Maria added with a laugh.

"How funny," Lauren said, but then she caught sight of Emily getting too close to the edge of the playset. "Oh, honey! Be careful!"

Lauren moved closer to where the girls were playing, and Maria followed. As they talked, Maria noticed that Lauren never took her eyes off Emily. She wasn't exactly helicopter-parenting, but she was being much more vigilant than Maria. To Maria, the playground couldn't get any safer. It was surrounded by a metal fence with a gate that only adults could open. The ground was covered with cushiony rubber mulch. Even the playset was made for very young kids with rounded edges and safe heights.

The girls raced up and down the slide, around the playset, and back again, with Lauren sucking in her breath any time they moved too close to the "edge." It couldn't have been higher than three feet off the ground, and Maria had to hold back a snort. Wrap the kid in bubble wrap if you're that worried!

Maria's phone dinged in her bag, and she pulled it out to check. When she saw what the alert said, her stomach plummeted. It was from her bank.

Overdraft alert. New balance: -$40.00

James didn't get paid again for another three days. How would she explain to him that he couldn't use his bank card for anything? Nausea hit her strong and fast. How could she let this happen again?

She put her phone back in her bag before Lauren could see it over her shoulder. As she did, she felt a crumpled twenty-dollar bill. It was the one she'd taken earlier, and even though she hadn't intended to use it so soon, she knew it could make a difference. She had another forty dollars in her wallet, so that would at least bring the balance back to green.

"Ariana, we have to go now," Maria called, her voice tight. "Mommy has to run an errand." To Lauren, she added, "I forgot that I need to run by the bank."

"We should leave now, too," Lauren said, waving Emily over. "Ready to go, sweetie?"

Emily nodded, while Ariana wore a threatening pout that made Maria tense. She couldn't handle a tantrum right now. Not when she wanted to throw one herself.

"I want to play more," Ariana said, refusing to put on her backpack.

"Don't start this," Maria said in a low voice. "You can play here again tomorrow."

Lauren and Emily were already moving toward the gate.

"I want to play!"

"Let's go, Ariana," Maria said, and she knew she should take the time to convince her without resorting to forcibly removing her from the playground.

Ariana's face scrunched up like she was about to cry. "No!"

Maria whipped toward Ariana. "Don't tell me, 'no.' We're leaving. Now."

She handed Ariana her backpack, but Ariana shook her head. All Maria could think about was that negative balance sitting in her bank account. That any moment, James might decide to go buy a drink, or a snack, or gas— or anything at all—and realize that she'd let this happen to their bank account *again*.

Suddenly, Lauren was by her side. She squatted down next to Ariana. "Ariana, your mama has to go to the bank now, but did you know they give out suckers?"

Ariana's eyes lit up. "Like Dum Dums?"

Lauren nodded. "Exactly like that."

"Okay, let's go, Mommy," Ariana said as she took the backpack from Maria's hands.

Maria was left feeling grateful and inadequate at the same time. Lauren had made it look so easy.

"You looked like you could use some help," Lauren said with a nod toward Ariana who was now happily walking toward the car with Emily.

Maria shot her a relieved smile. "I did—thank you."

"You're welcome. I'll see you tomorrow," Lauren said, using her key fob to unlock the car for Emily.

Ariana waved goodbye to her friend and practically jumped into Maria's car. "I can't wait to get a sucker!"

Maria made a mental note that bribery worked better on her daughter than threats—unsurprising, since she was the same way.

Her mind quickly shifted to calculations to try and figure out if that little bit of money would last them the rest of the week. Her car didn't need gas, and she had just gone grocery shopping the other day, but she wasn't sure about James. There were also bills that came out of their account automatically that she usually forgot about.

I'm disorganized as hell, she mentally berated herself. What kind of adult was she? She couldn't even keep track of their bills. James was making more than he ever had, but the account was negative.

Her mother was right: she was a natural-born screw up.

But at least she had that extra twenty dollars. It wouldn't go far, but it was enough to make the account positive again.

Now she'd just have to figure out how to tell James he couldn't use his bank card for the rest of the week.

LAUREN

L auren had planned to make dinner tonight. She had gathered the ingredients for a chicken and vegetable casserole, but when it came time to make it, she couldn't summon the energy. All she kept thinking about was what she saw on Wesley's phone that morning.

Can't wait for this weekend.

The text was suspicious enough on its own since Wesley supposedly had a fishing trip, but the heart emoji had shredded her insides. She felt gutted.

The possibility that he wasn't just a neglectful husband who spent his weekends hunting or fishing instead of with his family, but also a total *creep* who snuck around behind his wife's back put Lauren in a state of shock. She hadn't even been able to say anything to him yet.

It made her think unpleasantly of Sarah Anne. Her friend with the perfect little life at home who was risking it all to sleep with another preschool dad. Was Wesley sleeping with someone like Sarah Anne? A woman who was married with kids? Somehow, that made it so much worse. Especially when Wesley could be sleeping with his own wife.

In her mind, she screamed obscenities. She demanded an explanation. She threatened him with divorce.

But then she thought: I'm supposed to ovulate again in two weeks. I can't miss this chance.

She may have wanted to scream at Wesley and smash his phone to pieces, but she wanted a baby. And he was the easiest source of sperm.

So now she'd have to pretend like she hadn't seen the text until she got what she wanted from Wesley. But that sure as hell didn't mean she'd have to fix him dinner.

Emily had eaten a peanut butter sandwich and apples, and she was playing outside in their fenced backyard while Lauren watched from the sofa. She scrolled through Instagram, pausing as she came to a recent post from Sarah Anne.

It was another coffee art photo, with the foamed milk of the latte creating little hearts on the surface of the coffee. Lauren checked to see if the location had been tagged, but it seemed like Sarah Anne had learned her lesson. When she scrolled past the hashtags, though, she saw that Sarah Anne had tagged the name of the coffee shop.

With a groan, Lauren closed Instagram. If Sarah Anne wanted the world to know where she was at any given moment, that was her problem. Lauren had done her duty as her friend and warned her.

In another part of the house she heard the front door opening. Her whole body tensed as she listened to Wesley throw down his wallet and keys on the kitchen counter. She could picture him looking around the clean kitchen and noticing there was nothing cooking on the stove or in the oven. Her lip curled in a sneer.

"Lauren?" he called, his footsteps heavy.

Lauren swallowed the acid that had risen from her stomach. "In here."

"Now I see why I didn't get greeted at the door," he said with a smile and nod toward the backyard where Emily still played. "I'm glad to see her outside, though."

"It's better than her watching Mickey Mouse all day," Lauren said, trying to respond as she normally would. As he continued to watch their daughter, she searched his face. Was there a change that came over someone when they started cheating? Would she be able to sense it? That text didn't mean something was happening now, but it was definitely an indication that something would happen in the future.

Lauren saw the bulge of his phone in his back pocket, and her heart rate picked up.

"What should we have for dinner?" Wesley asked. "Or did you have something planned?"

"Emily already ate," Lauren said, "and I'm not hungry."

"Well, I am. I've been working all day," he said.

She shot him a look. "So have I."

He didn't have to know it wasn't really true. She thought of her checklist on her phone:

-Grade and turn in papers for English 101

-Grade and turn in papers for Creative Writing

-Catch up on bills

She'd only completed maybe 25 percent of those papers for the first class. Both classes required her to read over student essays, and after the first few, the words swam on her computer screen. She couldn't concentrate.

But for once, she'd been glad Emily and Wesley weren't at home. She'd stared at her checklist, breathing harder and harder. The tears had come fast and hot, and before she knew it, she was sobbing. She sobbed so hard she threw up, like a toddler throwing a tantrum.

It was only having to clean up her vomit that had snapped her out of it. She'd thrown herself into cleaning instead, which was why their kitchen was now immaculate.

"Are you listening to me?" Wesley demanded. He wore an incredulous look like he couldn't believe she was ignoring him.

"What did you say?"

"I said I'll order a pizza. What do you want?"

"Nothing," Lauren said.

Wesley sighed and crossed his arms. "What's wrong with you?"

Lauren heard her heart pounding in her ears as she swallowed the words she wanted to say.

I've been trying to get you to have sex with me to have another baby.

But it turns out you're probably cheating.

Which means you're not having sex with me. You're having sex with her.

And you don't care whether I get pregnant again or not.

Instead, she said, "I'm just not hungry."

He shook his head in an exasperated way that brought the heat of anger straight into her cheeks. "Fine. I'm going outside with Emily."

Lauren watched Emily's face light up as she noticed Wesley. Her little legs pumped as she ran and threw herself into his arms. He scooped her up for a hug and a kiss, spinning her around the way she liked. They were both beaming.

Lauren couldn't help but notice that he greeted Emily with physical affection, but not his own wife.

But most of all, she noticed how happy they both seemed together, and she wondered how he could not want another little girl just like her.

———

Later that night, after Lauren had read Emily *Goodnight, Little Bear* twice, rocked for ten minutes, and carried her to bed, she went downstairs. Wesley was in the living room, watching recaps of college football. Lauren stood in the archway of the room, looking at their perfectly matching dove-gray furniture accented with cheery yellow floral pillows. Wesley had another room to display his hunting trophies, but every other space in their house was bright and floral and undeniably feminine.

Had it pushed him away? Maybe he wanted a woman who loved sports and stalking helpless animals. Maybe he wanted a woman who didn't gag at the smell of freshly-caught fish.

Well, Wesley will just have to live with it. He knew who I was when he married me.

At the commercial, Wesley turned slightly to put his beer down and saw her standing in the doorway. "There's pizza left if you want some."

"I'm still not hungry," Lauren said and Wesley let out a big sigh and shook his head.

He paused football recap and turned so his arm was

resting on the back of the sofa. "Is this some sort of protest thing?"

Lauren stiffened. "Is *what* some sort of protest thing?"

"You not eating. Is this about my hunting trip this weekend?"

"Wow. You really do think everything is about you, don't you? Well, this may be difficult for you to understand, but try to keep up: I'm really just not hungry. As in, my stomach is full."

His eyes widened. "Damn. Are you on your period, or what?"

Lauren laughed, but the sound had no humor in it. "Not that you would have any idea about my cycles—in fact, it seems like you go out of your way to stay ignorant about them—but *no*, I'm not on my period. I actually finished it a day ago."

He snorted into his beer. "Doesn't seem like it."

Something dark and ugly rose its head inside her, and she fantasized slamming her hand into the back of his head. She could almost see his face landing in his beer glass, coating it with foam. Her hands curled into fists at her sides.

Instead, she turned around and left the room. She knew he wouldn't follow her—too much effort. At the top of the stairs, she turned right to go check on Emily. When she peeked into her room to find her sleeping peacefully, a few muscles in Lauren's shoulders relaxed. Emily was curled around her pink bunny, snug in her princess bed. Emily's room was excessively feminine—not like the more neutral nursery at all. But Emily had always liked princesses, unicorns, and the color pink. It was the room Lauren had always wanted as a child, too. With Sarah Anne's help, she'd carefully picked every piece of white furniture from

Pottery Barn in Emily's room and used pink as an accent color in the bedding and rugs. The walls were painted a pink so pale it looked cream-colored, which made the pink duchess satin drapes pop. The drapes were Lauren's favorite feature of Emily's room. She loved how they stretched all the way to the floor.

Her eyes followed the line of the drapes to the hard-wood, and she noticed one of Emily's baby dolls laying there. It was one that was made to look and feel like a newborn, with a scrunched-up face and soft body. Lauren picked it up off the floor, thinking she should put it with Emily's other toys.

The size reminded her so much of Emily as a newborn. She was tiny like this. Lauren could almost smell that new-baby smell of milk and baby shampoo. Her arms cradled the baby doll like they would a real baby. Something low and deep inside her quivered. Would she ever hold her own newborn again? Sometimes she could still feel a baby move inside her. Phantom movements instead of phantom pain. She cradled the baby doll closer to her chest.

Still holding the baby doll, she backed out of the room quietly. She left Emily's door cracked and padded down the hallway. Before she made a conscious effort to go there, she arrived at the nursery beside her room. She went inside and closed the door. The sun hadn't set yet, but it was on the other side of the house. In here, it was cool and dark.

She settled into the rocking chair, cradling the baby doll gently. The rocking motions soothed her and made the boiling rage she felt toward Wesley cool slightly.

She ran through plans in her head. There were so many, but right now, she thought of Wesley. She knew she had to talk to him about the text, otherwise her anger would just grow until it was a living thing. Even now, she didn't know how she would sleep beside him tonight.

She thought again of Sarah Anne and the threatening text she'd received. All because Sarah Anne had turned her location tag on. Wesley didn't even have an Instagram account, but that didn't mean the woman who texted him didn't either. Lauren just had to get a name. If she had that, she could dig around online until she found something.

When he was asleep, then. He didn't even lock his phone. She could pick it up when she heard him snoring and carry it to the bathroom where he would never bother her.

Her eyes fluttered closed with relief. It felt so *good* to have a plan.

Even if it was snooping on her own husband.

SARAH ANNE

Sarah Anne woke up to the sound of screaming. Since Mark was in their closet calmly putting on his clothes for work, she knew it was only Sophie. She often woke up screaming or crying over "emergencies," though none of it was ever anything to worry about.

Sure enough, Sophie came barreling into their bedroom like a rhino. Sarah Anne had never understood how a child that tiny could make so much noise, especially in the morning.

"Mama!" Sophie sobbed, coming to Sarah Anne's side of the bed.

"Hm?" Sarah Anne said, not even bothering to open her eyes. She hoped Mark would appear from the closet and solve the problem before she was forced to get up.

"Mama," Sophie said again, shaking Sarah Anne's shoulder.

Sarah Anne opened one eye and sighed. "Sophie,

you're naked as the day you were born. Where are your clothes?"

"I couldn't find anything beautiful to wear!"

"You have drawers full of clothes. They're all beautiful."

"They're not! I want my purple dress!"

"It's in the wash, honey," Sarah Anne said.

Mark chose that moment to come out, one hand adjusting his tie as he grinned at the furious Sophie. "What's wrong with my baby girl?"

"I don't have anything beautiful to wear," she said again, tears shining prettily in her blue eyes.

"Your child ought to come with a warning for how high maintenance she is," Sarah Anne said, finally throwing the covers off and getting out of bed.

"I'll have cards printed for her that we can hand out to future boyfriends," Mark said, and Sarah Anne snorted as she scraped back her bed head into a messy bun.

"Daddy, you have to find me something beautiful to wear!" Sophie demanded when she realized neither parent was listening.

"Daddy has to go to work," Mark said in a fake apologetic voice. Sarah Anne knew he was relieved to be escaping the morning battle.

"No!" Sophie wailed, dissolving into tears.

"All right, come with Mama. I think your rainbow dress is clean," Sarah Anne said, beckoning Sophie off the floor.

Instantly, her tears stopped. "Okay."

With a chuckle, Mark headed out of their room. "Love you, girls. Tell Jackson whenever he decides to get up that I'll play ball with him when I get home."

"Bye, honey," Sarah Anne said.

Just when he'd stepped out of their bedroom, Sarah Anne's phone vibrated. Her heart rate jump-started in response. Logically, she knew the text could be from anyone. Sophie's school frequently texted early in the morning.

Only she knew it wasn't.

She walked over and picked up her phone gingerly, like it was a snake. From the other room, she heard Sophie calling for her.

"Just a minute, baby," Sarah Anne said, and her voice sounded strained to her ears.

She unlocked her phone and brought up the message, heart pounding. When she saw the photo, she let out a groan of distress. This time, it was a picture of Hampton and her kissing on his front porch. She was wearing her favorite bohemian blue top with the plunging neckline and white shorts, which meant this picture was taken yesterday.

Right after they'd had sex.

Sarah Anne's breaths came faster. There was no accompanying message. Just the picture. But wasn't it enough? It meant someone knew she was there with Hampton. Did the person know their routine of going to the coffee shop after drop-off?

Sarah Anne racked her brain. Had anyone been hanging around in their car at drop-off? All she could remember was looking over at Hampton's shiny sedan. There may as well have been no other cars there as reliable as her memory was.

Sarah Anne put her head in her hands. Her mama always said she was dangerously oblivious.

You're going to be one of those poor women who gets jumped getting into her car because you never even look around you.

Her mama was the opposite. Her eyes darted around the parking lot like a hunted animal. She locked her car the moment she closed the door.

Well, it wasn't the first time Sarah Anne should've listened to her mama.

She thought of this morning with Mark, his casual joke about Sophie. The warmth of his familiar body beside her while they slept last night.

Not for the first time, she thought: *I need to end this with Hampton.* But then she went to the preschool and saw him, and it was like she was a teenager again. All she could think about was him.

Sophie came into her room then, completely dressed. "Mama, don't I look beautiful?"

As she watched her little girl spin around in front of her full-length mirror, she thought, *I'm going to be good today. I'll ask Lauren and Maria if they want to get together instead.*

She would be strong and resist Hampton. Even if her abdomen was already fluttering at the thought of seeing him.

"You do look beautiful," she said to Sophie, pushing back the panic the message had caused. "Now let's get you and your brother ready for school."

———

It turned out Maria and Lauren couldn't do anything with Sarah Anne after drop-off, so they made plans to take the girls to the park right after school. Sarah Anne had smiled and brushed it off, but inside, she panicked. How would she resist Hampton now?

I should get in my car and leave before he can even talk to me, she thought, and she went so far as to get in her car. But she sat, scrolling through her phone instead of driving away.

He came to her window with the smile that tore her up inside. "Hey, beautiful," he said, "I'm so sorry, but I can't meet you for coffee today."

Her gaze snapped to his. She'd been preparing herself to turn him down, so when he said he couldn't meet her, she was suddenly filled with doubts. Was he sick of her already? Did he want to end this? Is it because she hadn't answered his texts fast enough?

"I've been called into the office early. One of the other doctors is sick."

Sarah Anne searched his face for any sign of duplicity. That was the thing about sneaking around. You couldn't ever really trust the person you did the sneaking with. Lord have mercy, that sounded like something else her mother would say.

"Well, that's okay, I'll just get my coffee to go," Sarah Anne said, tossing her hair over her shoulder. "Without you."

He grabbed his chest like she'd stabbed him. "You know I want to be there." He leaned closer. "It's all I could think about last night."

She could smell his clean-soap smell, and it took her right back to yesterday with him. His mouth on hers as his fingers touched her in the way that made her back arch. His hands cupping her breasts as she rose above him.

"Don't you dare get me all hot and bothered before taking off for work," she said, giving him a look.

He held up his hands. "You're right, I'm sorry. I can't help it. I just see you, and it's all I can do not to kiss you right here in front of everyone."

"Well, you better not."

"You haven't had any more of those weird texts have you?"

Sarah Anne's stomach dropped. She opened her mouth to tell him about the message, but then she thought of how he'd react. What if he said they should call the whole thing off? They should, but was she ready for that? "No, just the one."

"This might be a good thing that I'm going into work. It throws off our routine. Still no idea who it could be?"

His laidback tone made her bristle. It didn't matter as much if he got caught—he was divorced. It had the potential to destroy Sarah Anne's life, but she knew no one would blame him. People would say Sarah Anne had come on to him, that she was the one who stepped out of her marriage.

"I still don't know," she said.

When he walked away, she pulled out her phone and looked at the most recent text again. She hated the idea that someone was watching her when she didn't know it. Honestly, Sarah Anne wasn't sure she'd had an enemy her whole life. Even in high school. She was the type of person who could talk to anybody, so she'd never stuck to one clique or another. One day she might sit with the kids in drama club because she was singing in the spring musical, and another day, she might sit with the cheerleaders because she and two of her girlfriends cheered. Sarah Anne had a natural talent for putting people at ease, and she took full advantage of it.

So who was following her? And what had she ever done to them?

13

MARIA

The text came while Maria was in the middle of vacuuming a dining room rug, so she didn't immediately see it. It wasn't until the missed-text alert popped up that she looked at the screen. When she opened it, she let out a wounded cry and dropped her phone on the hardwood floor.

She picked it up like a snake-handler would carefully grab the tail of a serpent. The picture was still there. Texted to her from an anonymous number.

It was Maria's mugshot.

Below it read:

PETTY THEFT

"Shit," Maria said, her stomach clenching painfully. Who sent this? What did it mean? There was no blackmail threat attached, nothing but the mugshot. Nothing to indicate what the anonymous texter wanted.

Maria forced herself to look at the picture again. She

looked young, with her hair scraped back in a tight ponytail and her eyes free from crows' feet—it was from ten years ago—but you could still tell it was her.

Her first instinct was to delete the picture, but she stifled that reaction. She needed to keep this for evidence.

What do you want? she texted back.

Better to get it over with sooner. The texter probably wanted what everyone wants: money.

Maria stared at her phone, waiting for a response while her stomach turned itself in knots. Five minutes later, there was nothing.

She had to keep cleaning the house, but she checked her phone every few minutes. She never received a response.

By the time she arrived at headquarters, she was a shaky mess.

Remember to do deep breathing as soon as you feel yourself get anxious, her old therapist's voice advised in her head. *When we get anxious, we take short, little breaths and generally forget how to breathe. Deep breaths flood your brain with oxygen and have a calming effect.*

Yeah, well, it wasn't working for her today.

In her head, she pictured dropping this bomb on James. Here they were, expecting a clean start in a new state, and her past was still coming back to haunt them. She'd already narrowly avoided having to tell him about their bank account. Somehow, they'd limped along until payday. Now, she was checking their online account every few hours.

As she dragged in her cleaning supplies, she panted again with shallow breaths—everything her therapist said going out the window.

"Hi, Maria," Diane said, holding open the door for her.

"I was just on my way to lunch. You can just leave the payments in the lockbox."

Maria struggled to smile. "I'll do that. Have a good lunch."

Diane hesitated, like she wanted to say something else, and Maria froze. She'd only had one other opportunity to keep some money for herself, so the company was only short forty dollars. Was that enough for Diane to notice?

In the end, the older woman did nothing but shake her head once and touch Maria on the arm. "Thanks for doing a good job."

She left, and Maria let out a shaky breath as the door closed behind her.

———

M aria had tried to tell Sarah Anne that she wouldn't be able to meet them at the park after school, but it turned out Sarah Anne didn't take no for an answer. Ordinarily, that wouldn't have stopped Maria from doing what she needed to do, but then Ariana heard Emily and Sophie cheering about going to the park.

So now Maria sat on a bench in the shade with Sarah Anne and Lauren while the girls played. Maria had turned her phone to silent, but winced every time she heard it vibrate in her bag, even though she knew logically it was probably just one of her cousins in New York.

"Can anyone see Emily?" Lauren asked, rising to peer around the play set.

"Honey, she's fine," Sarah Anne said with a laugh. "She's right over there on the swings."

This seemed to satisfy Lauren for the time being, but she kept her head turned in that direction, her eyes shielded by her dark sunglasses.

"So I have to tell y'all something," Sarah Anne said, turning to face them. Her eyebrows were furrowed as if she was worried, and it caused an answering spike of anxiety in Maria.

"What?" Lauren asked, sparing her a brief glance.

"I got another text." This time, Lauren turned to look at her.

"When?"

"This morning."

Just the mention of a text had Maria's breaths coming faster again.

To Maria, Sarah Anne said, "I got this horrible anonymous text that was a picture of…something I wouldn't want other people to see. And then, a week later, I got another one."

"I got one, too," Maria said, and she could hear the tremor in her voice.

Lauren and Sarah Anne both whipped toward her. "What do you mean?" Sarah Anne said, eyes wide.

"I got an anonymous text, and it was a picture of me I wouldn't want anyone to know about."

"What is going on?" Sarah Anne demanded. "How could you have gotten one too? What does this mean?" Her voice was getting increasingly more panicked.

Maria shook her head. "I have no idea. Why would we both get some creepy, anonymous text?"

"Lord, this is getting out of control," Sarah Anne said, her face pale. "When did you get it, Maria?"

"Just a couple of hours ago," she said, her mind racing. If Sarah Anne had received a threatening text, too, then it couldn't have been someone from New York who sent the mugshot to Maria.

"I thought it was someone from my past who sent it," Maria said, "but now that I know you've received a text like that, too…"

Lauren nodded, catching on quickly. "It has to be someone here that you both know."

"But who?" Sarah Anne demanded. "Maria just moved here!"

"I can think of one person who seems to really not like me," Maria said quietly, and Sarah Anne paused in her frantic fidgeting to listen. "Sissy."

Sarah Anne leaned back as though her body was stunned while her mind tried to process what Maria had said.

"Oh, I don't know, Maria…" Lauren said, shaking her head slowly. "She can be really nasty, it's true, but I don't know why she'd go to all this trouble."

"Did your text make any demands?" Maria asked. "Like blackmail for money?"

Sarah Anne shook her head.

"Mine didn't either," Maria said. "And don't you think that's weird? It would be a perfect opportunity for blackmail if the person needed money."

"What kinds of things has Sissy said to you?" Sarah Anne asked. "Sometimes she's just a little blunt, but I guess we've all gotten used to it."

Maria told them about her first embarrassing interaction with Sissy at the preschool. They cringed when she described how badly Sissy had snubbed her when she tried to introduce herself.

"I don't know what her problem was that day," Sarah Anne said with a shake of her head. "She must have been trying to rush back to her house to fix all those snacks to impress us with."

"This sounds like I'm just overly sensitive, but she also made a few mean comments to me at her house. It's just obvious that she doesn't like me and hasn't from the start."

"She has been pretty ugly to you, I'll admit," Sarah Anne said, "but I don't know what her problem would be with me."

"Well," Lauren said, her brows still furrowed like she was thinking hard, "there was that time when the girls were in K2 where she basically turned the whole school against that one mom just because she was getting too popular. Remember?"

"Lord, I forgot all about that, but yes. What was that woman's name? Shelly? Stephanie?"

"Sierra, I think," Lauren said. "Sissy didn't like how she was taking over all the big positions at the school like volunteer coordinator, and then she *really* didn't like when Sierra announced she was having her own end-of-the-year party."

Some of the color from Sarah Anne's face drained away. She grabbed hold of Lauren's arm. "I told her I was thinking of throwing a party at the play date! I meant a Christmas party, but I didn't say that then."

Lauren shook her head like Sarah Anne had just confessed to killing Sissy's dog.

"And something as small as that would set her off?" Maria demanded. "This is insane!"

Emily came over then, doing a little dance. "Mama, I have to go potty."

"Oh, okay, sweetie," Lauren said. "Let me get my antibacterial spray. We'll need it in those nasty bathrooms." Maria tried not to roll her eyes as Lauren rifled through her bag to retrieve the spray. A little ding came from her phone, and even the sound of someone else's text alert made Maria jump. As Lauren pulled out her phone, she glanced at the screen and froze.

"What's wrong?" Maria asked.

"I think...I think I just got one, too," Lauren said, and her face looked almost green.

Sarah Anne leaned over to look and sucked in a breath. "Is that—?" She cut herself off with a look at Emily, who still waited to go to the bathroom.

"Come on, Emily, let's go potty real quick," Lauren said woodenly. She stood slowly and put her phone back in her bag. "I'll be right back."

"Was it a text like we got?" Maria asked when Lauren and Emily walked away.

"Yes, it was from an anonymous number, and it just had a picture."

Maria didn't want Sarah Anne or Lauren to ask what her picture had been of, so she didn't ask about Lauren's either. Even though her imagination was conjuring all sorts of crazy things. Was Lauren having an affair like Sarah Anne? Hadn't she just been talking about wanting to have another baby with her husband?

Lauren and Emily weren't gone long, and when she returned, Lauren sat down heavily on the bench.

"Honey, I am so, so sorry," Sarah Anne said, touching Lauren's hand. "Did you know?"

And then Maria knew: the picture wasn't of Lauren at all.

"It was Wesley—my husband," Lauren said for Maria's benefit. "Kissing another woman." Her eyes were shiny with tears. "And no, I didn't know. Not for sure."

Sarah Anne hugged her while Maria looked on helplessly.

"Do you know who the woman is?" Maria asked.

Lauren let out a sound that was half-laugh and half-sob. "It's his secretary."

"I just cannot believe he'd do that to you," Sarah Anne said. "That woman isn't half as pretty as you. And her face looks old and haggard like she's been spending too much time in a tanning bed."

"His secretary at Mercedes?" Maria asked, and Lauren nodded.

"Wesley is one of the sales executives."

"He works in corporate where Sissy's husband also works," Maria said, and Sarah Anne and Lauren both looked at her.

"She could have heard the gossip from J.D.—that's her husband," Sarah Anne added to Maria. "This is a hot mess. I can't believe she would do this!"

"We can't confront her directly," Maria said. "If she can send these pictures to us, she can forward them to anyone."

"So what do we do?" Sarah Anne asked.

"We need to convince her that we're not women you should mess with," Lauren said, her expression grim.

"How?" Maria asked. The thought of going up against Sissy both churned her stomach and made the anger rise within her.

"The one thing Sissy has always cared about is that

preschool," Lauren said, "so it's the only way we can get back at her. We should do what Sierra did and take over all the important positions." She turned to Sarah Anne. "And I think you need to have that Christmas party."

"But didn't you say Sierra ended up leaving the school?" Maria said, jiggling her leg up and down like a drug addict.

"She can't go after us all," Lauren said, "especially if all the other parents are on our side."

"Yes, but how do we get them on our side?" Sarah Anne asked, voicing Maria's question, too.

"By throwing the most fabulous Christmas party we've ever seen. Sissy may have the most popular party at the end of the year, Sarah Anne, but you know it's because everyone just wants to get a look at her house and suck up. You're the better hostess. Sissy acts just like she did at that playdate: cold and aloof. You're the life of the party!"

Maria didn't know from personal experience if this was true, but she could already tell it was. She'd seen at the preschool. If Sarah Anne laughed, people naturally turned toward her with smiles on their faces. She was magnetic.

Sarah Anne tried to downplay Lauren's accolades, but Maria could tell that she agreed.

"Well, I'm in," Sarah Anne said. "I'll do anything to get her to stop."

"I think this will make her realize that we can take the whole school from her," Lauren said. "We'll take the one thing that she truly cares about hostage. And then when it's clear we have everyone on our side, we can go to her and say, 'Delete those pictures you have of us, or we're going to turn the whole school against you.' That'll get her attention faster than anything else."

Sarah Anne nodded eagerly.

But Maria couldn't help feeling like this was an easier risk for them to take. Their husbands were already well established at Mercedes, and they'd been at the preschool for years.

Maria had so much more to lose.

14

SISSY

Sissy frowned at the bruise on her upper thigh in the mirror. Just below her panty line, it was purplish-blue, with the imprints of J.D.'s fingers. She pushed away the memories of him holding her down after drinking. This wasn't the first time he'd been rough during sex, and she honestly couldn't remember the last time they'd done something she could consider love-making. At least it wasn't swimsuit weather, or she'd have a hell of a time hiding such a nasty mark on her skin.

She slipped on a simple white sheath dress, some heels, and a bright blue cardigan that made her eyes pop. With her hair in a chignon and pearls around her neck, she knew she looked the part of chairman of the board.

She went downstairs to wait for her guests. Her phone rang while she was setting out the hors d'oeuvres. It was Jackie, her cousin who had moved to Atlanta as soon as she could. Now she was a successful realtor selling million-

THE LIES BETWEEN US

dollar houses. But she loved gossiping about their family just as much as she did making money.

Sissy checked the time and decided the other board members wouldn't arrive for another twenty minutes, so she answered.

"Hey, Jackie," she said.

"Sissy! Girl, you won't believe what's going on with Ashley."

"I'm fine. How are you?"

Jackie snorted into the phone. "You know I don't have time for that! I'm on my way to show another rich couple a house. But I had to tell you this—I just got off the phone with Mama."

Her mama, unironically named Billie Jean, lived in a rusty old trailer not far from Sissy's own mother.

"How's she doing?"

"What's up with you wanting to know how everyone's doing? She's fine. I'm fine. You're fine. There. All caught up," she said in practically one breath. "Anyway, she said Ashley has a warrant out for her arrest!"

Sissy put the tray of appetizers down with a clink. "Are you serious?"

"As a heart attack. I looked it up myself. Some poor misguided soul put her in charge of the funds for Charity's dance team, and she was caught stealing. She was supposed to be making payments, but you know she owes people all over town, so she couldn't come up with the money."

Sissy groaned. She'd long ago blocked Ashley on her phone and all forms of social media since she nonstop begged for money. But this might blow up in her face if she ended up getting arrested. She might make the local news, and then someone might connect her to Sissy. The last thing she wanted was for people to know she came from trash.

"I know it. She's in a huge mess. She called me wanting a handout, but I took a page out of your book and blocked her. I haven't told you the worst part, though."

"It gets worse?" Sissy said with a shake of her head.

"Yes, one of Mama's customers is a bounty hunter, and he said all he has to do is show up at her work and bring her in."

Billie Jean worked at a barber shop, and she had some interesting clientele, so Sissy wasn't surprised. "Joke's on him, then. She never shows up to work."

Jackie snorted again. "True. She probably already quit."

"I really don't want this to be on the local news."

"I know. I'm sorry. But you know if the reporters hear anything about a warrant for a mama stealing dance money and a bounty hunter who wants to bring her in, they won't be able to resist. What do they have better to talk about?"

"Well, just so long as they don't figure out she's our cousin, I'll be happy."

"I know you're embarrassed of our humble beginnings, but I think you need to embrace it. You should be proud of where we came from."

Sissy rolled her eyes. Jackie always accused her of being embarrassed, but she never wanted to listen to Sissy's true feelings. "I'm proud of *you*," she said, sincerely. Jackie was proof that you didn't need a man to make it. Even when "making it" meant escaping the trailer park.

"Well, be proud of yourself, too. I know I am. Being chairman of a fancy preschool board is pretty impressive."

"Speaking of that, the board members will be here

soon, so I have to cut this short. Thanks for letting me know."

"Have a good meeting! Wish me luck on this house showing. This couple has been pretty tight-fisted so far."

Sissy smiled. "Good luck."

They hung up, and Sissy had just enough time to fix herself some sweet tea and give the impression that she'd been born into this life instead of fighting for it desperately tooth and nail.

———

S issy suppressed a yawn as Heather finished her long-winded monologue about the preschool playground. She'd worked herself up so much that her frizzy brunette hair was escaping the bun meant to tame it. "We have to allocate some of our money for the swing set," she said, her hands emphasizing her every word. "The swings get too much sun, and the children are miserable. Plus, the metal might even cause burns! We have to put up another shade structure."

"Hm," Sissy said, like she was actually debating the merits of a shade structure or not, "but how much will it cost?"

"Only $2,500, which I think is a real bargain. That's just 10 percent of the total amount the McKinney family donated this month."

Sissy pretended to have an internal debate just to remind these women who had the final say. "Shall we vote on it? All those in favor, nod once. I have a headache coming on and can't deal with a chorus of 'ayes.'"

It was a unanimous decision in favor of the shade structure, which almost made Sissy regretful since it made Heather beam like an idiot. "Michelle, are you ready to give us your update?"

The preschool director nodded, a warm smile on her face. She was an older woman, but kept herself in perfect shape. Her dark hair was always beautifully curled, and she wore a long-sleeved white button-shirt, black pencil skirt, and heels that emphasized her long legs.

"I have great news to pass along today," she said. "The parents have been stepping up and volunteering for more positions than ever before. I didn't even have to send out a second round of emails!"

The other board members murmured appreciatively.

Michelle read over the list of positions that had been filled, and Sissy mostly let the names roll over her until she said, "Maria Gomez and Lauren Williamson have signed up to be room mothers for the K4 class."

Sissy's lip curled, but she hid it behind a sip of sweet tea. Could she never escape that New Yorker? Her timid, mousey personality wouldn't make a good room mother. Room mothers were like desperate salesmen: constantly asking for money.

"Sarah Anne Campbell has taken the position of volunteer coordinator, which I'm just so excited about," Michelle added. "I just love her. She has the best personality, and I know she'll be able to keep all the volunteers in line with a smile."

Sissy's eyebrows rose at the mention of Sarah Anne. She couldn't remember the last time Sarah Anne had volunteered for anything. Deep down, she felt a twinge of something...jealousy? Unease? Sarah Anne was nearly as influential as Sissy but in a different way. Where everyone fell over themselves, afraid to get on Sissy's bad side, Sarah Anne was a natural people magnet.

Michelle had finished her list, and the vice-chair was talking while Sissy contemplated how she felt about Sarah Anne having a more prominent position in the school.

"I have a sad announcement," Gabriella Jimenez, the vice-chair, said, interrupting Sissy's thoughts. "My husband has accepted a job in California, and we'll be moving next month."

"I'm so sorry to hear that," Sissy said and meant it. She'd always liked Gabriella, with her soft accent and ready smile.

The other board members said the same, but Gabriella waved them off. "I know it's sad, and I will miss all of you, but it's also good news. My family lives in San Diego, so we'll finally live close enough to see them regularly."

"Well, I'm going to hate filling your position," Sissy said, and she stood to give Gabriella a hug.

"I'll try to appoint someone before I go," Gabriella said. "I don't want to leave you with extra work."

"That would be great, but if it gets to be too stressful with the move, then don't worry about it. I can do it."

Gabriella smiled at her. "I'm going to miss you, my friend. We need to be sure to have lunch many times before I go."

"I'll miss you, too. And of course we must have lunch."

As the others took turns giving Gabriella one-armed hugs that wouldn't smudge their makeup or mess up their hair, Sissy's phone made a little chime that indicated a text.

She glanced down at it and saw that the number was withheld. *Damn it, Ashley,* she thought. Her cousin must have gotten another phone that Sissy hadn't blocked.

When Sissy opened the text, there was a picture of the entrance of her mama's trailer park. The beat-up old sign read: Misty Acres. Sissy's grip on her phone tightened. There was no message along with the photo, but she understood it just fine.

It meant: remember where you come from.

THE PRESENT

I n the beginning, my plan worked so well, I was
convinced I should have led a life of crime. The text
messages, especially, were the easiest to send.

But of course, I had help.

It started with a text message from an old friend. We
didn't get together in person much, but we texted regularly.
We'd actually grown up in the same neighborhood, but no
one remembered this. That wasn't unusual, though, since
no one paid attention to the things I said.

*You know when you told me you wanted the chance to get back at
her for all those things she said?*

Yeah…?

What if we helped each other?

You want revenge on someone, too?

*No, but I want to keep things the way they are now. This is the
only way.*

I'd agreed because I wanted to teach one of them a lesson and because no one was supposed to get hurt.

Neither of those things went according to plan.

We started with Sarah Anne. A child could follow her movements because she posted every aspect of her life on Instagram. Everyone who knew her knew about it. There was a running joke that if you wanted to know what Sarah Anne had for lunch that day, just check Instagram.

A simple Google search revealed everything I needed to know about Maria. I have to admit, it surprised me to learn of her life of crime. I wouldn't have thought she had it in her.

It wasn't a secret at Mercedes that Wesley was sleeping with his secretary. Everyone had been whispering about it for days. He didn't even try to hide it. It was the easiest thing in the world to follow him after he left work with her.

Sissy was harder. It took several tries following her on her boring errands until one day, she drove out to a trailer park. Now what in the world could the chairman of the board be doing out in a trailer park? Nothing good. I didn't even have to know for sure what it was.

Two of them were the real targets of the plan, and the others were just to create confusion.

Obviously, I had to send myself a text message, too. Just to be above suspicion. They never figured it out.

LAUREN

Lauren could see that Maria didn't like the idea of asking for money. Her whole body was stiff at the suggestion, and her brows remained furrowed. They sat at a local restaurant together, discussing the need to collect money from the other preschool parents.

The restaurant was called Honey Biscuit and served biscuits only. It had been Maria's idea—she wanted to "try a real Southern biscuit." Lauren felt Honey Biscuit was more hipster and less Southern. When the girl who took their orders said they asked you the question of the day and would call out your answer instead of your name, Lauren's lip had curled. Maria had laughed in surprise.

"What's the question of the day?" Maria had asked.

The girl with short, spiky hair at checkout had smiled. "What's your favorite animal?"

"A dog," Maria said without hesitation.

"And yours?" she'd asked Lauren.

"A dog," Lauren had said to be difficult.

The girl at checkout had frowned. "Oh, any specific type? So I can differentiate the orders?"

"Nope, just all dogs."

Maria had started to answer, but Lauren pulled her away. "Let's go find somewhere to sit."

They sat in a quiet booth that faced the kitchen, and Lauren kept an eye on the barista while she made her flat white coffee. She didn't want the girl to spit in it because Lauren had an attitude—though it was probably what Lauren would have done.

The barista had flushed when she called out "dog," and they both came to get their orders. Now Maria enjoyed a massive biscuit dripping with honey, and Lauren sipped her coffee.

"Anyway, are you sure we can send out an email asking for money like that?" Maria asked.

"All the parents are used to this, I promise," Lauren said.

Maria nodded slowly like she didn't quite believe her. "It just seems like a lot of things to be asking for money about at once."

"Well, we can't help that Miss Jenny's birthday is in November, too," Lauren said with a shrug. "So we need donations for a present for her, the Thanksgiving party at the end of the month, and then Christmas presents for both teachers plus funds for the Christmas party."

"You don't think that's too much? Can't we spread it out?"

"Not really," Lauren said, trying not to let her exasperation show. "Preschool ends the second week of December, and it's already the second week of November, so we only have a month to get all the teacher gifts and party supplies."

Maria still looked unsure, but she didn't argue. "So how much do you think we'll need to cover everything?"

"I think $500 should cover it."

"Get outta here!" Maria burst out, causing Lauren to lean back in surprise. "$500? You can't be serious."

Lauren gave her a look. "Do you think it won't be enough?"

Maria scoffed, a few biscuit crumbs landing on her shirt. "I'm saying that's a crazy amount of money. Too much."

"It's just the usual amount. One hundred dollars for gift cards and gifts for Miss Jenny's birthday, another one hundred for her Christmas gifts, one hundred for Miss Katie's Christmas gifts, and the remaining two hundred for the party supplies."

Maria gaped at her. "Where do you get the party supplies? Tiffany's?"

"There's a local party shop we go to," Lauren said with a shrug. "But I see what you're saying. I just remember this being the breakdown last year."

"Well, how about we give the parents the chance to decide how much they want to give? We can just leave out how much we expect to collect."

Lauren glanced down at her tablet, where she had typed out a budget. "And you think they'll step up and give enough money?"

Maria shrugged. "You said everyone is used to giving a lot, right?"

"All right. We can do that. I'll say in the email that parents can put their amounts in an envelope to give to you or me. We'll just pool it all together next week and see how much we have."

A strange look crossed Maria's face, like she was uncomfortable.

"Is that okay?" Lauren asked.

Maria glanced up quickly from her food. Yeah, it's fine. I was just wondering if a week gives us enough time to shop."

"It'll be cutting it a little close for Miss Jenny's birthday, but otherwise we should be okay."

Maria finished the last of her biscuit and wiped her mouth with a napkin. "Is that everything, then? I hate to run, but I've got a few things I have to do before I pick up Ariana."

"That's everything. I'll just finish up the email and send it out right away."

"Thanks, Lauren," Maria said.

"See you later," Lauren said with a smile, but her attention was already drifting back to her inbox. She'd noticed an email come in from the online university she taught for, and now she just wanted Maria to leave so she could read it.

Maria cleared her plate, and when she walked out the door, Lauren opened the email. It was an alert that she hadn't turned in her grades for the English 101 papers on time. Lauren's stomach sank. That couldn't be right, could it? She could have sworn she'd finished everything.

But then she thought of the past week of nights spent reading Wesley's text messages with the woman she now knew was his secretary, Tiffany. She'd read every dirty word his slutty new girlfriend had sent him.

Thought about you and got soooooo wet.

You looked soooooo sexy in that suit. Can you wear just a tie later?

She'd looked at every picture of them together that he'd stupidly saved on his phone.

And when the anger had boiled up from the depths of her, pouring out of her eyes in stinging tears, she'd gone to the nursery and rocked the baby doll she still hadn't put back in Emily's room.

Tonight, though, she would have to push all of that to the back of her mind. It was day fifteen in her cycle, and her fertility monitor said she was at peak. So she would have to fix him his favorite dinner of steak and mashed potatoes like she still loved him—did she ever really love him?—wear sexy lingerie underneath her clothes, and hope he hadn't already gotten some earlier that day.

For now, she'd try to salvage the grades for her class.

———

Lauren was chopping potatoes when Wesley got home. Emily squealed and ran to Wesley the moment he stepped in the door, but hearing his footsteps, Lauren felt her entire body bristle. She had no idea how she was going to relax enough for sex. *Think of a baby,* she told herself.

Lauren waited until he came into the kitchen. She wanted him to find her prepping for dinner so that he knew she was making an effort tonight. They'd mostly been living off pizza and takeout because Lauren couldn't bring herself to cook. Some nights, she couldn't even get off the couch.

"Hey," Wesley said as he came into the kitchen. Lauren forced herself to return his smile. "What are you making?"

"Steak and mashed potatoes."

"My favorite. I'm so glad you felt like cooking tonight. I didn't think I could eat takeout again."

Lauren smiled tightly. She couldn't believe she used to think it was so funny that he could barely toast bread. He used to nuzzle her neck and say, "My toast doesn't taste as good as yours."

"I was getting tired of eating out, too."

He came and pressed a kiss on her cheek, light stubble tickling her skin. "I'm going to go watch the news."

"Okay," she said over her shoulder with a smile. "You can also give Emily her bath in a few minutes."

"Sure," he said agreeably, but she knew she'd have to remind him again.

Though part of her was relieved he was no longer in the kitchen making her think of how fake their marriage was now, she couldn't help but miss the way he used to be. There was a time when she'd be cooking, and he'd stand at the counter, fetching ingredients when she asked, but mostly just telling her about his day. She couldn't remember the last time they'd done that.

How long had he been sleeping with his secretary?

She thought of his reaction when they first found out she was pregnant after Emily was born.

"Another sweet baby like Emily to love," he'd said, beaming.

Weeks later, she'd miscarried.

They had held each other on their bed, both crying for what could have been.

She nicked her finger with a sharp knife and just watched the blood bead up.

After the last miscarriage, he hadn't cried. "Maybe it

just isn't meant to be," he said, like he was giving up on their future child.

But Lauren wouldn't give up.

Over the summer, they'd gone to the beach once as a family, and he'd spent the rest of the weekends on fishing trips by himself. At least, Lauren thought he was by himself. For all she knew, he could have been having an affair that whole time. His text messages went back to late September, but that didn't prove anything.

"Mama, you're bleeding!" Emily said from beside her. Lauren hadn't even heard her come into the kitchen. The trickle of blood ran down Lauren's hand onto the chopping board.

"Oh it's just a little scratch, honey," Lauren said, reaching for a paper towel to staunch the bleeding.

Emily watched with wide eyes for a moment but then must have decided Lauren really was okay. "Can I have a cookie since I already ate dinner?"

"Sure," Lauren said, reaching for the clamshell of grocery store chocolate chip cookies. "After you eat that, tell Daddy it's time for your bath."

"Okay!"

Emily loved playing with her toys in the bath, so she could be trusted to relay the message. It would save Lauren from having to nag him.

When she turned back to her dinner prep, she noticed tears leaking from her eyes.

That cut must have hurt worse than she thought.

————

"That was all really good, honey, thank you," Wesley said later after cleaning his plate.

Lauren's appetite still hadn't returned, so she'd only managed to choke down half of her small steak and a few bites of mashed potatoes. She was on her second glass of wine, though. That still went down easily.

"I'm glad you liked it," Lauren said with what she hoped was a coy smile. It was hard to tell with the wine making her feel a little dizzy. "Will you help me clean up?"

He nodded and stood, taking in both their plates. Lauren grabbed her wine glass and his empty beer bottle before following him into the kitchen. She took a deep breath before slipping an arm around his waist. He smelled the same as he always did, like his woodsy cologne, and somehow, that made her heart hurt.

Standing on tiptoes, she kissed his neck. He surprised her by turning into her embrace and kissing her back. She had been half-convinced he would push her away.

"Ready for dessert?" Lauren asked in a throaty voice.

"What did you have in mind?" Wesley asked with the husky tone that meant she had already hooked him.

In answer, she just took his hand and led him out of the kitchen. Upstairs, it was quiet except for Emily's noise machine softly humming. She'd already been asleep for an hour, so there was no risk of interruption.

In the bright, floral bedroom Lauren had spent countless hours creating Pinterest boards for, they undressed and slid into bed together. Wesley touched her in all the right places, but it was like her mind was detached from her body. All she could think about was: did he touch *her* like this? It made her numb to sensation. She ended up faking her orgasm. He didn't notice, of course, because he never did. His orgasm—the one that counted—overtook him, and he spent the requisite few minutes holding her afterward. Her skin was crawling. She wanted to get away.

Eventually, she got up, went to the bathroom and prayed that even now a baby was taking root inside her.

Because she honestly didn't know how many more times she could have sex with her husband.

SARAH ANNE

Sarah Anne was working harder than she ever had, and honestly, she hated every minute of it. It turned out the volunteer coordinator had to stay on top of every volunteer job at the preschool, and there were like fifty of them. For someone who spent most of her time making Pinterest boards for the interior design jobs she did maybe two or three times a year, this was an extreme undertaking.

She couldn't even say if it was worth it. Sissy hadn't seemed to react, but Sarah Anne also hadn't received any more texts.

Now, when she should be meeting Hampton for coffee, she was having to track down Claudia, the head volunteer for the family meals.

"Claudia," Sarah Anne called with a wave and a bright smile she'd smacked on her face. Claudia was in the process of power walking to her car. She was dressed from head to toe in slick, black workout gear. Her dark hair was pulled back in a ponytail so severe her face looked Botoxed.

"Hi, Sarah Anne," Claudia said with a quick smile.

Sarah Anne knew Claudia was barely resisting the urge to jog in place and keep her heart rate up. She wanted to tell the poor girl she looked thin enough—any thinner, and she'd be too skeletal to even have a period anymore.

Sarah Anne had given up flat abs after having Sophie, but she'd never had a man complain.

"I just wanted to pass on the updated list of parents who will be needing meals soon," Sarah Anne said. "There are three on the list until after the holidays. Do you have enough volunteers to cover them?"

"There are five of us, so that shouldn't be a problem at all," Claudia said with a glance at the list. "We actually lost a volunteer, though. Gabriella was the vice-chair and volunteered to bring meals."

Sarah Anne was only half-listening once Claudia confirmed that the meals were covered, but she refocused her attention. "Where's Gabriella going?"

"Her husband got a new job, and they're moving."

"I hadn't heard that. Who's going to take her place?"

Claudia shrugged. "I don't think anyone has stepped up, but I think you'd be perfect for the job."

"Me?" Sarah Anne said with a laugh. "Why me?"

Claudia glanced around and leaned a little closer. "Because you're way more approachable than Sissy. The vice-chair can do everything the chairman can, and I know everyone would rather come talk to you than her. At least you smile and listen!"

"That's sweet of you to say," Sarah Anne said, while her mind worked ahead. This could be the real opportunity to get under Sissy's skin. She couldn't imagine how pissed Sissy would be if everyone started coming to Sarah Anne instead of her. Sarah Anne imagined a dramatic soap-opera-style showdown where Sissy finally confessed her true feelings about why she sent those text messages.

"Gabriella did, too," Claudia continued, "but she always ran everything by Sissy. I think she didn't want to make her mad."

"Well, can you blame her?" Sarah Anne said, and Claudia laughed.

"Just think about it," she said with a glance at her watch. "Thanks for the list, but I gotta head to my burn class."

"You're welcome," Sarah Anne said with a wave. "Have a good workout!"

After Claudia walked away, Sarah Anne immediately got out her phone and texted Lauren.

Found the perfect way to take over Sissy's school.

Lauren answered right away.

How?

Become the vice-chair.

Lauren just responded with a bunch of question marks, but Sarah Anne couldn't stop grinning as she put her phone back in her bag. She always did love a good drama.

Her grin fell away, though, when she saw Erica waiting beside her car. Sarah Anne instantly got a knot in her stomach. Erica's eyes were hidden behind black sunglasses, and she looked intimidatingly put-together in a black pencil skirt, expensive-looking blouse, and heels.

When in doubt, Sarah Anne turned on the charm. She wrenched her mouth into a smile. "Hi, Erica. How are you?"

"Well enough," Erica said, and Sarah Anne couldn't help but notice she didn't return the greeting. "Look, I'm not here to chat with you. I'm here because Hampton can't stop talking about you, and I know what that means."

Sarah Anne tried not to let anything show on her face, but she was sure she wasn't hiding her shock well. "Hampton and I have been friends a long time."

"Don't bullshit me," Erica snapped. "I don't have time for it. Whatever it is the two of you have going on, I want it to end. It's only a matter of time before it starts going around the school, and I don't want your sick relationship making things hard for Ava."

Sarah Anne's eyes were wide, and she knew she looked like a fish out of water. "Erica, I don't—"

Erica held up her hand. "I don't need to hear your pathetic excuses. You're not the first woman Hampton's become obsessed with, okay? I recognize the signs. It's no secret that most of the other parents here don't like me, and that's already been a problem for Ava getting left out of some play dates or parties if they know it's not Hampton's day to watch her. But if they know that Hampton is running around with a married woman from the preschool, Ava will become *persona non grata*. Got it?"

"I think you've got this all wrong, Erica, but I would never want to make trouble for Ava," Sarah Anne said.

Erica snorted. "Yeah, okay. You've always given me the impression you only care about yourself, so I'm not holding my breath you'll watch out for my baby. Just know that if you screw things up for her here, I won't hold back. I'll tell your husband all my suspicions first chance I get."

Before Sarah Anne could respond, Erica spun on her heel and marched away, leaving Sarah Anne shaken.

As she sat in her car, her heart beating furiously like she'd just run a mile, she thought about the anonymous texts she'd received . It *had* to be Erica. It was probably her insurance policy to make sure Sarah Anne would toe the line. She and Sissy were clearly working together since Erica didn't have time to follow Sarah Anne and Hampton around to the coffee shop. Sissy was the one who hated Maria, clearly, and maybe Lauren, too, so she and Erica must have come up with this plan to threaten them.

Sarah Anne didn't like Erica, but she knew she was right about Ava. More importantly, however, she didn't want Sophie to find out.

———

S arah Anne tried not to think about the horrible confrontation with Erica later that evening at Jackson's flag football game. She did what she did best: pushed it from her mind where she didn't have to think about it. She plastered a bright smile on her face and pretended to watch the game because, bless their little hearts, the kids' sports games always bored Sarah Anne to tears. Usually, she had to spend the entire time trying to keep Sophie from throwing a fit because *she* was bored to tears, too, but today they all had a reprieve because there were other siblings her age to play with. She was currently running out all her energy on the playground next to the bleachers, where Sarah Anne and Mark could still see her. To keep her mind occupied, she thought of the progress she'd made on the preschool board.

After Claudia's suggestion, Sarah Anne immediately put her name in for vice-chair. It would be voted on

Monday, but when she spoke to all the other board members—except for Sissy—they assured her no one else wanted the position and that they would gladly vote her in.

"You look like you're actually enjoying yourself," Mark said, leaning toward her on the bleachers. His eyes had that teasing light she always loved. "Do you know something I don't? Have money on the game?"

Sarah Anne laughed. "No, but I should do that from now on to liven things up a bit."

"Well, you're sitting there grinning like a cat who caught herself a mouse."

"I can't grin now?"

He put his arm around her shoulders and leaned toward her ear. "You know good and well what that self-satisfied look of yours makes me think of."

She pretended to look scandalized. "Look at you, talking dirty at a kids' game."

He chuckled and kissed her cheek.

"If you really want to know, I'm happy because I'm pretty sure I'm going to be the new vice-chair of the preschool's board."

He raised his eyebrows. "Whoa, slow down. I didn't know it would be news this exciting."

She elbowed him in the side. "It is! I'll have a lot of influence over the school."

"I do like a woman with power," he said thoughtfully, and she rolled her eyes.

"That's why we're throwing that big Christmas party—sort of a 'congratulations to me for becoming vice-chair.'"

"I thought it was for my employees?"

She waved her hand dismissively. "You know practically

everyone at the school works at Mercedes. This is killing two birds with one stone."

He grunted a confirmation before shouting for Jackson after he got hold of the ball.

Sarah Anne was about to say something else when Mark interrupted her. "Hey, isn't that Hampton?" he asked, squinting toward a man walking toward the bleachers. "I think it is. Hampton! Over here."

To Sarah Anne's horror, Hampton heard Mark and waved back. He started climbing the bleachers toward them. Sarah Anne caught Hampton's eye and gave a little shake of her head, but he just smiled benignly back.

Mark and Hampton shook hands. "I thought that was you," Mark said with a grin. "What brings you to the game?"

"My nephew plays," Hampton said with a nod toward a red-haired boy with freckles. "My sister had an event to go to tonight, so I got roped into bringing him for her."

"You're a good man," Mark said. He glanced at Sarah Anne as if noticing for the first time she hadn't said anything yet.

"It's been a good game so far," she said with a smile that she hoped hid her churning insides. She couldn't imagine a more uncomfortable scenario than the three of them sitting here together...save for Mark walking in on them having sex.

"Not as good as the game we had, huh?" Mark said to Hampton with a grin.

Hampton just shook his head and hid a smile.

"What game?" Sarah Anne asked.

"Golf, where I completely annihilated poor Hampton here," Mark said, still with that teasing light in his eyes.

Sarah Anne was too busy trying not to hyperventilate to find it cute.

"When was this?" she asked, smiling from one grinning idiot man to another.

"Last Friday," Hampton said, far too casually, like it wasn't a big deal to be hanging out with the husband of the woman he was *sleeping* with.

"Well, you two must have had a good time, and I had *no idea*," Sarah Anne said with a little glare in Hampton's direction while Mark watched the game.

Mark snorted, making Sarah Anne jump. "I had a good time anyway. I think Hampton was regretting it."

Hampton laughed good-naturedly at the ribbing. "The way I see it, you did me a favor. I've been wanting to get back into golfing."

"You can play with me anytime," Mark said, and Sarah Anne closed her eyes to suppress a frustrated sigh.

They were both idiots, and she wished she could strangle them. For a while, they all fell silent while they watched the game. Sarah Anne could feel Hampton's gaze on her, but she ignored him.

"I'm going to check on Sophie," Mark said, nodding toward the playground where she and some other girls played.

"Tell her to stay on this side where we can see her," Sarah Anne said, but only because it was what she would have said if she wasn't completely eaten up inside.

She waited until Mark was a good distance away, and even then, she didn't turn to face Hampton.

"What do you think you're doing?" she demanded.

"Right now? I'm sitting here with you, enjoying the game."

"Do not play with me, Hampton. I'm not in the mood. I *meant*, what are you doing playing golf with my husband?"

"Jealous?" he said with a grin she could see out of the corner of her eyes. "And if so, of whom?"

"You're being coy again, Hampton, and I don't like it. I can't believe you would just casually play golf with him knowing what"—she cut herself off for a moment to be sure that Mark was still on the playground before continuing—"what we've been doing. If he ever finds out, he's gonna kill us both."

"That's a little dramatic, don't you think?"

"No," she snapped, knowing it was but not liking him pointing it out. "Look, if y'all start hanging out, he's going to be twice as hurt if he ever learns the truth."

"I get what you're saying, Sarah Anne. I do, but I was looking at it in a different way. I thought he wouldn't suspect someone he played golf with, and honestly, I like Mark."

"Well, I do, too. But you can't be friends with him. You just can't. It's too odd."

"I really liked his golf course though."

She groaned and risked a glance at him. "Shut up. You better not be serious."

He wasn't able to answer her, though, because Mark returned from checking on Sophie. "What did I miss from the game?" he asked.

Hampton gave him a surprisingly detailed play-by-play while Sarah Anne tried to look happy to be there. She couldn't help but notice, though, that Hampton never said he'd stop hanging out with Mark.

Sarah Anne gripped her cell phone tightly in her lap. She hated that she couldn't continue her conversation with

Hampton. She didn't get a chance to ask him what he thought about Erica threatening her in the preschool parking lot either. Sarah Anne liked to settle things right then and there. She never went to bed angry because she always made sure her husband knew *exactly* how she felt. Her thoughts were boiling up inside her like a swarm of bees.

She didn't like that Hampton hadn't taken her warning seriously. She didn't want Mark involved.

The more she thought about it, the more it disturbed her to have that intersection between her married life and her affair. Along with the text messages, things were getting too risky. What if Mark found out? She didn't want to hurt him, and he wouldn't understand why she'd done this. *Sarah Anne* didn't even understand why she'd risked her marriage and happy life on this affair. Seeing Mark and Hampton together made her heart flutter with panic. Mark was happily talking to Hampton, thinking he was his friend, when all the while, he was sleeping with his wife. She didn't want Mark to find out the truth and feel like a fool. She didn't want to let Hampton destroy her marriage. She knew what she had to do, but the thought of it made her stomach churn.

Somehow, she had to end it.

MARIA

After sautéing the garlic cloves and tomato paste with the back of a wooden spoon just like her ma used to, Maria added the cans of crushed tomatoes to her spaghetti sauce along with fresh basil. The smell instantly took her back to her ma's cramped kitchen, and for a moment, she had to pause in her stirring against the onslaught of homesickness.

I should call my mother, Maria thought, but she knew she wouldn't. Not yet.

Her mother was like a detective. She'd ask how Maria was doing, or some other innocuous question, and then she'd somehow be able to detect that note in Maria's voice that meant she was unhappy. That things weren't going so hot here.

That they were up to their eyeballs in debt.

Again.

Maria put the wooden spoon down on the spoon rest and turned to look at the living room full of furniture. She and James had gleefully picked it all out at the furniture store. They bought everything from the display living room, even the artwork. So now her living room had a navy blue sofa, love seat, chair, end tables, coffee table, rug, lamps, drapes, and four yellow and blue prints that looked like mosaics and made Maria feel like a world-traveler when she'd never been out of the country.

They shouldn't have bought any of it, but James had just gotten his first big paycheck—the one from working overtime. If Maria was smart, she would have saved for it first instead of putting it all on their nearly-maxed-out credit card.

But there was another part of her—the part that was responsible for all her stupidest financial decisions—that wasn't sorry at all. She *loved* this room. It made her feel like she was finally an adult.

Her looming debt problems reminded her that she currently had an envelope full of money in her purse, though none of it was hers. It was money accrued from parent donations for teacher presents and every other stupid-expensive thing Lauren wanted them to pay for. Apparently not demanding a specific amount from parents had some sort of psychological effect on them and they weren't sure how much to give, but they were terrified of giving too little. Consequently, they donated a ridiculous amount.

If they couldn't find Lauren to give the money to after school, they gave it to Maria, and her envelope had $500 inside. Cash. That no one had a record of. And when

Lauren had texted asking how much money Maria had collected so far, she told her it was about $300.

She hadn't decided yet that she would actually sink that low and straight up steal from the preschool parents, but she always liked to keep her options open.

She might need that money.

Maria was still staring at the living room, idly stirring the sauce, when James got home. Ariana didn't even emerge from the playroom where she was currently binge-watching Disney.

"That spaghetti smell takes me right back, baby," James said with a grin as he leaned over to kiss her.

"It might not be as good as Ma's," Maria warned, "but I did my best."

"It's better than what these Southerners think passes for Italian food around here."

"I know that's true. How was work?"

"Good. I like working on these fancy cars. It's better than having oil dripping directly in my eyes at a filthy garage."

"Yeah, I bet."

He peered around into the living room. "Where's Ariana?"

"Watching Disney until her eyes bleed."

"That's okay. I wanted to talk to you about something."

Maria tensed as she put the heavy pasta pot on the stovetop to boil. "Yeah? What about?"

"I got a weird call today at work."

Her heart started pounding, all kinds of scenarios going through her head. Had her boss found out about her stealing and wanted to talk to James about it? What about that anonymous text of her mugshot? James knew about her arrest, but she didn't want him to know she was being threatened here.

"It was from a collections agency." His dark brown eyes bore into hers. "Tell me that was just a scam call."

She couldn't, so she didn't say anything at all.

He plunged a hand through his thick, black hair. "Not this shit again, Maria. Not here."

Maria had that shaky feeling that always made her feel like an animal caught in a trap. "Screw you, James. Like you're so perfect."

He reeled back in shock as she turned to the boiling pasta water.

"Hey, you're really gonna talk to me like that? I didn't run up the credit card bill again!"

She let out a bitter laugh. "Yeah? Well, you were right there with me buying the furniture with it."

His eyes widened. "You told me that we were good! That we could afford it!"

That shaky feeling in her stomach increased until she was forced to put her hand there to hold in her insides. "You can check the balance, same as me."

"I'm sorry I took you at your word, Maria," he said, his voice gruffer with his attempt to restrain himself from yelling. It was the one thing she knew he tried not to do. He didn't want to be like his father. "You swore we wouldn't have credit card problems here. That you wouldn't—" he cut himself off with a shake of his head.

"That I wouldn't...what?" she demanded. "Mess everything up like I did before?"

He said nothing, and she closed her eyes and nodded. "Timer for the pasta goes off in five minutes."

She threw the kitchen towel down on the counter and

hurried to their room. She barely made it to the toilet in time to throw up.

The credit cards were the least of it.

He didn't know she was stealing again.

———

In their sparse master bedroom with its old bed and older dresser, Maria paced with one hand on her chest. Her breaths were coming fast and shallow. Part of her screamed that she couldn't breathe, that she was having a heart attack. Black spots appeared on the edges of her vision as she sucked in air like she was drowning.

She knew these symptoms. She'd had them ever since she was a teenager, but that didn't keep her mind from going into panic-mode.

Belatedly, she remembered the one good thing she'd done for herself since she'd moved here: she signed up for an online therapist.

She took out her phone and opened the counseling app. She'd talked with Kimberly, her therapist, a few times so far. At first, she'd been doubtful that the therapy would even be helpful online. But Kimberly turned out to be extremely responsive and validating. She gave Maria the feeling that she had a lifeline if she needed it.

And she definitely needed it now.

Hey, I just had an argument with James, and I'm kinda freaking out. Okay, I'm having a panic attack, I mean.

Maria paced while she waited for her therapist to respond, hoping she'd see the message. What if she was eating dinner? Or driving? Or doing a million other things besides being tied to her phone?

But after a few minutes, she replied.

I'm sorry to hear that, Maria. Panic attacks can be really frightening because it feels like you can't breathe, and it's hard to convince your mind otherwise. Are you doing your deep breathing?

Maria thought about her shaky, shallow breaths.

No.

Then be sure to breathe through your diaphragm rather than your chest. And slow those breaths down.

Maria did as she suggested—reluctantly, because she always felt like deep breathing was a crock of shit—but then slowly, she felt some of her panic ease.

It's better, Maria said after a few minutes.

Good. Do you want to talk about the argument?

Maria sat staring at her phone. *Did* she want to talk about it? It was one of those things in therapy that was like lancing a boil. She knew it would be painful at first, but in the end, it was the only way to heal properly. Kimberly couldn't help her if she didn't tell her what was going on. Maria had learned that the hard way before from previous counselors.

It was over our credit card debt. The collections agency called him at work today, and he's freaking out. This isn't the first time this has happened.

Any kind of financial stress can be really upsetting. Do you feel like he was blaming you?

Maria let out a self-deprecating scoff. *Yes, but it's mostly my fault. I knew the credit card was almost at the limit when we bought all the living room furniture.*

Kimberly was silent for a few moments like she was thinking about what she'd said, and Maria tried not to imagine that she was judging her.

And your husband can't check the credit card balance on his own?

Maria couldn't type a response fast enough. *That's exactly what I said to him! He can check the balance just like I can. He just never does. He trusts me with the finances even when he knows...*

She trailed off. Did she really want to get into this?

The therapist gave her a moment before prompting. *He knows...?*

Maria breathed deeply. *He knows I always end up overspending and getting into debt. And then once I'm in debt, I make really bad decisions.*

Being in debt can make anyone feel desperate.

Yes! Desperate. I feel desperate, and then I do horrible things.

Like what?

Maria's mouth went dry. She'd been dreading this question. She'd talked to a therapist before—it was part of her parole—but it never got any easier.

I steal things. It started out with inconsequential crap, like little trinkets at my friend's house or cousin's house—but then I graduated to big things. Like money.

Theft can be an extreme reaction to feeling like you're never going to get out of debt. Have you ever been diagnosed with kleptomania? It's very rare, but given what you've been through, it could be in response to your trauma.

I've never been diagnosed with it. But I was arrested for stealing before.

And just like that, Maria was eighteen years old again. She remembered the moment the cops arrived, her hands clutching the money she'd swiped from the pawn shop. She could still smell the gasoline in the air, the intense heat of the sun, and the way her tank top had clung to her back. For a desperate moment, she had actually thought about running. It was only the fear of getting shot that stopped her.

Have you stolen anything lately?

Maria thought of the soap from Sissy's house that had sparked it all here. The twenty-dollar bills she took every few days from her cleaning agency. She told Kimberly everything. Well, except for her desire to keep that preschool money for herself. She couldn't bring herself to admit that yet.

It sounds like you steal as a response to acute stress. When you were at that preschool mom's house, she hurt you and made you feel like you'd never fit in there. Not only did that hurt you personally, but I'm sure it made you think of your hopes for your husband, too. You desperately want him to succeed in his job, and you feel like this woman holds the key. And with the cleaning business, you kept the money after thinking about how much debt you're in. You took advantage of the situation when your boss wasn't there to watch you put the money up.

Maria didn't know how to respond. She just watched the words appear on her phone's screen, knowing that every one of them was true.

That being said, you can't do anything about the soap, but you can give the money back.

Maria flinched, knowing that the therapist was right. She'd told herself the same thing.

The problem is, Maria responded, *I spent it already.*

Then you'll have to save a little at a time and give it back. It's the right thing to do, and it will save you from getting fired or worse.

You're right, Maria said, but every muscle in her body was tight. *This has helped me so much, but I have to finish dinner.*

I'm here if you want to talk about the argument with your husband more.

I appreciate that, Maria said, fingers twitching to end the session as soon as possible. She closed out of the app before the therapist could say anything else.

The fact was she needed that extra cash.

And if she had to steal to get it, then she would just have to make sure she didn't get caught.

SISSY

Sissy marched into the preschool with Mary Elizabeth
trailing behind her. Her heels echoed in the halls, and
aside from the usual high-pitched little kid voices and
parent chatter, there was something missing. It wasn't until
she saw Sarah Anne holding court just outside the K4 classroom that she realized what it was.

No one had spoken to her, or even looked in her
direction.

She kept her head held high like it didn't bother her
because it didn't. She wasn't a child. She didn't need
constant validation.

But as she watched the others hanging on Sarah Anne's
every word, something mean coiled in Sissy's heart.

She delivered Mary Elizabeth to her classroom with a
distracted hug and kiss. "Have a great day, sweetie."

"We're just so excited about your Christmas party,
Sarah Anne," one of the moms was saying. Sissy eaves-

dropped while she pretended to be watching Mary Elizabeth in the classroom.

"Even your invitation was gorgeous," another said.

Sissy stiffened. She hadn't received any invitations from Sarah Anne.

"Oh y'all are just too sweet," Sarah Anne said, and Sissy's lip curled. She could tell Sarah Anne was just eating this up.

When Sissy finally turned around, Sarah Anne was still surrounded by her admirers. It was like high school again. And Sissy hated high school.

"Sarah Anne," Sissy said, touching her arm with a tight smile. "Can I talk to you for a second?"

Sarah Anne was all bright smiles. "Of course. I'll see y'all later," she said to her admirers. Sissy took note of who they were—mostly the gym-obsessed moms. They'd be cut from the party guest list come May.

Sissy and Sarah Anne moved toward the double doors that led out into the courtyard.

"You know, I should have been the one tapping on your shoulder," Sarah Anne said, tossing her golden-kissed hair over her shoulder. "Now that I'm your vice-chairman, you'll probably want me to share your workload."

Sarah Anne had won the vote for vice-chairman unanimously, but only because Sissy hadn't been able to vote. Gabriella had recommended her as the perfect replacement, and the others had followed like lemmings. No one seemed to care that Sarah Anne had zero qualifications.

Sissy turned to Sarah Anne. "I just have to ask you: why are you suddenly so interested in the board? I've never seen you so much as do volunteer work for the school before."

Sarah Anne tilted her head to the side. "Honestly, Sissy,

it wouldn't have even occurred to me, except I had *so* many parents come up to me to say that I should take Gabriella's place." She put her hand on Sissy's arm, and Sissy had to resist the urge to jerk it away petulantly. "Just between you and me, a lot of mamas have told me you can be a little intimidating to approach, and they would rather have someone they can relate to better."

Sissy reared back like Sarah Anne had slapped her. She couldn't remember Sarah Anne ever being that blunt. "Funny how I've never heard that before, Sarah Anne, considering I've been at this school for seven years now."

Sarah Anne just shrugged. "I guess no one was brave enough to tell you."

"And you are?"

"Well, the truth isn't always nice, right?" she asked with a smirk that made it clear she was proud of throwing Sissy's own words against her. "I figure I owe it to you considering how long we've been friends."

Sissy wasn't sure if it was her imagination or not, but Sarah Anne seemed to have put a funny emphasis on the word "friends."

"Mm-hm. We've been friends a long time. What's this I hear about a Christmas party then?" Sissy asked with a faux-innocent note to her voice. She was hoping to take some of that hot air out of Sarah Anne's sails.

"I'm throwing a big Christmas party for everyone at the preschool and for Mercedes employees," Sarah Anne said with an overly sweet smile. "Didn't you get your invitation in the mail?"

"I must have missed it."

"Well, now, I'm sure I sent it out," Sarah Anne said, her voice full of concern that Sissy didn't believe for a second.

"As soon as I get home, I'll mail another, okay? That way we can both be sure."

Sissy nodded, but she knew Sarah Anne had no intention of doing that. She just didn't know why. "What made you want to throw a party this year?"

"I think I told you before that I'd been thinking about having one, especially for the Mercedes employees, but I thought it would be fun to invite preschool parents, too, since so many work at Mercedes." Before Sissy could respond, Sarah Anne added, "I know you weren't crazy about that idea. You probably didn't want J.D. to look bad, so I get it."

Sissy crossed her arms over her chest. "What do you mean by that?"

"Oh, just that he's an executive but never throws a Christmas party. I've just heard some people say it's strange."

"You've been hearing a lot of things, apparently," Sissy said. "I don't think you've ever been so well-informed in your life."

Sarah Anne smiled tightly and gave another little shrug. "I've just had a lot of people open up to me lately."

Something wasn't right with Sarah Anne, and it was clear she had a problem with Sissy.

Sissy just didn't know what it was.

———

Earlier in the week, Sissy's mama had called, and amidst a flurry of coughing she had asked Sissy to take her to a doctor's appointment. Sissy had been silent for a full ten seconds before answering. Loretta never asked her to take her anywhere. If she had to go to the doctor, Loretta got her own sister to take her. They only had one ancient car between the two of them.

Now Sissy watched with concern as her mama walked slowly to her car. She would have gotten out to help her, but Sissy knew her mama would only wave her away.

Slower than molasses, Loretta opened the car door and slid in.

"Why they gotta make these cars so high off the ground?" Mama demanded, puffing. "I need a stool to get in here."

"I like being able to see all the other cars," Sissy said with a shrug. "So where are we going, Mama? Dr. Coleman's?"

Dr. Coleman was the physician Loretta had always had, and was now pushing eighty-five years old. Her mama trusted his advice implicitly, but his readiness to prescribe everything from Xanax to opiates always made Sissy question his judgment.

"No, we're going to a doctor's office near the downtown hospital. It's on Cobb street. I'll show you when we get closer."

"You don't know what it's called? I can just put it in my phone for the directions."

Her mama averted her eyes and shook her head. "Just drive toward Cobb street like I said."

Sissy sighed and put the car in drive, but she felt a tremor of unease. The doctors' offices near the hospital were for more serious conditions, and her mama had breathing problems.

"Did Dr. Coleman give you a referral to this doctor?"

"Yes."

Sissy glanced at Loretta, who was looking out the window, still avoiding her gaze. "What's this about, Mama?"

Loretta finally looked at her. "See? This is why I don't have you drive me anywhere. Then I gotta put up with all your questions. Why can't we talk about something else?"

Sissy swallowed her frustration. She figured she was about to find out what was really going on anyway.

"All right, fine. As long as you let me come in and see the doctor with you."

Loretta waved her hand. "If that's what you want to do."

Sissy nodded. After a few minutes of silent driving, she said, "I forgot to tell you that I heard from Jackie the other day."

"And? What did she have to say?"

"She said Ashley had a warrant out for her arrest and that some bounty hunter could go and get her at any time from work."

Loretta grunted. "And you're surprised? That girl's been trouble since she was born. Wild. Never slept."

"I've been checking the news and arrest records, but I haven't seen anything."

Loretta gave her a look. "I'll just bet you have. Wouldn't want news getting out that she's your cousin."

Sissy almost nodded her head in agreement until her mama's tone registered. She thought of the text message she'd received of the entrance to Loretta's neighborhood, but she didn't want to bring it up. No point in letting Loretta know that a text like that was even a threat.

"It's more like I don't want her begging Jackie and me for money."

"I thought I raised you better than that, Sissy. You don't help your family now? Too good for us, huh?"

Sissy gave her a sharp look. "It's one thing to help someone who can't help themselves, Mama. Ashley brings this on herself, and I'm not going to spend the rest of my life bailing her out. Jackie shouldn't have to either."

"Seems to me, if you don't want to be embarrassed by your cousin getting arrested, then you should just pay off the money she owes."

Sissy's hands tightened on the wheel. It seemed like no matter how hard she worked to escape the trailer park, it always tried to drag her back. She was about to tell her just that when her mama had a coughing fit.

"You okay?" Sissy asked when it seemed like Loretta could hardly breathe.

"Turn here," she said in between hacking coughs.

Sissy did as she said, and then her mother pointed toward a set of brick buildings. "Park there in front of that one."

Sissy put the car in park and stared up at an ominous black sign that read Greenville Oncology.

"Oh, Mama," Sissy said, but Loretta was already struggling to get out of the car.

"We're going to be late, Sissy."

Sissy felt like she was in a dream as she followed Loretta into the building. The receptionist told them the doctor would meet with him in his office in just a few minutes.

"You've been here before," Sissy said as Loretta sat down heavily on one of the chairs in the waiting room. Sissy was too mad to sit, so she stood there hovering at her mother's side.

"Yeah, I have. I had an exam already."

Sissy closed her eyes for a moment, fighting the urge to shake her mama. "You didn't think I'd like to know you'd been referred to an oncologist? And why? What do they suspect?"

"You're making a scene, Sissy. People might figure out you're from a trailer park."

"Mama," Sissy hissed as she sat next to her, "this is serious."

"You'll find out soon enough."

She coughed again, and Sissy knew it was her lungs. And those damn cigarettes she smoked by the pack.

The doctor came to get them himself, a balding, middle-aged man with kind eyes. Sissy's mother got to her feet slowly when he called her name, and pulled her arm away when Sissy tried to assist her.

"I'm not an invalid yet," she snapped.

"It's good to see you again, Ms. Woods," the doctor said. "I'm Dr. Adams," he added to Sissy.

"Sissy Harrison. I'm her daughter."

He nodded. "I'm glad you could come today. Now if you'll both follow me, we'll talk in my office."

The doctor was quiet as he led them the short distance down the hall, and Sissy kept her hands folded. She wished Loretta would let her put her arm around her or something; she knew she looked cold and unfeeling to others.

Dr. Adams's office was tidy and dominated by a large wooden desk with an expensive-looking computer system and a bookcase of leather-bound books. There were three plush chairs in front of his desk, and the doctor held out his hand for them to sit.

"How have you been feeling, Ms. Woods?"

Loretta gave him a long look. "How do you think?"

Dr. Adams let out a soft chuckle and nodded. "I'm sure you've been anxious to hear the results of your tests, but I also didn't want you to feel like I'm trying to rush you. If you'd like for me to just jump right in, I can do that. That's perfectly understandable, and I would feel the same."

"Yes, let's not drag this out," Loretta said, and Sissy winced at her sharp tone. That was a sure sign her mama was more stressed about all this than she let on. She always got testy when she was worried.

"You have stage two lung cancer," he said, his gaze holding hers steadily. "There is a tumor present in your right lung, but the good news is, the cancer hasn't spread to your lymph nodes. I recommend surgical removal of the tumor as our first line of defense."

Sissy had known he would say her mama had cancer, but still, hearing those words come out of his mouth had her heart pounding in her ears.

Cancer. It was such a dirty word.

"Your doctor was smart to refer you right away," Dr. Adams continued. "Because we've caught the cancer relatively early, the tumor isn't big enough that it requires radiation to shrink it first. We can go right in and remove it."

"And then I'll be cancer-free?" Loretta asked.

He nodded. "The five-year prognosis for stage two lung cancer like yours is good. A little over 33 percent."

Loretta let out a hoarse-sounding laugh. "Doctor, I might not be great at math, but even I know those ain't good odds."

Sissy had to agree with her. A 33 percent chance her mother would still be alive in five years didn't seem to be favorable odds.

"It may not sound good, but remember, we doctors like

to be conservative in our numbers. We can't go around promising you that you'll have a 90 percent chance of still being alive in five years. Not when there's always a chance of relapse, but I will say that your case looks very optimistic."

"So you think her prognosis is actually better?" Sissy asked, glancing at Loretta's drawn face.

"I do, but you'll have to make some drastic changes to your lifestyle. No exposure to respiratory irritants, which most definitely includes smoking."

"Sounds about right," Loretta said with a cynical smile, "I get to live, but I can't have any fun."

"Smoking cigarettes is hardly fun," Sissy said. "It costs too much, makes a big mess, and most importantly, it gave you cancer."

Loretta scoffed. "You can't prove that."

Sissy held out her hand for backup from the doctor. "Do cigarettes cause cancer?"

"Undoubtedly, they do."

"But did they cause *my* cancer?" Loretta demanded.

Sissy rubbed her forehead.

The doctor gave her a hard look. "I can't say for sure, but they certainly didn't help your lungs."

Loretta tried to laugh triumphantly, but it turned into a hacking cough.

"The cough is because of the tumor, but also because of the cigarettes. We need your lungs as healthy and smoke-free as possible before surgery, so I will ask that you quit smoking beginning right now."

Loretta set her jaw in that way she did when she was turning obstinate. Sissy could see what her mama planned to do: go home and ignore the doctor's orders.

Dr. Adams continued on about preparing for the surgery, which would be scheduled as soon as possible. He also prescribed medication for her mother's cough.

Every time Sissy imagined Loretta returning to her own home, apprehension twisted her insides. Her mama couldn't be trusted to follow any of these directions. She was distrustful of medication in general, and Sissy knew that the chances of her going home and following Dr. Adams's directions were about as high as her five-year prognosis.

But how could she possibly come live with Sissy? Not only would they constantly butt heads, especially when it came to the doctor's orders, but there were so many other reasons she didn't want her mother living with her.

Not least of all because Sissy wouldn't be able to hide the truth about J.D.

It's not because I'm embarrassed of my mama, Sissy told herself firmly. *It's because we haven't ever been able to live together and get along.*

Her other option was to convince Loretta to move in with her sister, but she could almost guarantee that Aunt Billie Jean wouldn't be able to keep Loretta from doing exactly what she wanted to do.

Sissy knew it had to be her, and she hated herself for even hesitating to suggest it to her mother. This wasn't bronchitis, this was cancer.

Her mama would have to come live with them.

Even if it was the last thing in the world Sissy wanted.

20

THE PRESENT

I'm lost in my own tormented thoughts when some of the others announce they're going to the hospital. They want to be there to offer their support. And I'm struck by their egotism. Like anyone gives a shit about you and your offer of comfort when the person they love most in the world lies dying.

It hits me again: the silence of drowning. She was there swimming, and then she wasn't.

Her eyes, unseeing.

Her chest, unmoving.

"Are you coming with us?" they ask me, and I stare, wide-eyed and confused.

Who would want me there? Didn't they see what I did? That it was my fault?

They should be chasing me away with pitchforks, but they're not. Because they're a pack of self-centered idiots.

I want to scream the truth about everything I did, but then it occurs to me: maybe I *should* go to the hospital.

I have a confession to make.

21

LAUREN

L auren was home grading papers when the call came. Usually, she screened all her calls and refused to answer if it wasn't on her caller ID, but this time, she needed an excuse to put down her grading.

"Mrs. Williamson? This is the nurse at the Fertility Clinic of the Upstate. Is this a good time to talk?"

It took Lauren a moment, but then she responded. "Oh. Yes. Yes, I can talk now."

"We've tried to get in touch with your husband for the past week, but we've been unable to. You're on the contact list, though, so we're calling you about his results."

"Results?" Lauren repeated dumbly. She was shocked that Wesley had finally agreed to go.

"Yes, I have good news for you. We couldn't find any fertility problems with you, but we do need to talk about your husband's results."

"Okay, so why am I having miscarriages if there aren't any fertility problems? Why aren't I pregnant?"

"I understand your concerns, and the doctor would be happy to explain it all to you in person. She would like for you to come to the clinic to discuss her findings. Is there a time you and your husband can come?"

"He's out of town this weekend, but we could probably come on Monday."

"Great. Should I put you down for Monday morning then? We have an opening at ten."

"That works," Lauren said, because even if it didn't, she would *make* him go.

As soon as she hung up with the fertility clinic, she called Wesley. He didn't answer, but when she heard his voicemail, she hung up instead of leaving a message. Usually, she would try again later, but not this time.

She called again and again, until finally, he answered.

"Lauren, what's wrong? Did something happen to Emily?" he demanded, sounding short of breath. In the background, she could hear birds singing and other forest sounds.

"No, the fertility clinic called. They want us to go talk to the doctor on Monday morning."

He was silent for so long she pulled the phone away from her ear to look at the screen. Still connected.

"Wesley?"

"You couldn't tell me this when I get back Sunday?" His tone was clipped, and she could imagine his nostrils flaring.

"What? Did I scare away the deer or something? This is important, Wesley! I just want to make sure you didn't have a meeting or something on Monday."

"I can make the appointment Monday," he said brusquely.

She opened her mouth to answer, but in the brief pause of conversation, she concentrated on the background noises.

Suddenly, she realized the sounds she heard—the ones she'd originally written off as bird calls—were actually the din of voices and faint music.

She felt like she'd been doused in ice water. "Where are you?"

There was a muffled-scrambling sound like he was covering the microphone while moving away. When his voice returned, the background noises had disappeared.

"Out hunting. I told you that."

"It didn't sound like hunting—I thought I heard voices in the background. And music."

Her heart was pounding with her suspicions.

"Oh, you just heard Henry and Will. We're sharing a deer blind."

There was something about his tone that just didn't sound right. She felt like her hackles were raised, and he wasn't an easy man to believe. She decided to use the situation to her advantage.

"So you'll come to the clinic with me?"

"Yes, I'll be there."

"Well, have fun *hunting*," she said, unable to keep the sarcastic note from her voice.

"Thanks, honey," he said distractedly. "Love you."

"You too," she mumbled before hanging up.

It only took a second to open Instagram and find Tiffany's account. It was at the top of Lauren's most searched for accounts.

The top post was of a lodge tucked into the mountains. Lauren immediately recognized the place and grimaced. It was a resort in the Appalachians that she and Wesley had been to many times. She loved the spa there, and he loved the hiking opportunities and rustic decor.

Lauren skimmed the hashtags, heart sinking with each one.

#vacationtime #longweekend #mybooandme

Her lip curled at the stupidity of the tags, especially the last one, while at the same time, each one seemed to drive a shard of ice into her chest.

She didn't have to see pictures of the two of them to know what was going on. A part of her wanted to drive up there and confront them, but the other part knew she needed to hear from the fertility doctor first.

Her period hadn't started yet. There was still a chance she was pregnant.

Lauren switched her phone off and climbed the stairs slowly. Her heart pounded so hard her chest shook, and her hands opened and closed into fists. She walked into their closet, and from above Wesley's dress shirts and ties, she retrieved a navy blue binder. Inside was his collection of baseball cards handed down from his father.

Lauren carried the binder downstairs with her, and on her way out to the backyard, she grabbed lighter fluid and a lighter. When she came to the old metal barrel they burned leaves in, she pulled out every baseball card save one and dumped it in. After a generous dose of lighter fluid, she lit the final card—a Mickey Mantle—and tossed it in. She watched for a few moments while they burned before carrying the binder inside, putting it into a black garbage bag, and adding it to their trash can outside.

157

———

Her period started that night. She stared at the tell-tale red, and after going through the motions of putting in a tampon, the sobs came fast and hard.

No one was there to see her fall apart, so she did—spectacularly. She fell on the bed and wailed, arms wrapped around her middle. Emily was already fast asleep, and she was a hard sleeper.

She thought of Wesley and his secretary at the lodge in the mountains, and her sobs turned to a flinty rage. She wanted to drive up there now and catch them in the act, humiliate both of them. Let Wesley know that she knew he wasn't on a hunting trip.

There was no point to sparing his feelings now.

Lauren imagined herself getting in her car and heading up 26 to Asheville. She would go to the lodge and march past all the things that reminded her of romantic stays with Wesley: leather furniture, warm lighting, roaring fires. She would convince the receptionist to give her Wesley's room number.

Her hand tightened on an object that dug into her palm. She glanced down at it and realized it was her key fob. Somehow, she'd gone all the way downstairs and grabbed her bag.

Her heart pounded, but she felt strangely detached, like she was wading through a dream.

I could be there and back before it's too late, she thought. And before she could stop to think more, she walked into garage.

At some point, she must have turned on the car, opened the garage door and backed out, but she didn't come to her senses until she was miles from home. Her phone had automatically connected to her car's Bluetooth, and suddenly, a call was coming through.

Completely on autopilot, Lauren pressed the button to answer.

"Lauren, you will not believe the conversation I had with Sissy today," Sarah Anne said in a rush, her voice coming through the Bluetooth perfectly. "I didn't know I had it in me to act that cold, but I just knew I had to give it back to her like she does everyone else."

Lauren heard Sarah Anne, but she couldn't process what she said. She could only think of Wesley and Tiffany in their hotel room, her hands on his body. Her seeing the birthmark he had just above his hip. Their bodies writhing together on the sheets.

"Can you hear me?" Sarah Anne asked, sounding puzzled. "Lauren?"

Awareness came back to Lauren in a rush, and she gasped. "Oh Jesus help me," she said.

"What? What's wrong?" Sarah Anne asked in increasingly worried tones.

Lauren pulled the car to a stop and bent over the wheel, breathing hard.

"Where are you?"

Lauren looked around the car, feeling the color drain from her face when she didn't immediately recognize the area.

"I don't know," she said, voice wavering.

"What do you mean? You're not at home?"

"No," Lauren said, and then she recognized the street she was on. She was about thirty minutes from her house.

Lauren let out a low moan. "Oh, Lord. Oh, Sarah Anne…"

"You have to tell me what's going on! I'm about to lose my mind over here."

"I think I already have," Lauren said in a panicky voice. "I-I just got in my car and drove."

"Well, that's not so bad, honey. I've done that before."

And that's when Lauren realized just *why* it was so horrifying that she'd left in the night.

"Oh God—Emily!"

Lauren put the car in drive and executed a dangerous U-turn without really making sure it was clear first. Other drivers honked angrily.

"Emily? What's wrong with Emily? Is she there, too?"

"No, I left her home—asleep."

Sarah Anne started to interrupt her with another placating remark, but Lauren didn't let her finish.

"*Alone*, Sarah Anne."

"Oh. *Oh.* How far are you from home?"

"Thirty minutes," Lauren said thickly. The tears had started again, swelling her tongue.

Lauren thought of Sarah Anne's home, only ten minutes away from her own. "I know this is a lot to ask, but is there any way you can go by and check on her? You're closer, and I would feel so much better knowing she was okay before I get there."

"You know I would do that in a heartbeat, but I'm not at home either. I'm on the other side of town."

Frustration rose so quickly inside of Lauren that it cramped her stomach. She could just guess where Sarah Anne was. She didn't ask because she didn't want to hear her excuses.

I can't check on your little girl because I'm sleeping with our kids'
pediatrician.

"I'm so sorry, Lauren," Sarah Anne continued, and
Lauren managed to mutter some sort of acknowledgment.
"Is there a neighbor you can call?"

"No. And let them know I left my own baby at home?
It's bad enough you know!"

"Now, don't worry about me. I know you've been under
a lot of stress lately, and it can be hard to make a rational
decision when you're hurting. Plus, I'm sure Emily's asleep,
right?"

"I hope so," Lauren whispered.

Lauren's hands were gripped so tightly on the steering
wheel that they hurt. Her anger was boiling over—at
herself, at Sarah Anne's attempts to calm her. What kind of
a mother was Sarah Anne that she was excusing such
behavior anyway? There was no reason that made it okay
for Lauren to have left Emily alone. What if Emily woke up
from a bad dream and couldn't find her? What if Emily
suddenly got sick and needed her? By the time she got back
home, she would have been gone over an hour. Plenty of
time for anything to happen.

Lauren's teeth chattered like she'd been out in the
freezing cold, but it was still warm in the car.

"Call me and let me know, okay?" Sarah Anne was
saying.

Sarah Anne probably wanted to get back to Hampton,
Lauren thought, running a red light and weaving through
the light traffic.

"All right," Lauren said.

"It'll be fine, honey. You'll see."

But Lauren knew she was just saying that to make herself feel better for wanting to hang up.

"Yeah, thanks a lot," Lauren said aloud when the phone call ended.

As she drove, her mind tortured her with what-if scenarios:

Emily had once tripped on the top step of their staircase and nearly tumbled the whole way down. What if she was lying dead at the bottom of the stairs with a broken neck?

Emily sometimes had bad dreams and would crawl into bed with them. What if she woke up, afraid and sobbing for her mother?

What if Emily was not in the house at all because she went looking for Lauren? What if she got lost in the dark?

She drove faster, barely pausing at stop signs, and it was a miracle that she didn't pass any cops. When she finally arrived home, she nearly scraped the roof of the car by not waiting on the garage door to fully open.

Lauren flew into the house and raced up the stairs. Her heart pounded in her ears so loudly she could hear nothing else.

When she got to Emily's door, she wanted to burst through it, but she checked herself at the last second. Slowly, she pushed it open.

Lauren sank to her knees with a muffled sob, all the breath escaping her in a rush. Emily was still fast asleep, curled on her side around her bunny. Lauren padded over to her and touched her soft cheek.

The sobs were bubbling up inside her again, so she backed out of her room and closed the door. Once she was in the quiet of her own bathroom, she gave into the need to cry, avoiding her face in the mirror because she was an ugly crier.

Emily was safe and sound in her bed despite the fact that she'd been left home alone for an entire hour. But even knowing she was safe didn't keep Lauren's mind from continuing to torture her with what could have been.

Lauren knew she'd lost her grip on herself tonight, but very quickly, her disgust at her own behavior turned outward. She thought of Wesley and Tiffany, completely carefree at the mountain lodge. They would get away with this little vacation—again—because Lauren hadn't been able to confront them. And until she met with the fertility doctor, she wouldn't.

It was enough to make her lose her mind.

22

SARAH ANNE

Sarah Anne tried not to be judgmental of her friends, but as she vacuumed her living room rug, she thought about Lauren leaving Emily in the middle of the night. Lauren hadn't called Sarah Anne like she said she would, so Sarah Anne had texted later that night to be sure everything was okay. She was proud of herself for remembering. Lauren hadn't answered her until an hour later, though, and all she said was, "She's fine."

It felt incredibly disloyal, but Sarah Anne had to agree with Sissy. Lauren was so obsessed with getting pregnant and having another baby that she didn't even appreciate the baby girl she already had! Not like Sarah Anne. She appreciated her babies every day. Hell, she was even up before them every morning, making pancakes and fruit.

Sarah Anne would have thought that Wesley's affair would be enough for Lauren to worry about, but clearly it wasn't. Lauren had texted Sarah Anne that morning and said she wanted to meet up to talk about what the fertility doctor told her. What was she even doing talking to a fertility doctor when her husband was sleeping with someone else? It was like that picture of Wesley kissing his secretary hadn't even mattered to her.

If Sarah Anne put herself in Lauren's shoes, there was no way in hell she'd think about having a baby with her husband if he was having an affair. She felt justified in saying this because *she* was the one sleeping around, and she would have thought Mark was nuts if he knew about it but still wanted to have another baby.

Sarah Anne glanced over at her phone with a grimace. The direction of her thoughts had reminded her of seeing Hampton at the game the other week. She'd managed to ignore his texts for an entire three days, but then she'd given in again when he practically cornered her at the preschool.

"I can't stop thinking about you," he'd whispered in her ear. "If I promise never to golf with Mark again will you answer my texts? You make me feel like a teenager—it's embarrassing. I'm a doctor for God's sake."

She'd laughed and then he knew he had her because she was weak-willed and pathetic. She'd always been like this with men. It was a miracle she was with someone like Mark, who was honestly too good for her. All her life, Sarah Anne had craved attention from men. Her daddy traveled all the time for business, and when he was home, he acted like the only one he had time for was Sarah Anne's brother. He went to all his games, but he never went to Sarah Anne's dance recitals or cheerleading competitions. No matter what she did, it was never enough to make her daddy pay attention.

But when she got to high school, she turned the heads

of all the boys. She was fun, blonde, and fit from cheerleading, and it seemed like every boy from the band geeks to the athletes wanted to date her.

So she did. She dated them all. Anyone who asked. Or she slept with them, and let their horny teenaged compliments fill up her self-esteem.

She'd never outgrown that need for attention either. She just got it from other moms, friends, and anyone who told her she was beautiful and fun and the *best mom ever*.

But she knew she was taking it too far with this affair.

All she had to do was tell Hampton it was over and that she didn't want to jeopardize her marriage, but she couldn't even do that. Last night, she'd forgotten to turn off her phone before bed, and Hampton's buzzing texts had caused Mark to turn over and ask her who was blowing up her phone.

It felt like having ice water poured over her spine, but she'd managed not to jump. "Oh, just a group text for the preschool board. These women are always panicking about something," she said with a laugh she hoped sounded natural and not unhinged.

He'd accepted it, though, rolling over with a nod and a laugh.

Sarah Anne had immediately turned her phone off, cursing her own stupidity.

She couldn't handle analyzing her own mistakes, so she chose to focus on Lauren's instead. Lauren's impending visit was the reason Sarah Anne was vacuuming. Normally, she detested the chore and was content to wait until her house cleaner came every week to do it for her. But Lauren had once said, "It's so pathetic when a stay-at-home mom has a dirty house. Are you so lazy that you can't even keep it clean when your kids are at school?"

Sarah Anne had smiled and laughed along with her at the time, but all the while, she'd felt secretly judged. She kept her house picked up, sure, and cleaned the kitchen, but she sure as hell didn't vacuum and dust regularly. Lord, she couldn't even remember the last time she mopped. Maybe a year ago? Two?

Lauren could be judgmental, was the point, and Sarah Anne didn't like to be found wanting.

When the doorbell finally rang, Sarah Anne was confident her house was pristine. *Let her make a comment about housekeeping* now, she thought. *I'll just not-so-subtly ask about the night she left Emily alone.*

But when she opened the door, she had a wide, welcoming smile in place. "Hey there! Come on in." She gave Lauren a one-armed hug and led her into the foyer.

Lauren was well-dressed as always in a cable knit sweater and dark skinny jeans, but even her concealer hadn't been able to hide the shadows under her eyes completely.

"Come sit," Sarah Anne said. "You look tired."

"Just stressed, I think," Lauren said, but she let herself be led to Sarah Anne's leather sectional.

"Coffee? Water?"

Lauren shook her head. "No, thank you. I think I'm still in shock from what the fertility doctor told me."

"Oh no," Sarah Anne said, eyes wide. "What?"

"She said that I don't have fertility problems. That, actually, my eggs look fantastic and so do the rest of my reproductive organs."

"Then why have you been having miscarriages? I hope she didn't just say she didn't know. That's so frustrating."

"No, she didn't say that. She does know. She said it's because of Wesley."

Sarah Anne's eyebrows shot up toward her hairline. "Wesley! What do you mean?"

"The doctor said he has this rare condition where over 50 percent of his sperm have unviable genetic material, so most of the time if his sperm fertilizes an egg, it won't give the right genes. Apparently, that means that the fertilized egg can never become a baby, but it takes my body a little while to realize that. So I get a positive pregnancy test at first, and then it ends in a miscarriage."

Sarah Anne shook her head. "I had no idea that men could be the cause of miscarriage!"

"I didn't either. And the doctor said it was kind of a miracle that I had a baby at all."

Lauren looked more than a little disturbed by the realization, but Sarah Anne couldn't help but think, *That's what we've all been trying to tell you.*

"It just made me think, 'If I had only married another man, then I would have another baby by now.'"

"Yes, but you also wouldn't have Emily," Sarah Anne said.

"That's true," Lauren conceded. "But it just makes me think of the future—like what the point of even being married to Wesley is."

Sarah Anne stiffened. It made her think of what she and Hampton were doing and what if Mark found out and said the same thing? She had a terrible moment where she wanted to make up an excuse to get Lauren to leave because she didn't think she could listen to this anymore.

"He's a good dad to Emily, though, right?" she asked instead because she hoped someone would say the same about her.

Sarah Anne is a fantastic mother, though, right?

"When he's around," Lauren said with such derision that Sarah Anne could see—just for a moment—how much the affair was torturing her.

"Have you asked him about his slutty secretary?"

Lauren shook her head. "Not yet. I just…haven't found the right time. But now that I hear this—that we're so incompatible that his body actually causes mine to miscarry —I probably will soon."

Sarah Anne watched anger ripple over Lauren's body, tightening her muscles and hardening her face. It made her look older, and Sarah Anne could see how this was eating away at her.

"Maybe I can divorce him now and find someone else before I get too old to have another baby," she said with a bitter smile.

"Lord, don't say that," Sarah Anne said with a nervous laugh. She couldn't quite tell if Lauren was being serious or not, but this was the last thing she wanted to talk about. It made her imagine a horrible scenario where Mark said he wanted to divorce Sarah Anne. "Surely y'all can work things out if you just talk it over."

Lauren fixed her with an eagle-eyed look. "Do you think you'll ever tell Mark what happened with Hampton?"

Sarah Anne glanced away, and she knew it made her look guilty. "I wouldn't want to upset Mark like that. In fact, I've decided not to invite Hampton to the Christmas party. I just don't think I can bear the stress of it."

"Won't he hear other parents talking about it?"

"He doesn't really pay attention to preschool gossip, so I doubt it. He tries to get in and out of the school fast because everyone knows he's a pediatrician and there are a bunch of moms who take advantage of that. The other day, I saw Kristie corner him and make him listen to her little boy cough."

"It's hard to pass up the chance for free medical care," Lauren said with a flippant wave of her hand. "So things are totally over with you and Hampton?"

Sarah Anne did what she always did when she didn't want to answer a question. Channeled her inner politician. "I just couldn't risk Mark finding out."

Lauren narrowed her eyes for a second like she wasn't buying it, but then she nodded. "How has it been going as vice chairman?"

Sarah Anne drooped. "Exhausting. These women are obsessive. They have me in this horrible group text message chain, and they rarely shut up." She glanced down at her phone. "In fact, I'm surprised we haven't heard my phone go off a million times since you got here. That's a small miracle."

"What do they talk about?"

"They just worry constantly about the perception of the preschool—like, is it getting enough social media attention to attract more families? Does everything about the school look well-maintained? Should we replace the rubber mulch on the playground?"

Lauren shook her head. "What about Sissy? I can't see her texting constantly."

"She actually did at first—just barking out orders, mostly—but now, I haven't heard from her in a while. I don't know what's going on with her."

"Probably busy stalking us to send more threatening texts," Lauren said with surprising venom. "Has she said anything to you that would make you think she's the one behind the texts?"

"She was pretty unhappy about me becoming vice chairman. For the longest time, she didn't add me to the group text. One of the other mamas kept talking about the rubber mulch on the playground, and she asked me what I thought. I told her I hadn't heard anything about it, and she said, 'We've been talking about it in the group text! Didn't Sissy add you?' Now I feel like she was doing me a favor by not adding me, so I don't know."

Sarah Anne was about to ask Lauren if she'd had any more threatening texts, but suddenly, she didn't want to know. It was as if speaking about it would bring it into being.

"That sounds pretty typical of her. She wants you to feel left out."

"She's the queen of that, for sure." Sarah Anne stood from the couch and stretched. "I'm going to go make some coffee. Are you sure you don't want anything?"

"Maybe a small cup if you're making it anyway."

Lauren followed Sarah Anne into the kitchen that was her pride and joy. Spotless white cabinets, white granite countertops, stainless steel appliances that were a pain in the rear to keep clean, and slate gray floors. Sarah Anne had a moderate interest in cooking and a considerable interest in having a magazine-cover-worthy kitchen.

"Have you stopped going to your favorite coffee shop?" Lauren asked, and though her expression was innocent, Sarah Anne couldn't help but bristle. Lauren knew good and well that's the place she went to with Hampton.

Sarah Anne shrugged one shoulder as she put the espresso pod into the machine. "Oh, you know. I go every now and then. Cheaper to use this at home, though."

"What can I do to help you with this Christmas party coming up?"

Sarah Anne waved away her offer. "You are too sweet, but I have it all covered. I decided to have it catered because it's too much trouble to try and prepare enough food for everyone. I'll probably have my cleaning lady come that morning, too." She laughed. "I pretty much just like to show up to my own party."

"Your parties are a lot more fun than Sissy's," Lauren said as Sarah Anne retrieved two coffee mugs with cheerful birds on them. "Everyone always seems to relax and actually talk to each other instead of fighting to talk to Sissy."

"Well, that's because everyone tends to drink more at my parties," Sarah Anne said with a laugh. "This party is already throwing Sissy over the edge, though. I could tell she was confused and more than a little aggravated that I hadn't sent her an invitation."

Lauren's eyebrows rose. "You didn't invite her? I thought that was the whole point! To get under her skin."

"I know, I know," Sarah Anne said with a groan. "I screwed up is what happened. I was just so mad at her about the text messages that I didn't even want her in my house. Now that some time has passed, I've calmed down a bit, but I didn't feel right sending the invitation out now."

Sarah Anne handed Lauren a cup of coffee, and as she retrieved some half and half from the fridge, the doorbell rang.

"That must be a delivery," Sarah Anne said over her shoulder as she walked back into the foyer.

Lauren followed after adding a splash of half and half to her cup.

When Sarah Anne opened the door, her back stiffened. "What are you doing here?"

Hampton grinned. "You didn't answer about coffee, so I thought I'd bring it to you." He held out a to-go cup of coffee and a brown paper bag that she already knew contained a cinnamon roll for her and a sprouted, gluten-free bagel for him.

"Well, I have company," Sarah Anne said in a hiss.

Lauren stepped closer to the door and waved. "Hi, Hampton." She took a sip of her coffee, unabashedly staring at the scene before her. Sarah Anne felt her blood pressure rise. Now Lauren would know she was lying about not seeing Hampton anymore.

"Hey, Lauren," Hampton said, without missing a beat. "If I'd known you were going to be here, I would have brought an extra coffee." He glanced at the mug in her hand. "Though looks like y'all have already made some."

"Well that's because we didn't know you'd come by," Sarah Anne said tightly.

"I just wanted to talk to you about that donation for the preschool my colleagues and I got together," Hampton said, and Sarah Anne was grudgingly impressed by his smooth lie. It would have been perfect, even, if Lauren didn't already know about the affair.

"I don't want to interrupt, though," he added. "I'll just call you about it later, okay?" He held up the brown paper bag again. "There's even a cinnamon roll that y'all can split."

"Thank you for this," Sarah Anne said, taking the proffered bag. "We'll talk later."

Normally, if it was anyone else, she would have insisted he come in anyway. She would have been smiling and charming. But right now, all she could think was, *Get out before Lauren sees you flirt with me.*

"Thanks for the treat!" Lauren called as Sarah Anne more or less shut the door in his face.

"It's so awkward to see him now, but at least we scored a cinnamon roll! Their cinnamon rolls really are the best," Sarah Anne tried to say breezily as she headed back toward the kitchen, clutching the bag.

"Was he really coming to talk about a donation?" Lauren asked, putting down her coffee mug to give Sarah Anne a pointed look.

"That's what he said."

Lauren huffed and crossed her arms. "I can't believe you're still doing this, Sarah Anne. I thought we were friends."

"We are! Of course we are."

"Well, you haven't even told me the truth. And, worse than that, you *know* what I've been going through with Wesley!"

"Honey, I know. And I feel awful for you about Wesley. But I don't see what that has to do with my own mistakes."

"Because it just makes me think about Wesley running around on me. Because I wanted to come here and escape it for just a minute. Because I think about you, happy with Hampton, having these little clandestine meetings, and it makes me wonder what Wesley and his slutty secretary are doing."

Sarah Anne could feel that her cheeks were flaming. She wasn't embarrassed, but she'd never been able to

THE LIES BETWEEN US

tolerate being scolded. "It's not the same at all. With Hampton, I mean."

Lauren laughed, but the sound was bitter. "Yeah? How?"

"It's not going to last, I mean. I swear I didn't even realize he was coming by. He's never been to my house before."

Lauren shook her head, and there were tears shimmering in her eyes. "Not going to last...so you're saying Wesley and Tiffany will?"

Sarah Anne's eyes widened, and she reached out to touch Lauren's arm. "No, that's not what I meant at all. I don't even know what I was trying to say, other than whatever it is Hampton and I are doing is different." She winced as soon as the words left her mouth, knowing it still wasn't the right thing to say.

Lauren nodded, arms clutched tightly around herself as the tears began to fall. "I don't even know why I care. He can't even give me what I want! And he killed my babies."

Sarah Anne leaned back at the vehemence in her voice. "The miscarriages, you mean? I'm sure they were hard on him, too."

"All I've ever wanted was a brother or sister for Emily so she didn't have to be alone like me. Do you know what it was like when first my dad and then my mom died? I had no one who knew them like I did. No one to turn to. Now I don't even have Wesley."

Her voice broke, and Sarah Anne stepped toward her, but Lauren just held up her hand.

"I should go."

"You can't leave when you're this upset! Stay, we'll talk or have a cinnamon roll."

"I don't want a cinnamon roll!" Lauren practically shouted. She grabbed her bag and keys while Sarah Anne stood momentarily stunned.

"I'm so sorry, Lauren," Sarah Anne said as she followed her to the door. "I know you're upset with me, but I really don't think you should be alone."

Lauren snorted before angrily swiping away her tears and yanking open the door. "I've always been alone."

Sarah Anne watched her hurry out to her car as her stomach churned. She knew she should have tried harder to stop her, but there was this horrible, selfish part of her that also wanted Lauren to leave. As a rule, Sarah Anne didn't like to spend too much time feeling guilty about something, and it seemed like that was Lauren's main goal.

A dark feeling rose inside Sarah Anne, alongside the pity she felt for her friend. *How dare she scold me like that?*

But Sarah Anne knew she wasn't being fair to Lauren. She'd never seen her so upset about something—not even her miscarriages.

23

MARIA

The day of Sarah Anne's Christmas party, Maria spent an hour on a panicky online chat with her therapist.

I stole from work again today, Maria typed. She didn't tell her therapist the rest of it—that she still had $200 of the preschool parents' money in her wallet.

There was a long pause, and then her therapist said, *Did you give the original amount back?*

Maria's stomach knotted. *No.*

What made you steal again today? What thoughts led to that decision?

Maria thought for a moment. What *had* she been thinking? *I just feel like our debt is this weight on top of me that I'll never get rid of. It makes my chest feel tight. Our bank account is also getting low again.*

It sounds like you felt desperate and panicky.

Maria's heart fluttered in response. *Yes.*

How much have you taken so far?

Only $100, Maria lied. The real amount was closer to $300, and they seemed to be burning through it no matter how much she added to the bank account. She kept the preschool parents' money in her wallet in case of an emergency, but there was no way she was going to admit that to her therapist.

You need to give the money back, Maria. Your problems will only get worse if you get caught. You don't want to lose your job or have your boss press charges against you. I know it's scary to hear, but I feel like it's my duty to encourage you to return it.

I understand. I have a job there today, actually, so I can do it then.

They'd discussed a few other things, and while she was talking to her therapist, Maria had every intention of returning the money. Even if it made her account negative. Her therapist was right: how could she risk her job, or worse, getting arrested for stealing?

Later, she told herself that as she vacuumed and dusted her elderly customer's house with all its many knick-knacks. She hated the house because of all the breakables that had to be carefully dusted around, but a fluffy long-haired cat that followed her like a dog almost made it worth it.

She scratched his head when he leapt up on the couch and meowed at her plaintively.

"You're going to have to move so I can clean these cushions," she told him, lifting him gently off the couch.

Once he was on the floor again, he circled her legs until he saw her bring the vacuum over. He wasn't a fan of the noise, so he scampered off for Mrs. Coffey's bedroom.

When Maria got to the third couch cushion, she paused. Shoved deep inside the couch was a twenty-dollar bill. She pulled it free and placed it in her pocket for safekeeping. Before she left, she'd leave it on the kitchen counter with a note for Mrs. Coffey.

Maria finished her scrubbing and cleaning and gave the gray long-haired cat a scratch before leaving. She gathered up Mrs. Coffey's check, and then remembered the twenty dollar bill in her pocket. With her brows knitted, she pulled it out and looked at the money that would mean so little to Mrs. Coffey.

She thought of the bills that never stopped coming and the preschool tuition that was due. She looked around at the house with its high-end appliances, leather furniture, and five bedrooms when Mrs. Coffey was the only one who lived here.

Tears stung Maria's eyes, and she crumpled the bill in her hand. She hated herself in this moment. Hated her weakness and her constant need for money.

A little jingle of a bell announced the cat's return, and he jumped up on the kitchen counter to be able to see Maria better. He watched her for a moment as tears spilled down her cheeks, and then he bumped his head against her arm. She scooped him up and hugged him close, crying into his soft fur. He purred like he loved every second, though she knew she was hanging onto him for dear life.

"I don't know why you even like me," she told him through her tears. "I ruin everything."

But he continued to purr like he didn't care just so long as she kept petting him.

After a few minutes, Maria put him back down on the floor, where he meowed a protest. She put the twenty dollars on the counter and retrieved a piece of paper from her bag. She scribbled a note to Mrs. Coffey about finding it in her couch cushions and then raced out of the house before that evil side of her convinced her to do otherwise.

She thought of that cat the whole way back to the cleaning headquarters and tried to hold onto the strength he'd given her. Did it mean she was crazy if the cat had given her more comfort than her talk with her therapist this morning?

I'm adopting a cat this weekend, she promised herself, even as she knew James would never let her. They needed the additional food and vet expenses like a hole in the head, but if a cat could provide free therapy, then wasn't it worth it?

She was still thinking about the warm comfort she'd received from Mrs. Coffey's cat when she turned in the payments. Her promise to her therapist echoed in her mind, but she thought of her depleted bank account. She didn't have an extra $300. She didn't even have an extra fifty dollars.

At least I'm not taking more now, Maria thought. *I'll save up and pay them back, and they'll never know it was missing.*

But then Maria thought of their mountain of debt and the bills that never stopped. She thought of James's paycheck that came every two weeks, but by the time payday rolled around again, they were broke.

She knew she could make all the promises in the world, but she wasn't going to pay back that money unless she was forced to.

She just prayed it didn't come to that.

———

Later that night, Maria had pushed all thoughts of debt and theft from her mind as she got ready for the Christmas party. She added red lipstick to go with her red cocktail dress that made her breasts and hips look fantastic. She had her playlist blasting as loud as she dared with Ariana asleep just down the hall, but music while getting ready always made her feel like a teenager again.

She heard James's heavy footsteps as he came into the room. "That a new dress?" he asked.

Maria glanced at him in the mirror. "I've had this forever," she said in a prickly tone.

He held up his hands in peace. "I was just asking. You look gorgeous."

He bent down and kissed the sensitive skin between her neck and the curve of her shoulder, and some of her tension relaxed.

"You don't look so bad yourself," she said, admiring his navy blazer and dark pants that showed off his muscular build. She knew none of the other dads at the preschool looked like James, which always made her feel bizarrely proud. Like she should be congratulated for marrying a hotter man than them.

"I have some good news to tell you."

Her gaze leaped to his in the mirror, and then she turned toward him. "What?"

"There's an opening at work for a corporate position that I qualify for. It would be a big promotion if I got the job."

"That's incredible! Have you applied yet?"

He laughed. "No, I just heard about it today."

"So whose ass do you have to kiss to get the job?"

"Well, J.D. Harrison has the final say on every hiring, but I think the person directly responsible is Mark Campbell."

"J.D. Harrison...that's Sissy's husband, right?" Maria asked with a frown.

"Yes, but Mark Campbell is Sarah Anne's husband, so maybe you could put it in a good word." He waggled his dark eyebrows at her, and she smiled.

"You know I will. Let me just finish getting ready, and then I'll be right down."

He nodded. "I pointed out all the controllers for the babysitter, so I think she's good to go."

As soon as James left the room, Maria pulled the top of her dress down enough to remove her bra. Then she went into her closet and fished out the one that pushed her cleavage so high it practically choked her.

She had a feeling an eyeful of breasts would come in handy tonight.

———

As James found a place to park on the long, circular driveway, Maria drank in the sight of Sarah Anne's house. It was surrounded by mature trees and thick bushes, and the large brick house was brightly lit with outdoor lights. The house had two porches on either side of the brick walkway that led to the front door, and Maria couldn't help but feel like the icicle string lights she and James put up on their own house looked tacky compared to the elegantly-lit wreaths above every window. As they got closer, Maria took in the enormous wreath on the front door, adorned with red birds and berries. Everything about the house shouted tasteful wealth, and Maria's stomach clenched with how badly she wanted one just like it.

She held onto James's arm as he rang the doorbell, fixing a smile on her face when she saw through the window that Sarah Anne was coming.

"Hey, y'all!" Sarah Anne said when she opened the door, a wide smile on her face. "Come on in." She was wearing a stunning emerald green cocktail dress with long, flowing sleeves that tapered at her wrists. The dress had a plunging neckline that bared her perpetually tan chest, but somehow, it looked classy and elegant.

She led them into a gray and white kitchen with shiny, stainless steel appliances that would be absolute hell to keep clean. Her pointy black heels rang out on the slate floors.

"Say hello to Maria and James, everyone," she said to the many couples gathered around the huge spread of food on the island.

There was a chorus of hellos, and Maria and James smiled and waved back.

"Let me get y'all drinks," Sarah Anne said, her arm sweeping out toward a well-stocked bar area with glittering crystal glasses. "No matter what you dream up, we've got you covered. Mark, honey, we have newcomers who don't have drinks in their hands!"

A handsome, trim man dressed in dark slacks and what looked like a cashmere sweater turned to them with a bright smile. He had lighter, wavy hair and with his touch of facial hair and laugh lines by his eyes, he looked slightly older than Sarah Anne. Still, they made a beautiful couple. Maria found herself comparing him to Hampton and thought that Mark had quieter handsome features, maybe, but his smile seemed more genuine.

"We can't have that," Mark said. "What would y'all like?"

Maria glanced at James, unsure what he would say. He drank beer, and that was about it. She'd grown up with red wine, but these seemed like cocktail sort of people. She had no idea what to say.

Sarah Anne put her arm around Maria. "You're like me, I bet. If there are too many choices, you get overwhelmed. Want Mark to just make you his specialty? It's delicious, I promise."

Maria nodded with a little sigh of relief. "That sounds great."

"Sure," Mark said. "And what about you, James?"

"I'll have the same," he said.

"Y'all are doing me a favor," Mark said over his shoulder as he moved toward the bar. "Any excuse to showcase my skills."

Sarah Anne smiled. "Mark was a bartender in college, and he still likes to reminisce."

Mark handed them both drinks with the strong smell of whiskey tempered by ginger, lime, and club soda. Maria wasn't a huge fan of whiskey, but when she took a hesitant sip, all she could taste was the ginger and lime.

"This is really good," she told Mark truthfully.

He beamed at her. "Glad you like it."

James made a noise of agreement, and Maria wanted to dig her elbow into his side. Would it kill him to show a little more enthusiasm? This was the man who could give him a promotion, after all!

She needed to enlist Sarah Anne's help with this, but there were so many people in the kitchen, she wasn't sure how to get her alone.

"Your house is beautiful," she told Sarah Anne. "I love the wreaths outside."

"Thank you! Did you see the tree? Mark insists on getting the biggest one that will fit inside the house every year."

"No, but I'd love to see it."

"Come on then," Sarah Anne said, beckoning her through the doorway to the living room. There in front of the bay windows was a tree that nearly touched the soaring ceiling above it. It was decorated beautifully in gold and red and topped with an enormous bow and ribbons that stretched down the sides of the tree. Maria thought of their cheap little tree they bought at Kmart that was decorated with random ornaments they'd collected over the years and a few Ariana made. It made Maria squirm with a mixture of embarrassment and envy.

"This is incredible," Maria said.

"Christmas is my favorite time of year, so I go a little overboard," Sarah Anne said with a laugh.

"I've always liked Christmas, too," Maria said. "When I was little, my mom would bake gingerbread and sugar cookies. It was the only time she baked—she cooked, but she didn't like to bake—so it was a really big deal to us."

"I love family traditions like that! Do you continue it and bake with Ariana at Christmas?"

Maria nodded. "Usually, but I haven't done it yet this year…" she trailed off, thinking of all the things that had kept her from enjoying the holiday season. "We've been so busy just moving in and getting settled."

Sarah Anne reached out and touched her arm. "Oh, I completely understand! I don't blame you. Moving can be so stressful, but I hope you've enjoyed living here so far."

"Definitely. James has really liked working at Mercedes, too. Actually," Maria said, trying to slide into the segue smoothly, "he just told me tonight that a corporate position came open that he can apply for."

"That's great news! Is he interested in working in corporate?"

"Yes, he's always wanted to be in management," Maria said, though that wasn't entirely true. James just wanted the best-paying job he could get. "He told me that your husband Mark can help with the promotion."

Sarah Anne's eyes widened. "Are you serious? Well, I'll just have to talk to him about it!"

"James said either Mark or J.D. Harrison could promote him, but I wasn't going to hold my breath hoping Sissy's husband would help us out."

"Lord, no, honey," Sarah Anne said with an exaggerated shudder. "You don't want Sissy finding out about that. It's funny, though. J.D. is nothing like her. He's loud, outgoing, and he's a lot of fun at parties. I was a little sad not to invite him."

Maria's eyebrows rose. "You didn't invite them? That's a bold move."

Sarah Anne laughed. "It is, isn't it? And I didn't even mean for it to be." The doorbell rang before she could say more. "Excuse me for a minute, okay? Mark acts like he's allergic to opening the front door."

Her heels rang out on the hardwood floors as she headed into the foyer, and Maria turned to go back into the kitchen. When she heard the door open but didn't immediately hear Sarah Anne's friendly greeting, curiosity got the better of her, and she turned back toward the foyer.

"Sarah Anne!" a deep, booming voice called. "Sissy tells

me that we didn't get an invitation in the mail to your Christmas party, but I knew Mark wouldn't want some women's argument keeping us from a Mercedes celebration. So here we are. I brought bourbon. You're welcome," he added with a laugh.

Maria walked around the corner just in time to see Sissy watching Sarah Anne with a cold smile as the man with the booming voice—J.D., Maria supposed—handed over a bottle of bourbon and came in the door. He was a large man, nearly as wide as James, only his bulk had less to do with muscle. He had dark hair shot with silver, and his face was ruddy. He was nothing like Maria would have thought Sissy's husband looked like. Beside him, Sissy looked as thin as a ballerina, clad in an elegant black-and-silver dress with dark heels and tights.

It seemed to take Sarah Anne a minute to recover herself, but then she said, "Well, none of that is true, J.D.! The invitation obviously got lost in the mail. And anyway, everyone at the preschool knew about it. Come on in, y'all. Mark's mixing drinks in the kitchen."

"Mark! How the hell are you?" J.D. called, stomping into the kitchen.

"That's true," Sissy said to Sarah Anne. "Everyone at the preschool does know about the party, and I expect everyone will be here tonight. I just *knew* you wouldn't have left out your old friend, especially now that you're my vice chairman."

Sarah Anne smiled tightly as Sissy followed J.D. into the kitchen.

Sissy brushed past Maria without saying a word.

SISSY

The invitation to Sarah Anne's Christmas party never came in the mail, but Sissy hadn't been surprised. Truthfully, she'd been too worried about her mama's health to care.

But then J.D. caught word of it at work. He'd come home asking about it, and when she told him they hadn't officially been invited, he'd demanded to know why.

"You two might have some ridiculous fight going on, but that won't keep me from going and having a good time. Mark will expect me to be there. I guarantee he doesn't have a clue what that crazy wife of his has been up to."

So Sissy had resigned herself to going to the party. She'd been on edge all week, nerves shot with worry over how J.D. would act. Normally, at their own end-of-the-year party, J.D. didn't drink much since it was during the day and with a bunch of little kids. A holiday cocktail party was something else entirely.

Sissy hadn't slept more than a few hours for the past couple of nights, and she'd had to use every makeup trick she knew to hide the dark circles under her eyes.

So now here they were, with that obnoxious New Yorker slinking around, listening in on their conversation before they'd even come in the door. Sissy just pretended she wasn't even there.

She had to admit that Sarah Anne had recovered quickly from the shock of seeing them at the door. She, at least, had some class. That didn't mean Sissy wasn't planning to corner her at some point tonight when she had a couple of drinks and demanded to know what the hell her problem was. The thought of that brought a smile to Sissy's face. She may not have any control over her husband's behavior, but nothing made her feel more confident than a good confrontation. Especially since most people she knew were complete cowards who spooked the moment she spoke to them directly.

Sissy watched with arms crossed as Mark fixed J.D. a bourbon on the rocks. A few of those, and they'd be on their way to a repeat of dinner a few weeks ago. Only this time, it would be witnessed by everyone at the preschool. A sweat broke out on Sissy's back, and she felt a bead trace uncomfortably down her spine.

She took a sip of her club soda and lime to try and cool off. Her attention shifted to others in the room. There were the usual exercise-obsessed moms, showing off their lean arm muscles and strangely muscular legs in short dresses.

That's not what men like, she heard her mama's voice say with a trademarked sneer. *Not enough cushion for the pushin'.*

Sissy gave her head a little shake to remove her mama's

words from her mind. Her mama could be crasser than a sailor.

A loud voice with a grating accent drew her attention for a moment, and she saw a man with dark hair talking animatedly to Mark, using plenty of hand motions. His accent was similar enough to Maria's that Sissy figured this must be her husband. He was handsome enough, if a little thuggish in appearance. And that accent was doing him no favors.

"Sissy!" a voice called, and she turned to find Michelle moving toward her, drink in hand. Sissy stifled a sigh. "I've been dying to talk to you about the doors. We've got to come up with a better system for keeping them locked. These volunteers just aren't cutting it. They feel sorry for anyone who looks the least bit stressed, and then they run and open the door—no proof that they're a parent or anything! They could be letting in a maniac to shoot up the school!"

Sissy listened to this monologue where Michelle hardly took a breath, and tried very hard to keep her eyes from rolling into the back of her head. Normally, she'd welcome a conversation about the preschool. But not when she couldn't keep darting her eyes back to her husband to try and judge from here how drunk he was, or when her mind was crowded with worries about her mama who *still* refused to stop smoking.

"Can you email me about all this, Michelle? I want to make sure I remember."

Michelle nodded but she took another gulping breath like she hadn't processed Sissy's comment yet. "Or maybe we should just bite the bullet and hire another security

guard? Is that in the budget? I'll have to check with
Stephanie."

"I think I saw Stephanie in the living room," Sissy said,
and Michelle whipped her head toward the doorway.

"Really? I'll just go talk to her now then!"

Sissy raised her glass with a smile in acknowledgment as
Michelle hurried away. In the midst of Michelle's verbal
assault on her ears, the doorbell had rung. Now Lauren and
her husband Wesley were entering the kitchen. Though her
blue dress flattered her pale complexion, Lauren had worse
bags under her eyes than Sissy. She must have lacked the
skill to hide them, or else she didn't care.

Sissy knew it was from Wesley sleeping with his secretary. J.D.'s receptionist had told her about it the last time
she'd gone by work. Honestly, she was surprised. All Wesley
had ever seemed to care about was hunting and fishing.
Having an affair seemed like the type of thing that would
take too much effort and keep him away from the things he
really loved to do. But maybe his secretary was just ridiculously good in bed.

Wesley joined Mark and J.D. at the bar, and Sissy
watched with a sinking feeling as Mark poured J.D. another
drink. It was going to be a bad night.

Sissy turned back toward the living room with the
intention of subjecting herself to more of Michelle's mono-
logues—if only to have a distraction—but then Maria
sashayed up to the men, whore-red dress cut low and perky
breasts on full display. Only Mark seemed to be able to
resist the temptation to ogle, but J.D. and Wesley honed in
like hunting dogs.

"James, I hope you've been telling these guys just how

much of a difference you've made since you got to work there," she said, laying a hand on her husband's chest.

"Nah, we didn't want to talk shop at a party," James said, trying unsuccessfully to deflect his wife.

"My husband has raised all the numbers on all your little reports," she said, wagging a finger at them.

Sissy almost winced for her. It was clear she couldn't hold her drink. J.D. grinned, though, because her wagging finger jiggled her breasts right under their noses.

"*All* of them?" J.D. asked in a teasing tone, taking a sip of his drink.

Maria looked confused for a moment. "Well, the ones that are supposed to have big numbers anyway. I'm sure he slashed prices everywhere else."

James looked like he wanted to crawl under the table and die.

"You'd be doing yourselves a favor if you promoted him," she said with a wheedling tone that made Sissy's lip curl. The men didn't seem to mind, though, because Maria was leaning so far forward they could probably see her nipples. "Did you know there's a job opening in corporate?"

"Maria," James said with a warning tone, "that's enough about work—really."

"Which job opening is it?" Mark asked, seeming genuinely interested, bless his heart. J.D. was still enjoying the view but not paying attention to her words. Sissy searched deep within herself, but she didn't even feel a flicker of jealousy. If Maria wanted to make herself look like a fool and throw herself on all the husbands here, then that was her problem. She should learn to hold her alcohol.

"Operations Manager," James said when all their gazes landed on him for an answer.

"That's something to think about," Mark said. "We do want to promote from within the company. Come talk to me Monday, okay?"

Maria threw her arms around Mark, nearly sloshing his drink on the floor. "Thank you!"

He just laughed good-naturedly, but Sissy had seen enough.

She turned away and headed back toward the living room. A whispered conversation in the alcove between the kitchen and dining room drew her attention.

"I just didn't think it was appropriate," Sarah Anne said in a tone of voice that made Sissy move closer to the alcove.

A low, surprised laugh. "It's a party for everyone, right?"

As soon as Sissy heard the voice, she realized what Sarah Anne's problem was. Obviously having her lover show up was a bolder move than Sarah Anne was prepared for. Sissy didn't know why she was surprised to see him, though. Everyone knew about the party, and Sissy knew for a fact she'd even spoken to Hampton about it in passing.

"Yes, but we've talked about this. It's awkward—"

"You look gorgeous, by the way."

Sarah Anne groaned.

"You know I love it when you moan like that," Hampton said in a teasing whisper, and Sissy rolled her eyes.

It was pretty ballsy of him to flirt with Sarah Anne like this right under her husband's nose. She wondered with a smirk what would happen if Mark just so happened to come looking for her now. She had to admit, it would be an amusing scene that Sarah Anne more than deserved after all her ridiculous machinations with the preschool.

"I'm serious, Hampton, if you're going to stay, then you need to go hang out with all the men around the bar. I don't want Mark to even see us together."

"I came here to see you, not Mark," Hampton said, and Sissy felt annoyed on behalf of Sarah Anne. He obviously didn't care what Sarah Anne wanted if he just brushed off her request like that.

So Sissy took matters into her own hands.

"Sarah Anne?" she called, walking toward the foyer as though she'd just started looking for her.

She heard a rush of whispering, and then Sarah Anne came around the corner with a slightly-harried smile. "Looking for me?"

"Yes, I wanted to talk to you about the upcoming board meeting. What do you think of having it at a restaurant instead of someone's house?" The board meeting was two months out, and Sissy hadn't even thought about it yet, which was unusual for her. She'd just been so busy worrying about her mama, but this seemed like a good excuse.

"That sounds great to me," Sarah Anne said with a shrug.

A loud greeting sounded from the kitchen, and Sissy saw Sarah Anne's attention shift in that direction for a moment. It seemed like Hampton had actually listened to her request to stay with the men. Sissy felt a burst of satisfaction that she'd extricated Sarah Anne from an awkward situation, even if she didn't realize it.

"Can I get you another drink?" Sarah Anne asked, her shoulders relaxing.

"I'm fine," Sissy said, giving her half-full drink a shake.

"I'm going to check on the others," Sarah Anne said, "but come with me. Which restaurant were you thinking of for the meeting?"

Sissy followed Sarah Anne back to her bright and airy kitchen where the men had camped out around the bar and the few women who were huddled around the snacks talked animatedly. Sissy noticed with unease that J.D. was no longer in there. Had he gone looking for her? More importantly, how much did he have to drink?

"I was hoping you could help me decide that," Sissy said.

"Somewhere downtown maybe?"

Sissy put her drink on the granite counter. "Downtown has some great places to eat. Let me go use the bathroom while I think about it, okay?"

"Sure. You know where it is, right?"

Sissy nodded. It was off the living room in the hallway, and it was the first place she knew to check for J.D.

But as soon as she got to the dim hallway, Lauren nearly ran into her. There was high color in her cheeks, and when she met Sissy's gaze, her eyes quickly darted away. The reason for it became obvious when J.D. strolled out of the bathroom, too, as though he'd followed her in there.

Sissy stifled a groan. Of all the women here, J.D. had to pick the one who was the most emotionally fragile. Although she supposed she shouldn't be surprised. He couldn't resist a woman like that. He'd proven it when he'd swept her off her feet—and out of the trailer park—at nineteen years old.

Before Sissy could react or try and salvage the situation, Maria and Sarah Anne came around the corner at the exact wrong moment. Sarah Anne was cut off in the middle of saying, "The bathroom is right over here," when she saw Lauren and Sissy standing awkwardly together. J.D. smiled at them all with a bold, "Ladies," and a nod of his head, he slipped away, leaving Sissy to clean up his mess.

"I couldn't help but notice J.D. was in the bathroom with you," Sissy said, never one to ignore the elephant in the room. Better to go ahead and face this—let Lauren know it wasn't her fault.

Lauren looked ill and didn't immediately respond.

Before Sissy could continue, Maria stepped forward, taking up even more space in the cramped hallway.

"Hey, don't blame her," Maria said, surprisingly bold, but one look at her flushed cheeks showed it was definitely due to drink. "It's not her fault your husband has been leering at everyone like some perverted old man."

Sissy smirked at Maria before glancing pointedly at her dress. "It's hard not to look when you've got your cleavage shoved right up his nose." Sissy couldn't help herself. It was all those years growing up where they all had to be tougher than junkyard dogs. If someone started a fight, she would be the one to finish it. It didn't help that Sissy already wasn't a huge Maria fan.

Maria reeled back. "Wow. Talk about victim-blaming."

Sissy shrugged. "Just calling it like it is, honey. And, by the way, you interrupted a private conversation between Lauren and me."

Maria obviously didn't like to be told a conversation was none of her business. Her eyes narrowed like a snake's.

"You know," she said, pointing her finger at Sissy, "one thing I'm sick of here is that no one says what they mean. No one will tell you to your face, Sissy, that we all know you sent us those horrible anonymous text messages, but we do. We know you did it."

Sissy's mind worked fast. Maria was intoxicated, yes, but she could tell from the way Lauren and Sarah Anne were looking at her that they believed it, too.

"You all think I sent you anonymous text messages? About what?"

Sarah Anne's face reddened, and she had trouble meeting Sissy's gaze. It wasn't hard to guess that Sarah Anne had received a message that had something to do with her affair. Lauren just looked furious. Maria's gaze was unsteady, but Sissy thought she saw a glimmer of fear deep down.

"About things we wouldn't want other people to know," Sarah Anne finally said.

"Yes, well, it wasn't me."

"Ugh, you Southerners," Maria said with a curled lip. "Why are you bothering to deny it? We know you eavesdrop and get all kinds of dirt on people."

Sissy smirked. "Well, that part is true at least. But y'all make it so *easy*."

She could see their anger rising as they glanced at one another, so before Maria could let loose with another outburst, Sissy said, "It wasn't me because I got a text, too."

They looked stunned. Maria even rocked back on her heels comically.

"You got a text?" Lauren asked, glancing at Sarah Anne uncertainly.

"Yes, I thought it was from my cousin. She's always asking me for money, so I blocked her number a long time ago." They shared another look that Sissy could see was judging her for being so cold, but she didn't care if they thought she was a cold-hearted bitch. Better than trailer-trash. "This text came from an anonymous number. It was just a picture, but it was something my cousin knows would upset me."

"Why would your cousin be texting us?" Maria asked, her brows screwed up in confusion.

"Bless your heart, honey," Sarah Anne said in an exasperated tone. "She's not saying her cousin is behind the text messages to us. She's just saying that's what she thought when she got her own text message."

"How do we even know you got a text message?" Lauren asked with a skeptical arch of her brow. "You could be lying."

Sissy's eyes narrowed. "Why did you even think I would send you these text messages in the first place? What's in it for me?"

They were silent, and then Sarah Anne said, "Well, everyone knows you can be...blunt. And sometimes even a little mean? And we knew you'd heard about some of our secrets—you heard us talking at the playdate."

"If I'm so blunt and mean, then why didn't I just tell you what I thought to your faces about these 'secrets'?" Sissy demanded.

Sarah Anne's mouth opened and closed. "Well... that's...that's a good point, actually."

Sissy threw up her hands. "Y'all don't know what you're talking about!" Something suddenly occurred to her, and she whirled on Sarah Anne. "Is that why you had a sudden interest in the preschool board? And your attitude problem the other week? You know, I can't believe I'm saying this, but Maria's right. You should have just confronted me about this earlier."

They had the decency to look sheepish, except for Maria, who looked like she was struggling to follow the conversation. Her drunken behavior reminded Sissy of J.D., and as if on cue, a burst of raucous laughter came from the kitchen. If he was still laughing and joking, there was time until he turned mean. But his mood could turn on a dime.

"This is a bad thing that it's not Sissy, though," Lauren said, arms folded protectively over her chest. "It means it was someone else."

And Sissy knew they were all thinking the same thing: Then who?

THE PRESENT

K nowing my daughter is safe at home with our neighbor doesn't make it any easier to leave. I imagine them at home now; no doubt she's complaining about the party being cut short. None of the kids understand what happened. They're too little to bear such a burden, and some parent with more sense than me moved them into the house before the paramedics even arrived.

I think of the ambulance and that terrible ride to the hospital. Just the thought of it makes my breaths change to sobs as tears sting my eyes. I know I should go to the hospital, too. The others invited me to ride with them, but I couldn't do it. They left only minutes ago shooting me strange looks before leaving. I almost laughed because it's the least I deserve. I stand with one hand on my car door, shaking. The urge to just go home right now and pretend this never happened is so strong I can't stop picturing walking into my house, going up to my room, and hiding like the coward I am.

You have to go there and face them.

Nausea rises as I wrench open my door and fall into my seat. I press the button to start the ignition. I don't know where I'm driving until I'm halfway there.

When I park and get out, my knees nearly give, and I stumble as though drunk.

I can't do this.

The hospital looms above me, sign blazing reproach- fully as I walk toward the revolving glass doors. I imagine them all in there, having figured out what really happened. What I did.

They will turn toward me, faces showing various signs of disgust and horror. How could I let this happen? What kind of person does such a thing?

I wrap my arms around myself protectively as I inch toward my inevitable judgement. I glance up at the sign above me.

The words of the hospital's sign are written in red, and they are the last thing any parent wants to see.

Children's Hospital.

LAUREN

The morning after the Christmas party, Lauren awoke with a splitting headache. It pounded and throbbed along with her heartbeat and made her eyesight blurry. She hadn't drunk that much in a long time, but after they all found out Sissy wasn't responsible for the anonymous texts, Sarah Anne had fixed them drinks and insisted they hash out a plan. Maria and Sissy had continuously given each other nasty looks, but they'd managed not to fight the whole time.

Secretly, Lauren thought Sissy had a point about Maria's dress. It was a little low-cut, and she was shamelessly throwing herself at the men from Mercedes all night. Lauren was surprised Wesley hadn't copped a feel or followed *her* into the bathroom.

Lauren still couldn't believe J.D. had approached her like that. She imagined him in the hallway, brushing just a little too close. Lauren's first thought had been: *I wish Wesley could see this.* She wanted to hurt him. Make him jealous. So she'd done something she never would have only a few months ago: she slipped into the bathroom and left the door not only unlocked, but cracked just a bit. She stood at the sink, washing her hands to pass the time, knowing that J.D. would take the bait.

One knock on the door, and then he came inside with her. As his body filled the small space, Lauren's heart had pounded. She couldn't believe she was letting this happen. He smiled at her, but it wasn't a predatory or leering smile. It would have been charming if she wasn't shaking at the thought of another man touching her.

But then he hadn't done anything at all. He pulled something from his wallet, and she realized it was his business card.

"Word is, Wesley has been running around on you. If you ever want to even the score, then give me a call." He pointed to his cell number typed in bold.

Lauren could feel the heat radiating from her face and neck, but she took the card. "Maybe I will," she said, in what was supposed to be a flirty tone but ended up just sounding kind of belligerent.

"I hope so. You're a beautiful woman, and Wesley would do well to remember it."

She wished she could say she'd flirted with him or said something witty, but all she did was nod once and slip out the door. That was when she'd run into Sissy, fully expecting her to tear into her. J.D. had sailed on by without a care in the world, and Lauren had felt that same rage raise its head inside her. It was frustration at seeing a man get away with murder while she twisted on the noose for the smallest offence.

Sissy hadn't brought it up again, though, that whole night. It was as if she was used to such behavior from him and didn't care. Lauren found that both shocking and disturbing, but she also found herself envying Sissy just a tiny bit. She wished she didn't care what Wesley did either.

But they'd also been too distracted by the text messages. Once Sissy had been crossed off the list of suspects, they didn't know who to blame.

"I think we should look at people who might hate us without us even knowing," Sarah Anne had said. "Like Hampton's ex-wife. We all know her from preschool, so there's the shared connection."

By the way her eyes blazed when she said that, it seemed like Sarah Anne just wanted an excuse to blame Hampton's ex-wife. *All you have to do is stop sleeping with him,* Lauren had thought.

"It could even be Wesley's secretary," Maria added in a stage whisper. She'd glanced at the doorway that led into the kitchen as though she could see through walls.

"Well, I guess there's a connection through Mercedes," Sarah Anne said, though it was clear she preferred her own suggestion.

"It's never the most obvious person, though, is it?" Sissy asked with an amused smile, like a cat watching mice fight over a piece of cheese, knowing it will gobble up the winner.

"That's only in books and movies," Lauren had said. "In real life, it has to make sense."

"Like a scorned lover or an ex-wife," Sarah Anne said with renewed conviction.

The conversation had ended with numerous drunken theories, such as Sissy's cousin being behind it all because she wanted to make Sissy look like the villain in all this. They'd just agreed to let Sarah Anne try and find whether or not Hampton's ex-wife might have motivation to send them the texts. And Lauren volunteered to investigate Tiffany. It wasn't like she didn't already spend plenty of time stalking her on Instagram.

Now that it was morning, she didn't open the app because she could hear Wesley in the bathroom. They'd been able to sleep in because Wesley's mother kept Emily for them last night for a weekend sleepover. Lauren wished she hadn't drunk so much so that she could actually enjoy sleeping in. As it was, she couldn't even remember getting to bed last night.

With a groan, she got up to brush her teeth. Wesley was brushing his at his sink, and she noticed with a stab of annoyance that he didn't look nearly as haggard as she did.

"I forgot to tell you I'm going hunting with John and Will today," he said, casually, like this wouldn't upset her, even though they fought constantly about it.

She wheeled toward him. "You've been hunting almost every weekend for the past few months!"

"It's deer season," he said with a shrug.

Before she'd even thought it through or decided she really wanted to do it, Lauren said, "Except I know you're not going hunting every weekend."

He turned to look at her. "What do you mean?" His tone was neutral like he was trying to keep calm, but Lauren wasn't fooled. She saw the telltale tic in his jaw muscle.

"For one thing, where are the deer you've killed? Where's the venison? This time last year, our freezer was full. Are you that terrible of a hunter?" She knew that last

comment would incite him—he couldn't stand any asper-
sions being made about his hunting prowess.

"There haven't been as many deer this season," he said
lamely. Even Lauren knew it was a weak excuse. She was
insulted he couldn't manufacture anything better, so she
decided to drop a bomb on him.

"I know you've been sleeping with your secretary,"
Lauren said. "I even know you went to a mountain lodge
together for a weekend getaway while I stayed at home
watching your little girl."

He looked like a fish out of water. Eyes wide, mouth
opening and closing. *What a complete idiot*, Lauren thought.
*He seems shocked that I know, even when he did nothing to cover his
tracks.*

"That's insane, Lauren! Is this because of the miscarriage? Do you think you're dealing with postpartum
depression?"

Lauren laughed. "Oh *now* you care about my emotional
health! When I was actually drowning under the weight of
my own grief and depression, you were nowhere to be
found! But when it comes to an excuse for why I might be
accusing you of having an affair, you're suddenly worried
about my well-being."

She stepped closer to him until she could smell the mint
of his toothpaste. "I know about you two because your
slutty secretary posts too much on Instagram. I know
because everyone at Mercedes knows you're sleeping with
her. And I know because of this." She pulled out her phone
and showed him the loathsome picture of him kissing
Tiffany.

He rocked back on his heels, stunned. "Where did you
get that?"

"Someone sent it to me. Anonymously. Threateningly, I suppose, though I actually appreciated the heads-up."

He was tensed for a fight but then all of a sudden, the air seemed to go out of him, and his shoulders bent forward, deflated. "How long have you known?"

"Oh, for several months now."

His eyes widened. "And you didn't say anything?"

"It's up to me to bring it up, then? You just would have kept going indefinitely? Guilt-free?"

"No, that's not what I meant," he said, clearly floundering.

And suddenly, Lauren hated him. She hated that he thought she was stupid enough to believe he was hunting every weekend or that she'd never hear about him sleeping with his *secretary* when everyone at Mercedes knew.

"I didn't say anything because we were still trying to have a baby together, and I thought there was still hope. But when I heard that horrible news from the fertility doctor, I realized it's been hopeless all along." She met his gaze. "So it doesn't really matter if you're sleeping with someone else, does it?"

His face turned thunderous, and he stalked out of the bathroom. Lauren felt her blood pressure rise another point. He was the one sleeping around on her, but he thought he could just walk out in a huff?

She followed him into their bedroom. "Yeah, that's right, don't try and talk about it with me. Just run away to your slutty secretary."

He paused with one hand on the doorknob. "What's there to talk about? All you care about is having another baby, and you've made it clear I'm useless in that regard."

Lauren knew they were balanced on the edge. She

needed to say something to keep them both from plummeting, but she couldn't do it. *It's true,* she thought. *You're useless to me.*

He shook his head at her, pulled open the door, and left.

———

With Emily still at her grandmother's house for the rest of the weekend, Lauren could allow herself to completely fall apart.

She felt that desperate urge to destroy the things Wesley cared about most, but instead of giving in, she opened up their wedding album.

As she looked into their smiling faces, she didn't think, *Where did we go wrong?* She thought instead, *I wish I had never met him.*

His broken sperm would have never killed off her babies, and maybe her mind wouldn't feel so fractured now. Maybe she would have been happy and normal. Maybe she wouldn't feel the need to rock a baby doll in a nursery that may never see another living baby.

She thought about the way they had met. It was at a cookout thrown by a friend she no longer even spoke to. He told her he liked to fish, and Lauren had said her fondest memories were of her daddy taking her out on his boat. He'd invited her right then to a day on his fishing boat, and she should have told him the truth: her daddy had owned a pontoon boat, and she hated everything about fishing. The smell. The boring inaction for hours on end. She even hated the taste of most seafood.

But he was handsome and charming and most of all,

interested in her. It had been a long time since she'd met anyone. She'd dated her high school boyfriend until her last year of college, and she'd only broken up with him then because he had forced them to. He had met someone else and wanted out of the relationship. Story of her life, she guessed.

All she'd ever wanted was a big family. Even in college, she chose a major that would give her a career she could do from home: creative writing.

When she and Wesley started getting serious fast, she remembered just feeling relieved. *Good, now I've found the man I want to marry, so I can get started having babies.*

She'd be surrounded by laughing children and never feel lonely again. She wanted to completely erase her own childhood from her memory. It wasn't just the loneliness. As an only child, her parents treated her like a miniature adult. She never went to extracurricular activities or birthday parties, and they included her in all their grownup discussions. Including stresses at work like her father frequently getting fired and financial struggles like living in a house they couldn't afford.

She wasn't allowed to cry or be grumpy or act silly—or be a child in any way. The end result was that she was often trapped in her room, anxious and fearful about things she didn't understand and couldn't control. But Wesley had given her the key to her escape. When she met him, she was still living at home, saving money for a house.

Only a month later, they moved in together. Three months after that, they were married. Two years later, she finally got pregnant with Emily. Everything seemed to be falling into place...until four years went by, and she still hadn't had another baby.

But now she knew why. All she could think of as she looked down at their smiling wedding picture was every painful thing this marriage had brought her. All the weekends spent alone because Wesley was out hunting and fishing—actually hunting and fishing as opposed to the running around with his secretary he did now. The painful miscarriages. The loss of her dreams. And now, of course, the affair.

Did I ever love him?

The question made her close her eyes tightly. She wasn't sure. She loved being a mother, but she'd never been happy being married. Not the way she thought she would be. And now, it was too easy to wish pain on him. She wanted to hurt him in every way she could—make him pay for all the hurts she'd endured. Did other wives think like that about their husbands? She didn't think so.

Even though Sissy had seemed to hardly care that her husband had been hitting on Lauren. She hadn't brought it up again after they'd talked about the text messages, and Lauren hadn't known whether to feel relieved or confused. Did J.D. frequently hit on other women at parties? Did he and Sissy have an open relationship or something? Or did Sissy just think that Lauren would never accept his advance?

Before Wesley's affair, and more importantly, before the discovery that Wesley's sperm was causing her to miscarry, Sissy would have been right. Lauren would never entertain stepping outside her marriage.

But now...

She thought of the empty house and the fact that she had no idea where Wesley was or when he'd return.

In the same way that she had gotten in the car and

driven halfway to the mountains, she got up and went to her room. In the pocket of the skirt she wore last night was a business card. She pulled it out and stared at it.

Before she could think about what she was doing, she grabbed her phone and dialed.

It rang twice, and then he answered.

"J.D.? It's Lauren."

SARAH ANNE

With preschool closed through the holidays, and Sarah Anne busy with cookie exchanges and present-buying and family visits, she and Hampton went for two months without seeing each other. She was feeling smug and proud of herself for resisting, but it didn't take long before February rolled around, and she was falling right back into old habits.

It only took one flirtatious moment at her car after drop-off, and then they were texting each other nonstop again.

One Saturday, Mark volunteered to take the kids to the park and out to lunch to spend some time with them. God help her, but Sarah Anne's first reaction was to tell him she'd be out running errands all day, and then to call Hampton.

Hampton was also kid-free that day, though his ex was supposed to be bringing his daughter later in the afternoon.

So Sarah Anne picked up their favorite coffees and rolls and went straight to his house.

She wished she could say they did something other than have sex. But they didn't. They were all over each other like horny teenagers, and afterward, Sarah Anne lay there, suffocating under waves of guilt. Hampton happily drank his coffee and ate his roll, but she couldn't even stomach it. This was what happened every time. She craved the sex and was absolutely desperate for it, but the minute it was over, she resigned to never do it again. All too soon, though, the cravings for their wanton time together would return, and she would succumb to it. Over and over. It was an addiction. She knew this, but she didn't know how to help herself.

Later, Sarah Anne wondered if what happened next was God answering her.

As they lay naked together in Hampton's big bed, with his Bose stereo playing his favorite playlist, they heard the worst sound:

Footsteps.

And not only footsteps, but an excited child's voice calling, "Daddy! Daddy!"

They moved so fast Sarah Anne got tangled in the sheets, and Hampton stumbled for his door. He stepped in front of it just in time to block some of the view into the room, but not all. Sarah Anne could see Ava's little face, bright-eyed and flush-cheeked.

"Ava! Hi, honey," Hampton said, awkwardly. He'd managed to pull on his pants, but Sarah Anne was still trapped under the covers. She desperately wanted to hide in the bathroom, but she didn't dare get up.

"What are you doing, Daddy?" Ava asked, trying to

peer around her daddy and into the room. Sarah Anne pulled the covers up higher. "Is someone else here?"

"This is my friend, honey. We were just talking," he said lamely. "Hey, is your mama out there? She decided to bring you early, huh?"

He grabbed a shirt and moved closer to Ava until he was able to close the door behind him. Sarah Anne's heart beat as fast as a rabbit's as she sat frozen, listening.

"She's going to the store and I *hate* going to the store, so I asked to come here instead."

"Good idea," Hampton said, the sound of his voice beginning to travel down the hall. "Let me go and speak to her, and then you can watch your favorite show."

"I can?" she asked excitedly. You could never underestimate the power of bribery with young children. "Yay!"

Sarah Anne waited another moment to be sure they were gone before climbing out of bed and getting dressed in a hurry. Not that she could go anywhere until his ex left. Why the hell did she have a key to his house?

She tried to imagine how much Ava had seen from the narrow strip of doorway, but she thought Hampton had blocked a good bit. She hadn't called out to her or asked what a naked lady was doing in his bed, after all.

The problem was her car. She wondered if Erica would recognize it, or if Hampton would be able to convince her it was someone else's. Erica could be vindictive, and she might tell people at the preschool that she'd seen Sarah Anne's car over here just to stir the pot.

Sarah Anne's stomach roiled. She'd always been a bit of a thrill-seeker when she was younger—fast cars, roller coasters, sex with way too many different guys before she was even eighteen—but she didn't like this feeling of nearly being caught. Her whole life was balanced on the edge.

As soon as she heard the front door shut, she grabbed her bag and left Hampton's room. Ava was in the living room, glued to the big TV in there while something bright, happy, and distracting played on Netflix. Sarah Anne found Hampton in his bare kitchen with its basic appliances and paper plates.

"I am so sorry about this," Hampton said in a hushed voice. "I had no idea they'd be here this early. Apparently Erica knocked, and when I didn't answer the door, she just let herself in."

"Why does she even have a key, Hampton?" Sarah Anne demanded.

"Just for emergencies."

Sarah Anne groaned. "This could be really bad. Did Ava get a good look inside your room? Did she see me in the bed? Lord, this could completely traumatize her!"

"I don't think she could see around me. She's distracted with the TV right now, so she hasn't had a chance to say anything. I don't think she will. You know how kids this age are. She'll forget all about it in just a few minutes."

Sarah Anne snorted. "Yeah, until Erica reminds her! My car is in the driveway, remember?"

"Oh, she asked whose car it was, but I told her it's a friend helping me redecorate, and you were in the back, measuring Ava's room."

Sarah Anne looked around Hampton's boring kitchen and thought of the rest of his house, free from decorations and just containing the bare basics of comfort. She laughed. "Oh yeah, that's believable. So, what, now I have to redecorate your house?"

"That wouldn't be such a bad idea. It's at least a good front for our scandalous behavior," he said with a lurid wink.

"And all of that might be true if your poor daughter hadn't witnessed us in bed together—*naked*."

"She didn't see anything," he said, exuding his typical nonchalance. "And even if she did, I'll work on her. *Doctor* her memories."

"Ugh, no dad jokes, please. I can't take it. All right, I have to go. Now, before she sees us talking together in the kitchen."

She shook her head and turned to leave, but he grabbed her around the waist and pressed a kiss to her cheek.

"Text me later, okay?"

She softened marginally. "Have fun with Ava—I mean that. She's so excited to see you. Turn off the TV and take her somewhere fun."

"I will," he promised.

She nodded and smiled—even allowed him to kiss her one more time. But when she walked out to her car, she felt this terrible fluttery sensation that she knew was rising panic. There was no way any of this would end well.

———

Sarah Anne barely got to her car before her phone rang. She jumped, knowing who it was before she even looked at the screen. She thought about not answering, but she was more afraid of what Erica would do if she didn't.

She pressed the screen to accept the call.

"I warned you," Erica practically snarled into the phone.

"I was just helping him with decorating, Erica," Sarah Anne said weakly.

"You think I'm an idiot? I'm a fucking lawyer. Not only can I tell that you're both lying, I'd have to be a complete moron to think you weren't there to sleep with him. Not least of all because Hampton is colorblind and has never cared what a house looked like so long as it had a nice TV."

Nausea rose fast and hard. Sarah Anne couldn't say anything as she blinked back tears. She hated Hampton in that moment. Hated that he had seduced her into getting herself into this mess.

"What are you going to do?"

"I'm going to call up Mark, obviously. Maybe he'll be able to get this under control."

"Oh, Erica, please," Sarah Anne said, her voice breaking pathetically. "You said you didn't want Ava to know about all of this—"

"Well, it's too late for that, isn't it? You were in his bed!"

"She didn't see anything!" Sarah Anne swore, praying to God it was true. "Just, as a mother, I'm asking you not to tell Mark. I don't want my kids to know."

"You should have thought about that before you slept with Hampton."

"Please, Erica. It won't ever happen again."

"I have to go now," Erica said. "I have things to do."

"Hampton isn't married right now, Erica, so he's free to be in a relationship with someone else. It's not like we were making out on school property or something. We were at his house, on the weekend, and he didn't realize you would bring Ava early. But now you're talking about screwing with *my life*. You have no right to talk to my husband. I'm going to end it with Hampton, but it'll be my decision whether or not to tell Mark about my affair. Not yours."

Erica made a soft sound into the phone that sounded like a laugh. "That isn't a bad argument. As someone who argues for a living, I respect that."

Sarah Anne's heart leapt to her throat. "Then you won't tell Mark?"

"I didn't say that. Look, I really do have to go."

"Erica, wait—"

But she'd already ended the call.

"Damn it!" Sarah Anne yelled, hitting the heel of her hand on her steering wheel.

———

When days went by and nothing happened, Sarah Anne began to relax. She hadn't seen Hampton outside of pickup and drop-off since that weekend, and she'd even managed to ignore all his text messages. She was feeling proud of her restraint, and to celebrate, she was fixing her family's favorite meal—chicken fried steak with mashed potatoes and a salad. They would all sit down to eat it together on the back porch since the night was unusually warm for February.

"I set the table, Mama," Jackson said, coming into the kitchen with Sophie at his heels.

"I helped!" she said, and Jackson shook his head but wisely kept his mouth shut.

Sarah Anne smiled and gave Jackson a kiss on the top of his messy sandy-brown hair. "Well, thank you both, then."

Mark came into the kitchen with a beer in his hand.

"This looks amazing, honey." He grabbed the salad bowl and the plates. "Should I go ahead and bring these out on the porch?"

"That would be great," Sarah Anne said as she loaded up another bowl with the potatoes.

Once they carried all the food out to the table, they said the blessing and started eating. Sarah Anne watched them with a smile as she sipped her wine, smug in the knowledge that she'd made the food herself instead of getting takeout again.

"Did y'all have a good day at school?" Mark asked, and both kids started talking over each other to answer. They were still at that sweet age where they wanted to talk to their parents, and Sarah Anne wasn't looking forward to the grunts and eye rolls that would accompany adolescence.

After going through the highlights of his day, Jackson said, "I need to practice for the game on Saturday."

"That's no problem, buddy," Mark said. "We can throw the ball around after dinner."

"Ava told me Mama was playing a game," Sophie said, and at first, her words didn't register on Sarah Anne. She was cutting into her steak and thinking about Jackson and his daddy throwing around the football later.

Mark grinned. "Yeah? What game was she playing?"

"She was playing a game with Dr. Hampton," Sophie said casually, as if she wasn't dropping a bomb on the table.

Sarah Anne froze and nearly dropped her fork onto her plate. Here it was, the moment she'd been dreading all week. The bullet she'd naively thought she'd dodged.

"Ava was probably talking about Dr. Hampton and

me playing tag with you girls on the playground," Sarah Anne said, hiding her nervous smile behind a sip of wine.

Mark still had no clue this was such a dangerous topic, so he was happily eating his steak, thinking Sophie was going to regale them with one of her funny stories.

"No, she said you were at his house. And you were in his bed! What kind of game is that, Mama? Hide and seek?"

Sarah Anne had the distinct horror of seeing things register in Mark's mind. He'd been chewing a piece of steak, but now he swallowed hard and every muscle in his body tensed. Even Jackson stared at her.

There had been many moments in Sarah Anne's life where she desperately wished there was some sort of magic wand that could turn back time. That could completely erase a moment. This was one of them.

It felt like she would throw up her food all over the table, but she knew if she acted completely defensive, she could make this so much worse. If it weren't for the wine, her face wouldn't have a drop of color, so she was thankful for small favors.

"Oh honey, Ava's just confused. I know for a fact that Dr. Hampton's new girlfriend has hair the exact color as mine."

"So Dr. Hampton was playing hide and seek with his girlfriend?"

Sarah Anne shrugged. "I guess so."

"Weird game to play while your daughter is home," Mark said, but Sarah Anne didn't dare look at him. She was too afraid he was staring at her accusingly.

Sarah Anne just let out a little snort to keep from

releasing a peal of nervous, high-pitched laughter. Mark would be suspicious for sure if she did that.

"They should have let Ava play, too!" Sophie said and then went right back to eating and talking about her dance class.

When Sarah Anne dared to glance at Mark again, he had resumed eating. That had to be a good sign, right? It would be hard to eat if you thought your wife was sleeping with your kids' pediatrician.

"I'll have to ask Hampton about his girlfriend next time we golf together," Mark said. "Hopefully she's less uptight than Erica."

Sarah Anne smiled in relief. "No kidding."

"I'm finished, Daddy," Jackson announced, obviously bored with the conversation topics at hand. "Ready to go throw the ball?"

Mark took one more bite and nodded. "Sure. Let's take our plates to the kitchen first, though, okay?"

Sarah Anne's heart swelled. It was the little things like this that reminded her why she loved Mark so much. He always wanted to be sure the kids were raised right. That they did their chores and appreciated all the many things they had.

This is a sign from God, Sarah Anne thought, even though she hadn't been to church in months and was pretty sure God had forgotten all about her considering that she was running around with Hampton. But she was taking this close call as a warning that she had done the right thing by ending it with Hampton.

She smiled at Sophie. "How about I get your bath ready? Do you want to play with your mermaids?"

Sophie's face lit up. "Yeah!"

Bathtime was still fun for Sophie, full of bubbles and toys. She also liked any opportunity to be pampered—a child after Sarah Anne's own heart, honestly.

"Okay, bring in your plate, and then I'll start your bath," Sarah Anne said.

Sophie looked like she was about to protest—she didn't like helping out as a rule—but then she clearly thought better of it. "Okay, Mama."

Sarah Anne's phone chimed as she carried the bowls and plates into the kitchen, and her stomach clenched when she saw she had a text from Hampton. Without even reading it, she quickly deleted the entire thread.

All Sarah Anne had to do was think of that horrifying moment when her own daughter had been talking about her in bed with Hampton, and she lost all desire to even text with him.

"Come on, Mama," Sophie said, already racing toward the stairs.

"Coming!"

Sarah Anne looked down at her phone. Should she block his number, too? What if he texted her again tonight, and Mark heard? Mark might be more suspicious than usual after that close call.

But...she couldn't just block him. She should at least talk to him about all of this first, right?

"Mama, come on!" Sophie yelled again from the top of the stairs, and that made up Sarah Anne's mind.

She'd talk to Hampton about this tomorrow. In the meantime, she'd just have to make sure Mark didn't look at her phone. That shouldn't be a problem since he'd never once shown any interest in looking at it.

The rest of the evening had been so pleasant that it was hard to believe it had almost ended in disaster. Sarah Anne tended to live in the moment rather than torture herself with what-if scenarios, so she'd happily let it all go and just enjoyed giving Sophie a bath before watching Mark and Jackson play ball.

They'd played until dark, the golden light catching in their hair until it faded away and the air had cooled. Sarah Anne sipped her wine and felt that comforting satisfaction that everyone else was content and didn't need anything from her. The kids weren't whining or demanding anything. Mark looked relaxed playing with Jackson. It was just a really lovely night.

She should have known not to trust it.

After the kids went to bed, Sarah Anne and Mark typically watched TV together. But tonight, Mark had a phone call from one of his salesmen at work as soon as he finished putting the kids to bed. Sarah Anne cleaned the kitchen, took a shower, and then was getting ready for bed before she even saw Mark again.

She didn't realize he was acting strange toward her until they were alone.

"How did your call go?" she asked, and Mark grunted out an answer while he spread toothpaste on his toothbrush.

He was looking down at his phone while he brushed his teeth, so he didn't even make eye contact.

Unease settled heavily on Sarah Anne's shoulders. "It didn't go well?" she tried again.

"No, it was fine," he said, still mindlessly scrolling on his phone while he finished brushing his teeth.

She would ordinarily ask what was wrong, but she didn't dare right now. She knew what it could be, and it terrified her to think of him expressing concerns out loud.

She could feel the itch to push him into arguing with her, but she suppressed it. Sarah Anne hated leaving things unresolved. She didn't like going to bed with a problem, but in this regard, it was simply self-preservation to pretend everything was fine. She pictured the way Mark had been smiling and laughing with their son. Surely he wouldn't have acted so carefree if he believed his wife was having an affair, right?

She pulled out her book—a calming beach read—and read a few chapters without really absorbing any of the words. Her heart pounded and her mind raced, but she forced herself to look outwardly relaxed. Mark eventually came to bed and continued to look at his phone.

When Sarah Anne decided she'd had enough pretending to read, she reached over to turn the light off, and her phone vibrated with a text. She knew who it was from without even looking. Beside her, she could feel Mark tense. She hurriedly dismissed the notification before turning off her light. But two more messages made her phone vibrate again, and she winced in the darkness.

"More group texts from the preschool board?" Mark asked, only this time, Sarah Anne could hear the sarcastic note to his voice.

"Probably," she said with what she hoped was mild frustration. "I'll just turn it off so it doesn't keep bothering us."

"Yeah, I bet you will," Mark said, not entirely under his breath.

Sarah Anne powered off her phone and then rolled away from Mark, laying there in the dark stiffly. She didn't know how she'd ever go to sleep.

She listened hard for Mark's breaths to deepen, but they never did. And then, in the quiet dark, he said, "Was that true about you and Hampton in bed?"

She jerked as though slapped. "Of course not! I told y'all that poor girl was confused."

"How could she mix up her father's girlfriend with you?" Mark asked quietly, as though he'd been wondering that all night.

"They haven't been together long," Sarah Anne said, her throat so tight it was hard to push the words out. "I don't even know if Ava has met his girlfriend. I know Hampton didn't want to introduce them until it got more serious."

It was a sad fact of Sarah Anne's life that she'd always been a decent liar—as long as no one could see her face. Her face always gave too much away. And the darkness of their room hid any telltale signs that she might not even be aware of. Things like touching her face or not making eye contact.

"Hm," Mark said, and Sarah Anne had to stop herself from pushing him to say more. She waited quietly instead, like an innocent wife with nothing to hide. "It just scared me to hear that, you know? And coming out of our baby's mouth. I can't think of a worse way to find out something like that."

Tears stung Sarah Anne's eyes so suddenly she was afraid she'd give it all away by weeping. "Well, it was just as horrible for me. I can't imagine what the school is saying now if that's what Ava believes. That's probably what the board was texting me about tonight, but I couldn't face it."

Mark was quiet, as though digesting what she'd said. "I hope no one else is talking about it."

"I'll find out tomorrow, I'm sure."

He didn't say anything else, but he reached over and touched her shoulder like he did every night to say good-night. Sarah Anne leaned into his touch like a cat and was disappointed when he rolled over to go to sleep.

What was I expecting—sex?

Disgust at herself rose quickly. She was lucky he wasn't continuing to ask questions.

That was twice tonight that Sarah Anne had narrowly missed disaster, and she knew she'd have to make sure Hampton understood things were truly over between them. No more late-night texts.

But, God help her, she didn't know if he'd listen.

28

MARIA

Maria's day at work began like any other, so deceptively peaceful that she felt almost hopeful. She hadn't stolen money in a week, James might be getting a promotion at work, and there seemed to be a lull in even the collection agencies' rabid desperation.

She should have known it would never last.

After she finished cleaning her last house for the morning, she loaded up her car and got in. That's when she saw the missed calls. When she looked at the number, her stomach plummeted. She knew it was a collections agency, and she couldn't bring herself to listen to the voicemail.

Maybe we can take out a loan, she thought, her hands tightening on the steering wheel. If she looked at herself in the mirror, she knew her face would look haggard.

She had no choice now. She'd have to tell James just how bad it was. That they were regularly overdrawing their bank account. That she'd have to cut all non-essential expenses like cable and eating out.

That he had to get that promotion to keep the new house they'd bought.

Her mind was still trying to work out ways to get more money coming in when she arrived at the cleaning agency. Maybe she could ask her boss for more work? If she worked faster and harder, she could squeeze in another house every day before picking up Ariana. Or maybe she could see if any customers needed evening cleanings that she could do once James got home.

She dragged out all her equipment and started hauling it into the building.

"Maria, is that you?" Diane's voice called from her office.

"Yes," Maria said as she shoved the vacuum back in the storage closet.

"Come see me when you put that stuff up, all right?"

Maria paused with her hand on the closet door, her whole body tense. "Sure."

Maria procrastinated as much as she could, bringing things in one at a time to delay going to see Diane. She wasn't sure what she wanted to talk about, but Diane had never called her into her office like that. She usually just came out and said what she was going to say. The fact that she seemed to want do it in an official capacity made Maria's mouth run dry.

When there was nothing left to bring in, Maria walked slowly toward the office. She had this terrible moment where she imagined just hopping in her car and leaving, but she managed to stop herself. What if Diane wanted to talk about something good?

It never works like that, Maria thought cynically. *It's always worse news than I imagined.*

"Hi, Maria," Diane said, and her voice sounded resigned. Maria stiffened. "Do you have the customer payments for today?"

"Yes, they're right here," Maria said, pulling them from the little pouch she carried for the purpose. She resisted the urge to say, *You can count it up if you want to.* Somehow, she felt like that would only heighten Diane's suspicion.

"Thank you," Diane said when Maria handed the money over. Diane looked down at the checks. "The reason I wanted you to come talk to me is that I noticed we're a little short on payments for the past few weeks." She took out a spreadsheet, and Maria squirmed in her seat.

Damn, she should have known the payments would be tracked.

"I contacted the customers, but they assured me they'd given their full amounts." Her watery-blue eyes bore into Maria's. "It was only the customers who paid in cash, and it was twenty dollars missing here or there. If it had been only one person, I might have suspected they were just trying to cheat us out of our full payment. Except it wasn't just one, and they were only your customers, Maria."

Why hadn't she put the money back like her therapist told her to? That had been months ago, and she not only never replaced the stolen sum, but she even took a few dollars more.

Her stomach bottomed out until she was sure she'd be sick. Still, she kept silent. She wouldn't volunteer anything until Diane asked her directly.

Diane sighed as though frustrated by what Maria was making her do. "Maria, did you take some of the customers' money?" She glanced down at the spreadsheet. "By my calculations, we're missing a total of $340."

Did it add up to that much already? Maria rubbed her sweaty palms on her pants.

"I have a problem," Maria said, so quietly that Diane leaned forward across her messy desk.

"A problem?"

"Yes, I-I have a problem with stealing." There, she said it.

Diane closed her eyes for a moment and leaned back. "Do you have the $340 to give back?"

Maria thought of the money in her wallet that she'd been hoarding. "Yes."

But they wouldn't make their mortgage payment again this month. It would have to be turned in late—when James got paid.

"On you?"

"Yes," Maria said, struggling not to break down. Or throw up. Either was possible at this point.

"If you give me the money back—today—I won't press charges against you," Diane said, and Maria nearly whimpered with relief. "However, I can't allow you to keep working with us. Not when you're going into customers' homes alone. It's a liability—I'm sure you understand."

"Yes," Maria said because it was all she trusted herself to say. "The money is in my car. I'll get it for you now."

She got up stiffly and walked to her car with shaky legs. Adrenaline pumped through her body, demanding she run far, far away from this situation. But of course she couldn't.

She pulled her slim black wallet from her purse and retrieved the money. She tried not to think about the bills waiting for her like an anvil over her head. She tried not to think about what this job loss would mean for her family.

A loan. They'd have to get a loan. What other choice was there? They had to get their expenses under control.

She shuffled back into the cleaning agency, cash tightly gripped in her hand. When she handed it to Diane, tears welled in her eyes.

"I'm so sorry," she told Diane. And she was. There was something terribly wrong with her—she knew that. She'd ruined everything up in NY, and moving down here was supposed to be a new opportunity for her. But she'd messed that up, too. Almost immediately. It was pathetic.

"I know you are. I can see it on your face, honey. And you've been a great worker, so I'm sad it had to end like this. Maybe...maybe see a therapist, huh?"

Maria didn't even bother telling her she *was* seeing a therapist already, but even that hadn't helped save her from herself. She nodded instead.

Maria stood and made the walk of shame out to her car. Her mind was scurrying around like the rats that used to infest her New York apartment, but she didn't know what to do.

Bizarrely, she thought of Sissy's giant house. Of Sarah Anne's fancy car and gourmet kitchen. They weren't struggling to afford their mortgage and furniture from Rooms to Go. Neither of them had ever struggled a day in their lives. She hadn't seen Lauren's house yet, but she assumed it was more of the same. Maybe she had to deal with a little disappointment over not getting pregnant right away, but at least they weren't struggling financially. At least Lauren could afford to feed her daughter! It made Maria grit her teeth with the need to scream.

It made her want to lash out at them with their petty little concerns. She wished she had stolen more from Sissy when she had the chance. She should have gone up to her bedroom and stolen jewelry.

As she drove back to her own house in shame, Maria cried ugly tears. She hated all of them. Everyone at that horrible preschool.

But most of all, she hated herself.

———

I *'m thinking about running away,* Maria typed to her therapist after James and Ariana were asleep. She was shaking and ashamed of herself.

Sometimes we all feel like escaping our lives, so I don't want you to panic. How do you feel like running away would solve your problems?

Maria looked over at the bag she had packed. She'd already told her therapist everything that had happened in a panicky rush, but she hadn't brought herself to tell James she'd lost her job.

I've made everything worse. James wouldn't have blown all that money on our house and furniture if it hadn't been for me. He can just concentrate on work if I'm not here, draining every paycheck.

And what about Ariana? Who would take her to school?

Maria choked on a sob. She couldn't think of her baby sleeping peacefully in her bed in the next room.

James could pull her out of that expensive preschool and just take her to the Mercedes daycare.

And couldn't you do that? Couldn't you take Ariana out of the preschool to save money?

If I'm still here, I can't do that. I would have to keep trying to network and get James a better job.

Is this something James has asked of you?

Maria snorted through her tears. The opposite was true. *He's begged me not to, actually. I think I really embarrassed him at the Christmas party.*

Then I'm not sure I understand why you've taken this on yourself. Ultimately, you don't have any control over whether or not James gets promoted.

If I'm here, I still have to try.

Or you feel anxious?

Maria looked down at her arms, where she'd been furiously scratching them.

I feel anxious any time I think about our finances, or James's job, or my spending. But when I steal something or try to get James a promotion, then I feel better for a little while. Like I actually did something to help.

And this is what you think will happen if you leave? That you'll feel like you did something positive to help?

Yes! Exactly.

I think this is your anxious mind lying to you, Maria. I think everything will get much, much worse if you leave. James will be confused and upset—maybe even angry at you—but worst of all, your daughter won't understand why her mommy left. She'll start to blame herself like all small children do.

Maria gripped her head, rocking herself. *This makes me want to steal. Like really steal like I used to. I even wished I'd stolen something better from Sissy's house.*

Having that desire is like obsessive compulsive disorder. You feel compelled to act on these behaviors—like stealing or pushing your husband to get a promotion—because it makes you feel more in control and relieves your anxiety.

Maria could feel the truth in what her therapist was saying, but she also didn't want to hear it. She wanted to run away. Maybe if she returned to New York, her family would be better off. James would get them back on track.

You should wake your husband, Maria. Tell him you're really upset about everything and you're scared you're going to do something you regret. Let him help you. Don't try to handle this alone.

I'm talking to you, aren't I?

And I appreciate that. I'm proud of you, and I also think you contacted me tonight because you don't really want to go through with this. You want someone to stop you. But I'm also not there in the room with you. Sometimes you need someone to touch your shoulder, look you in the eyes, and say, "Don't do this."

I'll think about it. But for now, I'm going to go.

Please wake James, Maria.

Maria didn't want to hear it anymore, so she closed out the app. It was just that simple. Now she didn't have anyone arguing with her or trying to change her mind.

She grabbed her packed bag as she stood. The house was warm, and she was fully dressed, but she shook all over. Her teeth made a horrible chattering noise.

Silently, she crept down the stairs to her purse and keys.

She gathered them up and moved toward the garage. On her way, her eye caught on a drawing Ariana had brought home that day. It was hung beside the refrigerator, which was right beside the garage door.

It was a crayon drawing of Maria holding Ariana's hand.

"I made this for you, Mommy," Ariana had told her proudly earlier, and Maria had only half paid attention. But now, she collapsed on the floor in front of the drawing, sobbing.

Everything her therapist said ran through her head, and

all she could think about was what Ariana would say in the morning when she found out her mommy was gone.

It was a long time before Maria dragged herself off the floor. She put away her purse and keys and made her way back up to her bedroom.

After taking a deep breath, she went to James and gently shook him awake.

He rolled over and sat up when he saw her tear-streaked face.

"James? I have to tell you something."

29

SISSY

After her mama's surgery, it was just easier if she stayed at Sissy's house to recover. This way, Sissy didn't have to drive out to the country every day to make sure she was taking her medicine and not smoking up a storm. The problem was that Loretta didn't want to be there. She hated living at someone else's house. Loretta had her own bedroom suite to herself, but even this didn't keep her happy.

What she really wanted was a cigarette, and the way she snapped at everything that breathed, Sissy was tempted to give it to her.

"I can't stand that cat of yours, Sissy," Loretta said from the recliner they'd bought for her bedroom. "It's always slinking around, and it keeps getting on my bed."

Most of the time, Sissy forgot they even *had* a cat. To her, the fluffy Persian was a sign of wealth. Sure, Princess Jasmine hated everyone and couldn't stand to be petted, but

Sissy could relate to that. She wished she could be more like the cat.

"Just keep your door shut, and she won't come in here," Sissy said.

Loretta huffed. "What are the kids doing?"

"They're outside playing. Do you want me to call them in?"

"Hell no! To do what? Watch me watch TV?" She snorted.

"I could help you go outside, too. It's finally nice and warm, and all the flowers are blooming."

Loretta gave her side-eye. "Can I have a cigarette out there?"

"No. I told you: I don't even have any in the house."

"I need to go home," Loretta said with a groan.

Sissy didn't even bother to respond to that. She said it several hundred times a day. "Fresh air will be good for you, and it's so nice on the porch. You can help me plan for the party."

Her mama looked at her sharply. "What party?"

"Don't worry—it's not for you," Sissy said with barely-concealed annoyance. "It's the end-of-year preschool party I throw in May. I only have about six more weeks to finalize everything."

"I hate parties, so I don't know what help I'll be."

Sissy strode over to her mama's recliner and put her hands under her arms. "All right, get up. You're going outside. It's good for your lungs."

"I'm sure all that pollen floating around is great for my lungs," Loretta said with narrowed eyes, but she allowed Sissy to help her up.

They made it down the stairs, and then out onto the

back porch. The happy sounds of the kids playing, the birds singing, and the light breeze made the muscles in Sissy's back relax. She loved spring. Their lawn, the one they paid so much for, seemed finally worth it as the azaleas, dogwoods, and crape myrtles bloomed. The pool was still covered up at this point, but soon, the maintenance company would come to treat it and get it ready for the party.

Loretta plopped down heavily in a cushioned chair that overlooked the yard. The kids were near the back of the property by the playset and treehouse. They were safely contained by the privacy fence but still hidden away by all the shrubbery and trees—just the way Sissy liked it.

"When will that husband of yours be home?" Loretta asked, her tone fond. She'd always liked J.D. But then, Loretta always liked *any* man better.

"Late," Sissy said, rubbing her arms even though the air outside was warm. Late was not good. It gave J.D. too much time to get up to something—like drinking. Somehow, at the Christmas party, they'd avoided disaster. He'd been pretty drunk, but instead of getting agitated and mean, he'd turned lecherous. Hitting on Lauren hadn't been ideal, but Sissy would take that over berating and belittling her in front of everyone she knew.

She'd asked him about it when they got in the car later that night, but he'd only laughed. "You know I can't resist a vulnerable woman," he said with a wink that made her stomach turn. He was talking about all the girls he used to get with before he started dating Sissy, but honestly, it was his type of choice for affairs, too.

Whatever had happened with Lauren at the party in

December, it hadn't continued, or if it had, Sissy hadn't heard anything about it—which was all she cared about.

Loretta had no idea what J.D. was really like, and Sissy wanted to keep it that way. She didn't want to hear her mama's reaction, and there was a big part of her that was sure Loretta might even take J.D.'s side. She'd never had her head on straight when it came to men.

The medicine her mama was taking made her tired, though, and she went to bed early. Hopefully, she'd be fast asleep before J.D. even got home.

"He's a good man, Sissy. Just look at this yard. You do whatever you can to keep him."

Sissy rolled her eyes behind her sunglasses. Loretta liked to pretend that she'd always been a fan of J.D., but this was most definitely not the case. It went on the list of Things They Didn't Talk About. Disturbingly, it wasn't J.D.'s abusive tendencies that used to bother Loretta. In fact, Sissy wasn't sure that Loretta would even think the way he acted was a problem. Not if it meant living in a house like this.

The truly sick thing, though, was that Sissy agreed with her mama: she had to do whatever it took to keep J.D.

———

Later that night, after Loretta and the kids had gone to sleep, Sissy was reading in bed. She was so deeply engrossed in her murder mystery that she didn't hear the front door open, so she didn't know J.D. was home until he walked into their room. Normally, Sissy would have already turned out the light before he even got home. This way, he would think she was asleep and would hopefully just stumble to bed without bothering her.

But it didn't work out that way.

As soon as he walked in the door, Sissy threw her book down in surprise. With her bedside light on, there was no chance of pretending to be asleep.

"Waiting on me?" J.D. said with a leer. "I don't believe it."

He bent over to kiss her sloppily, reeking of alcohol. She struggled not to wrench away in disgust, but so many horrible memories were surfacing. This wasn't the first time J.D. had pressed himself on her, stinking of whiskey, yet her recoil and accompanying thoughts were unusual. She wondered if it was because Loretta was here.

After all, it was Loretta's drunken boyfriends who had fondled her in the dark. Beginning when she was only thirteen.

So even though she knew logically that it was her husband—even though she could see him in front of her— she thought of the nameless men who snuck into her bedroom after Loretta had fallen asleep. The men who stank of sweat, alcohol, and tobacco. The men with dirt permanently wedged under their fingernails.

She couldn't help it. She shuddered violently.

She knew J.D. had noticed when he straightened slowly, almost agonizingly. When she met his gaze, his eyes were blazing with booze and indignation.

"I disgust you? Is that it?" he said, his voice dangerously calm.

"No, of course not," Sissy said, but she felt her limbs quiver.

The most shameful thing was that they quivered as much from anticipation as they did from fear. It had been something she'd sought out a therapist for years ago. The sexual trauma of her youth had caused her to have bizarre sexual desires. Things like bondage fantasies and borderline rape. No matter how hard she worked to suppress it, J.D. could still trigger that response in her.

He leaned down close to her face. "Then good thing I already fucked tonight. That's what you really like, isn't it? When I just leave you the hell alone and get with someone else."

Yes. And no. It was true Sissy tried to avoid sex as much as possible. She didn't like the memories it stirred in her, and she hated the weird desires even more.

He let out a groan of disgust. "How did I end up married to someone as cold as you? Even that ice-queen friend of yours is a better lay."

That got Sissy's attention. She sat up in a rush. "What did you say?"

His eyes glittered. "Finally got a rise out of you? Yeah, that's right. That friend of yours—Lauren—couldn't wait to text me. Said she was tired of her husband shooting blanks."

Sissy jerked like she'd been slapped. "This is a new low, J.D.," she said without thinking. "Seriously. Even for you."

"What the hell else am I supposed to do? My own wife doesn't give me what I need."

"You didn't have to go sleep with one of my friends!"

He sneered at her. "Like you even care about that. You just don't want it getting out at your precious school—tarnishing your reputation as the perfect board president."

No longer content to lay in bed and listen to this, Sissy launched herself up. J.D. immediately shoved her back down and climbed on top of her. Her heart pounded as they struggled, and she pushed him away so fast and hard that he knocked into her nightstand. The lamp went crashing to the hardwood floor.

"Now look what you did!" J.D. shouted, and another hot wave of alcohol blew in her face. It took her straight back to her claustrophobic, dark bedroom when she was a teenager.

"Get off me!"

From outside their bedroom door came a voice calling, "Sissy?"

They both froze as they slowly remembered that there was another adult in the house with them now. One who didn't sleep as soundly as the kids.

"Sissy, I just need help going to the bathroom. I can't see in this damn hallway."

"Coming, Mama," Sissy said, and she was proud that her voice sounded halfway normal. J.D. got off her abruptly and stalked toward the bathroom. If she stayed gone long enough, he'd be in bed passed out when she came back in the room.

Loretta waited for her right outside Sissy's bedroom door. She had a look on her face that Sissy had always hated as a child. It was the one that said she knew *exactly* what was going on, and they were going to have words about it.

"I wasn't asleep," Loretta announced as Sissy turned on a dim hallway light for her.

"Why? Is your medicine keeping you awake?" Sissy asked mildly.

Loretta gave her an exasperated look but kindly held her tongue until they'd made it to the bathroom together. As soon as the door shut, her mama turned to her.

"I heard a crash and shouting, and I thought to myself,

'We must be under attack because I *know* Sissy and J.D. wouldn't be talking to each other like that.'"

Sissy leaned back against the counter and didn't say anything.

"I've had a lot of men get drunk and shout at me, Sissy, so don't think for a minute I don't know what it sounds like."

Sissy let out a sigh and shook her head. "I'm surprised you're even saying that, considering how much you think that man walks on water."

"Does he beat you?"

Sissy flinched at her blunt choice of words. She thought of the bruises from his rough treatment, especially during sex, but she wouldn't call that a beating. She remembered the boyfriends that used to beat her mama, and there were times when her face had swollen so badly she couldn't see or walk for days. "No."

"Well, that's not so bad. Just shouts and gets a little rough?"

Sissy felt suddenly ill. She stared at the decorative hand towel and nodded.

Her mama surprised her by looking concerned. "Have my grandbabies ever heard him shouting at you? I don't like the thought of that."

Sissy snorted. "You didn't seem to mind when it was your own daughter."

"Yes, but these are my grandbabies, and they haven't grown up like you. This isn't the type of house you'd expect to see treatment like that."

"You think it only happens in the trailer park? That's the most ignorant thing I've ever heard. As long as there are powerful men with women who are willing to put up with their bullshit, violence will happen everywhere."

"And you're one of these women?"

Sissy met her mama's gaze. "Your boyfriends taught me how to take a beating."

"Mercy, what an exaggeration. I may have brought some terrible men into the house, but none of them ever hurt you."

Sissy gripped the counter hard enough to turn her knuckles white. It wasn't as if Loretta didn't know the truth. She did. One of the first things Sissy's therapist had her do was confront her mama about the sexual assaults she endured as a teenager. Loretta had broken down and cried —the first Sissy had ever seen her shed a tear. She told Sissy she was a terrible mother who had even worse taste in men, but that she hadn't regretted getting Sissy out of their broken-down neighborhood the only way she knew how: by pushing her on every rich man she could find as soon as she hit puberty.

"You know that's not true," Sissy said.

"We've been down this road before, and I don't want to relive it with you. I did what I had to do to get you out of my rusty old trailer." She gestured at the elegant bathroom with its ornate fixtures and marble counters. "Now look where you live."

"And you think that's thanks to you?"

"Well, yeah. Who made you take a job at that golf course restaurant? I knew it wouldn't be long until you were invited to one of those fancy parties. And then you met J.D."

Sissy said nothing. She knew Loretta felt that putting

Sissy in the path of rich men exonerated her from what had happened when Sissy was younger.

Loretta met her gaze with hands on her hips. "Well? Are you one of the women with a rich husband who secretly beats her?"

Did rough sex count as a beating? Sissy wasn't sure anymore, and she knew that was messed up. "Not in the way you're thinking," Sissy admitted.

"And my grandbabies? They haven't seen or heard anything?"

Sissy shook her head. "They'd sleep through a hurricane. He only gets like this after a late night drinking."

Loretta nodded. She knew all about men who couldn't hold their drink. "Then wait a few more minutes. He should be passed out by the time you go back in there."

Sissy didn't admit that she was counting on just that. She gestured toward the water closet. "Didn't you need help going to the bathroom? You haven't used the toilet yet."

Her mama huffed. "Since when do you have to help me on and off the toilet? No, I couldn't sleep, so I was walking the halls, and I heard that loud crash from your bedroom. Thought I was doing you a favor."

"Yeah, thanks for that," Sissy muttered. Loretta had distracted J.D., it was true, but there was this huge part of Sissy that didn't want anyone to know this shameful part of her life. Not even her own mother.

Thinking about why J.D. had come home so late struck Sissy like an arrow, and she suddenly wanted this horrible night to end. "If you don't need my help, I'm going back to bed."

"Go on then," Loretta said with a shooing motion. "Don't let me keep you."

Sissy just nodded wearily. "Night, Mama."

When the bathroom door closed behind her, Sissy walked quietly back to her room. J.D. was snoring soundly as she entered their spacious bedroom, and her shoulders dropped in relief.

She padded over to their bed, her footsteps muffled by the thick rug. She looked down on his sleeping face. This wasn't the first time he'd stepped out on their marriage, and it had never really bothered her before. She had issues with sex, and she preferred he sought it from other women.

But Lauren was different.

Lauren was a fellow preschool mom, and her daughter had come here for play dates. That was enough of a boundary in Sissy's mind.

She could understand J.D. being drawn to Lauren's vulnerability. She wore it like a black cloak that anyone could see. But she couldn't understand why Lauren had done this. Wasn't she just complaining about not having another baby with her husband? Was this to get back at Wesley for having an affair?

Sissy felt some of the color drain from her cheeks. That was a scary thought. She didn't want Lauren to think she could throw sleeping with J.D. in Wesley's face. That would be a disaster! It would be all over Mercedes in seconds, and from there, it would spread through the preschool.

Sissy couldn't allow that to happen.

THE PRESENT

The others turn to me as I enter the waiting room, and though I feel as though I have a scarlet letter branded on my chest, they give me grim nods of greeting. I would be more comfortable if they had pointed and demanded, "What are *you* doing here?"

But they don't know what I've done. The terrible part I've played in all of this.

"We're waiting to talk to her parents," one of them says —to me, I think.

I nod and tighten my arms around my abdomen where I try unsuccessfully to keep myself from shaking. Eventually, they will come from those ominous double doors, and it'll be time for my reckoning.

When I don't say anything, they continue the conversation I assume they were having before I walked up.

"I texted my friend who's an ICU nurse since they won't tell us anything."

"Will they give you an update? Or is that against HIPAA?"

"Oh, it's definitely violating privacy, but she said she'd call when she could. She knows we're desperate to find out what's happening."

Nausea rises inside me, and I glance around for the nearest toilet.

Before I decide if I need to start walking toward the bathroom, a cell phone rings out. "Shh! This is my friend who works here."

Everyone freezes, and my mind is temporarily silenced. We watch her face as she listens to the caller. Behind us, in the waiting room, a woman starts crying. We don't know her, but it seems like a bad sign.

I return my attention to the phone call and what I can glean from her expression. Her every facial muscle is contracted in a grimace, and I know whatever the nurse tells her is not good.

The nausea crawls up to my throat, and I have to swallow it back down. This girl—this child—could die still. I know it. She was breathing when the ambulance came, but I know the dangers of drowning.

When she hangs up the phone, her face is pale. Her voice wavers. "She said they're not sure if she'll survive right now—she's in ICU in a coma. And if she does live, she might have brain damage."

Some of the others start crying, but my stomach takes the news hardest of all. I run to the bathroom.

Before I can even get to the toilet, the drink and appetizers I had earlier come back up in a burning mess on the floor.

LAUREN

Wesley didn't move out of their house, but he started sleeping in the guest room after the Christmas party. The first night she spent in their bed alone, Lauren kept bracing for an onslaught of emotions. Pain, confusion, anger, sorrow. *Something.* But there was nothing. She just felt a terrible, gnawing emptiness. It wasn't because she was detached from her husband—she had lost him a long time ago. It was because she didn't have a baby.

Now it was March, but Lauren's feelings hadn't changed. Wesley continued to sleep in another room and run around with Tiffany. And Lauren still didn't have a baby.

But she had a plan to change all that.

She opened up her fertility app on her phone and looked at the calendar. Tonight, it said. Tonight was when she'd be the most fertile and had the best chance of conceiving. It made her think of texting Wesley months ago, naively thinking they could make a baby together. Naively thinking he *wanted* to make another baby with her. She knew better now.

A reminder about the play date she was supposed to bring Emily to today popped up. It was spring break for the preschool, so Sarah Anne had suggested they meet at the park to let the kids play. Lauren closed the reminder. She didn't want to think about kids right now. Not when she was about to send out a text to a man who wasn't her husband.

She knew exactly what to say to get his attention—she knew what type of woman he liked, and she was happy to play the part.

I'm feeling lonely and neglected. Want to meet up tonight? Same place?

It wasn't long before she saw the dots indicating he was texting back.

I know a great cure for loneliness. Meet you there at 6?

I can't wait to see you.

The last text wasn't true, but she knew he wanted to hear it.

That task finished, she went to check on Emily. She could hear that she was still in her playroom, but she wanted to be sure she hadn't gotten into anything she wasn't supposed to—like the paint.

"Is it time to go to the park yet, Mama?" Emily asked when Lauren entered the brightly-colored room. She was standing in front of her play kitchen, serving up food to her dolls. She was such a maternal child that it made Lauren's heart twist whenever she watched her play. Emily would adore a baby sister or brother—she knew it.

"Almost," Lauren said with a smile. "After lunch, okay?"

"Okay," Emily said, but then her eyebrows furrowed. "Mama, why did Daddy sleep in another room?"

Lauren stiffened. She hadn't thought Emily would ever notice. She went to bed long before they did, and Wesley was usually up and dressed for work before she came out of her room. She didn't know what would happen with Wesley, but she didn't want Emily to worry.

"How do you know he slept in there?"

"He was in the room this morning in his pjs."

"Oh, well, he just had to get something from in there, honey. He didn't sleep there. That would be silly."

Emily looked profoundly relieved. "He didn't?"

Lauren shook her head. "I don't want you to worry about it, okay?"

"Okay, Mama."

When Emily returned to playing with her kitchen and dolls, Lauren went to her own private sanctuary—the baby nursery. She sat in the rocking chair and stroked her belly.

With luck, it wouldn't be long before it grew round and big again.

Now that she wasn't relying on a man with broken sperm, she knew she had a chance.

And neither man had to know the truth.

———

S arah Anne was annoyingly cheerful when Lauren and Emily arrived at the park later. She threw her arm around Lauren for a perfume-scented hug, bangles on her wrist jingling away.

"Hey you. How have you been?"

Lauren smiled back and tried not to pull away from the

hug too quickly. She wasn't a hugger. "Good. Busy with grades, but good."

Sarah Anne said something else, but Lauren had gotten distracted by seeing Sissy on one of the benches. She closed her eyes for a moment. *Damn it, Sarah Anne.*

"What's the matter? You look worried," Sarah Anne said.

"Did you invite Sissy here?"

Sarah Anne glanced over in Sissy's direction and waved her hand dismissively. "Well, sure. After she told us she wasn't the one sending those texts, I figured why not," she said with an annoying laugh. "I invited Maria, too, but she said she was busy today."

Sarah Anne was one of those people who couldn't stand small, intimate gatherings. She wanted a crowd. Maybe it was a consequence of her cheerleader days in high school, but whatever the reason, Lauren hated it. Lauren was the opposite and got easily overwhelmed with a bunch of people in one place. It was worse that it was Sissy, though, considering Lauren had a date later to sleep with her husband.

Lauren glanced over to where the three girls were playing with each other on the playset. At least they all got along—not like when Maria's poor little girl was with them and Sissy's daughter picked on her.

"I guess it's true we have nothing to be mad at Sissy about anymore," Lauren said, but she thought about Sissy's penchant for thoughtlessly cruel comments. Maybe she shouldn't feel so bad about sleeping with her husband.

"Not for the text messages anyway," Sarah Anne added with a laugh. "So how have you been surviving spring break?"

They walked back toward where Sissy was sitting on the bench, and Lauren tried not to let her irritation at the question show. She hated when other parents asked that. Like it was so miserable being around your child without some form of school to get rid of them for a few hours. Lauren had always thought it was cruel to the kids. She thought of her own childhood, of her mom laughing with her friends about being "stuck" with Lauren for the summer. More often than not, Lauren was sent away to summer camp so her mom could "get rid of her" for a few weeks. She never wanted Emily to feel unwanted like that.

"We've just stayed busy," Lauren said.

"We're talking about ways to survive spring break," Sarah Anne told Sissy when they were finally within earshot again. "We were supposed to take a trip to Disney, but Mark couldn't get off. Don't y'all usually head to Disney about this time, Sissy?"

Sissy looked a million miles away. She seemed to pull herself back to the conversation slowly. "Yes, but...we decided to go in the fall instead."

"That's smart," Sarah Anne said with a nod. "Fewer people than spring break."

Sissy nodded, but Lauren wasn't sure that was the real reason. Could she be upset about J.D.? She definitely hadn't acted like it at the party. And considering what J.D. had said...

Sissy and I have an understanding. Basically, I have sex with women who want to have sex, and she doesn't have to.

It had honestly turned Lauren's stomach to hear, but she didn't have any other prospects. She'd briefly considered a hookup app but then decided she didn't want to risk being raped and killed. This was a much safer option.

With Lauren distracted by her plans for later that night and Sissy dealing with…whatever it was she was dealing with, Sarah Anne was left to carry the conversation more or less by herself. Luckily, she was well-suited for such a task.

"I've given it a lot of thought, and I really believe Erica is to blame for those text messages. She hates me and knows we're all friends, so she wanted to make us think it was one of us to turn us against each other. I'm just sad it worked. We shouldn't have thought it was Sissy when there was someone like Erica around. And she's a lawyer, so she has all kinds of resources."

Sissy had nodded while Sarah Anne talked, but Lauren could tell she wasn't really listening. Lauren thought Sarah Anne just wanted Erica to be guilty since she was Hampton's ex.

"What do you think, Lauren?"

"Erica has always been cold to me—I'll give you that," Lauren said. "She mocked me to my face for working from home. She said even if I had a side job like online teaching, I was still just a housewife."

This got Sissy's attention. "Women who say things like that are jealous of those of us who chose to stay home."

Lauren shook her head. "I really don't think she's jealous of me or anyone else who stays at home. She seems like the type of woman who just naturally despises people who live a different lifestyle than she does."

"She does seem to hate everyone," Sarah Anne said with a laugh. "Always walking around with that pinched face."

Their conversation was interrupted by Sophie running up to Sarah Anne. "I have to go potty," she announced.

"Sure, honey. Be right back," Sarah Anne said to them.

Sissy turned to Lauren after Sarah Anne had walked away. "I understand you and J.D. have been sleeping together."

Lauren stiffened in horror, her eyes immediately searching the area for their girls. She couldn't believe Sissy had come right out and said that.

"He told me," Sissy added when Lauren still hadn't responded.

"Then you don't need me to tell you," Lauren said finally.

"I just want to warn you since you seem like an emotionally fragile type of person," she said with a distasteful curl to her lip. "J.D. never sticks with a woman long. He likes the chase, but he gets bored quickly. Soon enough, he'll start ignoring you and finds some other fragile woman to have sex with."

Sissy clearly thought she was imparting shocking information to Lauren, but the opposite was true. She knew exactly what type of man J.D. was, but it was also what made him so perfect for her goal. It was obvious Sissy was attempting to intimidate her.

"If he goes through women like tissues, then what makes you think he won't do the same to you one day?"

Sissy smiled a catty smile. "Because he needs me. The elegant, put-together wife that he can bring to events on his arm. The one that makes him look like a successful VP. One day, I might not look so elegant anymore, and he might lose interest, but don't worry about me. I know how to take care of myself."

Lauren met her green-eyed gaze. Sissy was elegantly dressed as always, but there was always something underneath that suggested she was an alley cat pretending to be a Persian. "Well don't worry, I don't see this lasting long."

This had to have been the most awkward conversation Lauren had ever had with anyone.

"Then why are you even bothering? Are you trying to get back at Wesley?"

Lauren's brain was slow to form a response. This was not something she thought she'd be talking about with Sissy. "Yes, I want to show him how it feels."

Sissy nodded. "I can't argue with that. I'm just not thrilled you chose my husband to do this with. It's not something I want circulating around the preschool."

Lauren didn't know what to say. An apology didn't seem to be appropriate. In the end, Sarah Anne's return saved her from replying.

"Have you been talking about the party?" Sarah Anne asked, cheerfully ignorant of the awkward vibe she was returning to. "And do you need help with anything, Sissy?"

"No, I arranged for the catering already and extra tables and chairs to be delivered. I'm having a company do it all this time so I don't have multiple deliveries."

"That's the way to do it. What's on the menu?"

"A build-your-own taco station for the kids and fajitas with shrimp and steak for the adults, plus just about every side item you can think of."

"Yum! This means some sort of margarita is the signature drink, right? Lord, I'll be wasted twenty minutes in," Sarah Anne said with a laugh.

Lauren laughed, too, but she knew that was all too true. Sarah Anne was the type who became silly and ridiculous after one drink. It was probably why she didn't drink at all during her Christmas party.

"Maybe Lauren will have one!" Sarah Anne added. It was easy to tell that she'd been the friend parents warned about when they discussed peer pressure. She couldn't stand that Lauren rarely drank.

"I doubt it," Lauren said with a smile. She hated the way drinking made her feel out of control.

"It would just be nice if I wasn't the only one making a fool out of myself."

"Believe me, there will be plenty others," Lauren said with a wry smile.

Sarah Anne's phone chimed, and she glanced down at it with a frown. Lauren peeked at the name and saw it was a text from Hampton.

"You're still carrying on with him?" Lauren couldn't help the note of disgust in her voice. She knew she had stepped outside her marriage, too, but it was different. For one thing, her husband had slept around first. For another, she had a plan. Sarah Anne was just needlessly risking everything.

Sarah Anne looked up guiltily and put her phone back in her bag. "I've tried to get him to stop texting me, but he won't listen."

"Actually, I wanted to talk to you about that," Sissy said. "Miss Jenny told me Ava and some of the other girls were talking about you and Hampton playing a game together in his room."

Lauren whipped her head toward Sarah Anne. She hadn't heard this yet, but it was shocking. Sarah Anne had become so careless that even the kids knew?

Sarah Anne groaned and covered her face. "Yes, Sophie told me at dinner the other night. In front of Mark."

Sissy just shook her head. "Is it true?"

"I was at Hampton's house when Erica brought Ava over early. That's why I said she could be behind the text messages! I didn't tell y'all before, but she threatened to tell Mark about our affair."

"Then what were you doing over there?" Lauren demanded. "Did you want to get caught?"

Sissy gave Lauren a sharp look. "You're one to talk."

Sarah Anne just looked back and forth between them. "What do you mean?"

Lauren stiffened, willing Sissy not to say anything.

"I mean you're not the only one stepping outside her marriage," Sissy said, and the urge to smack her boiled up inside Lauren so fast her hand twitched.

Sarah Anne looked dumbfounded. "What?" She turned to Lauren questioningly.

But Lauren only shook her head. She didn't have to explain herself to someone who spent the entire school year sleeping with her daughter's pediatrician. It was a miracle she hadn't been caught earlier.

"Well, okay…I don't understand, but it doesn't sound good. Believe me, you don't want to be in my shoes right now. I told Mark that Ava was confused because Hampton had a girlfriend with hair like mine, but I don't know how long that's going to hold up. Especially since Mark said he was going to ask Hampton about it next time they played golf."

Sarah Anne looked miserable as she fiddled with the strap of the leather bag in her lap, but Lauren couldn't summon an ounce of sympathy.

"This isn't a good look for vice chairman of the board," Sissy said, with a disapproving gaze that set Lauren's blood on fire. "I told Miss Jenny it had to have been a misunderstanding and smoothed things over for you, but I honestly don't know how you can continue to be on the board."

Lauren made a noise of disgust. "Wouldn't want it to reflect badly on your precious school, right?"

"Thanks for sticking up for me, honey," Sarah Anne said, "but I think Sissy is right."

Lauren stood abruptly. "I wasn't sticking up for you—believe me. I warned you from the beginning this was a horrible mistake. No, I just can't stand Sissy's holier-than-thou attitude."

Sissy met her gaze with a flinty stare. "Maybe you can't make it to the party after all. That's a shame because I know Emily was so looking forward to it."

Lauren smirked at her. "Oh, we'll be at your party. You can count on that. You wouldn't want me to be spreading things around the school that I've learned about the chairman of the board, after all. Because remember, I have nothing to lose. Nothing at all."

Lauren waited until understanding dawned in Sissy's eyes, and she knew by the set of her jaw that Sissy realized she'd been outmatched.

Lauren gathered Emily up and marched away, glad that her daughter was more obedient than most kids her age about leaving suddenly. She wanted to be able to savor her victory.

32

SARAH ANNE

It was funny how you often got the worst news when you were having the best time.

Just two weeks after the park play date, Sarah Anne was on a rare date night without the kids. She and Mark had gone to dinner, and now they were seeing a movie. It was some thriller that Mark really wanted to see but that Sarah Anne didn't really care about. She just loved the movie-going experience. The smell of popcorn, the dark, soothing theater, the candy. She even loved watching the trailers.

Mark sat to her left, completely enthralled by the plot twists and action scenes, and Sarah Anne had polished off her box of Raisinets and was halfway through the popcorn. Caloric content never even crossed her mind. To her, going out meant indulging. It wasn't like they got to do it very often. She'd never understood women who went out to eat and completely denied themselves the food they wanted by ordering a salad. Sarah Anne liked salads, but she refused to pay for one.

When they'd gone to their favorite steakhouse, Sarah Anne had ordered a sampler appetizer with three types of fried food. Mark hadn't said a word. He'd been too busy enjoying the fried foods right along with her. That was one thing about Hampton that was hard for her to tolerate: he was a health food fanatic. He didn't eat processed foods, steered clear of gluten, and rarely ate out—except for coffee. He would have watched her eat those fried appetizers in judgy silence.

Thinking of Hampton reminded her that she was forced to block his number for tonight. She didn't trust that he wouldn't text her—even though she'd begged him to stop. Sissy had been right at the park; she couldn't let this get out in the preschool. She also couldn't believe Lauren had acted like that toward Sissy—that wasn't like her at all. She wondered if it was because of the stress of Wesley having that affair and not being able to give her any more children. Although, why Lauren would even want more children with him was beyond Sarah Anne's comprehension.

Lord, I'm a hypocrite. At least she admitted it. Maybe it was like thinking you were crazy. If you thought it, then didn't that mean you really weren't?

Sarah Anne couldn't remember ever seeing Lauren storm away like that. She'd asked Sissy what that was all about, but Sissy had only shaken her head and refused to answer. So of course Sarah Anne had texted and called Lauren, but Lauren ignored her. It made Sarah Anne desperate to know what Lauren was holding over Sissy.

You wouldn't want me to be spreading things around the school that I've learned about the chairman of the board, after all.

Like what? But neither of them had said. Sissy for obvious reasons, but Sarah Anne was more than a little frustrated that Lauren hadn't shared with her. She felt like she told Lauren everything, and she thought Lauren confided in her, too.

A huge explosion on the screen temporarily drew her back to the movie, but then she saw her phone light up in her bag. Her stomach dropped. She had blocked Hampton, right? Surely it wasn't him, but that was always her worry when she was with Mark. At least since her own daughter had dropped that bomb at the dinner table last week.

She tried to resist the lure of her phone, but she couldn't stand not knowing.

She waited until a scene was lighting up the whole theater and then pulled her phone into her lap.

When she saw the first picture, she didn't understand what she was looking at. She saw the message was from an anonymous caller again, and suddenly, the candy and popcorn churned in her stomach.

She opened the message, and at the top, she saw it was actually a group text. It included Lauren, Sissy, and Maria.

She recognized the horrible picture of her and Hampton kissing. Immediately, she deleted it. She risked a glance at Mark, but he was totally wrapped up in the movie.

The other pictures were ones she'd never seen. One was a picture of a mug shot, which Sarah Anne realized with a jolt was Maria. It said she'd been arrested for theft. There was also a picture of Lauren's husband kissing his secretary. The third picture was of an entrance to a run-down mobile home neighborhood. By process of elimination, Sarah Anne knew it had to do with Sissy. Was that what Lauren had been talking about when she left the park? Why were they suddenly all receiving these text messages again? Was this Erica's revenge for finding her at Hampton's house?

Sarah Anne hurriedly closed the message. No one else had responded, and she didn't think they would. That's probably what the anonymous texter wanted: to get them riled up. Well, Sarah Anne wouldn't give them the satisfaction.

It was terrible of her, but she immediately Googled Maria and what must have been her maiden name. Not much came up, so she added theft plus New York. That brought up an old report on Maria robbing a pawn shop. Sarah Anne wasn't sure how surprised she was. There'd always been something about Maria—like she had a secret.

Then she Googled the name of the mobile home park and found out it was about a thirty-minute drive outside of town, way out in the country. But what did it mean to Sissy? Did she have a lover there or something? Sarah Anne almost snorted out loud. No, that didn't fit at all. If Sissy had a lover—and who knew, Sissy might even be asexual— then he certainly wouldn't live in a trailer. He'd be some powerful corporate executive somewhere. Although... wasn't that basically a description of Sissy's husband? Maybe she wanted someone totally different. Maybe it was even a woman! A stripper living out in the country.

That didn't seem to fit either, but Sarah Anne knew you could never really tell what someone was like behind closed doors.

"That was such a good movie," Mark said beside her, and she realized that the credits were rolling. He gave her a look. "Did you even watch any of it, or were you on your phone?"

"I just looked up a few things after I finished my popcorn and candy," she said with a flirty tilt to her head that she knew he loved.

He groaned good-naturedly as they left the theater. "Well, you missed an amazing ending."

"I'm sure."

"At least you didn't fall asleep this time."

"I did my best, honey."

"Just try and stay awake a little longer," he said with a suggestive waggle of his eyebrows. She laughed and leaned into him.

He didn't have to ask her twice. But as they walked out to their car, Sarah Anne found herself looking around the parking lot suspiciously. Why had those text messages been sent to all of them?

And who sent them?

———

S arah Anne unblocked Hampton later that night after Mark had passed out after sex. She knew from experience that not even the house falling down around him would wake him now.

Where have you been? His text said.

Dinner and a movie.

Going on dates without me now?

Sarah Anne sighed. They'd been over this. *I thought we agreed that we couldn't do this anymore.*

So why are you texting me at midnight?

Sarah Anne gritted her teeth. She didn't know why. It

was a sick compulsion, and if she didn't do it, then she'd toss and turn and compose text messages to him in her head.

I'm texting you back so you won't blow up my phone.

Want to get coffee with me tomorrow?

No, I don't.

I don't think I can do this. I can't watch you at the school every day, smiling at everyone but me. I have to keep seeing you.

Sarah Anne felt that shameful tug low in her abdomen, the one that fed on being wanted. The one that craved another man's attention.

Well, it's already spread around school about us—thanks to Erica. And Sissy made it clear she'd kick me off the board if we did anything else to give people reason to gossip.

Honestly, Sissy's threat had horrified Sarah Anne. Not because she was afraid of getting kicked off the board, but because she didn't want everyone to *know* about it. Sissy had said she'd smoothed things over, and Sarah Anne was sure she did to cover her own butt. The thought of everyone at the school suspecting that about Sarah Anne—and thinking little of her—though, was eating her up inside. Not only that, but she was afraid Sophie would hear more about it on the playground. She might innocently repeat it to Mark again. And this time, Sarah Anne was sure Mark would figure it all out.

Would that be so bad? I thought you didn't even like being on the board. This is the perfect excuse to step down.

Sarah Anne shook her head. *An affair is the perfect excuse? That's crazy and you know it. Your daughter walked in on us! And then she told MY daughter! That was enough of a wake-up call for me.*

Hampton didn't text back for several minutes, and she

thought she'd finally gotten through to him. She rolled over and got comfortable, letting her eyes fall closed. But then her phone vibrated again.

I'm supposed to play golf with Mark soon.

That thought seemed to come out of nowhere, but Sarah Anne's muscles tensed.

You told me before that I should tell him about having a girlfriend if he asks, but what if I didn't do that?

Sarah Anne sat up. *What are you saying?*

I'm saying why should I lie to my friend for no reason?

So that you don't completely ruin my marriage for one thing, she texted back hurriedly, her stomach twisting.

The only reason I'll lie to him is to protect our relationship.

Fine, then do it to protect us if you have to think of it that way.

I'm saying…we have to be in a relationship for me to tell your husband what you want me to.

Sarah Anne clutched her phone. She was wide awake now. *Are you seriously threatening me right now?*

I'm just telling you how I feel.

And you think saying that is going to make me want to get back with you?

Meet up with me tomorrow, and we can talk about it in person. We shouldn't be texting about it.

Sarah Anne had to throw off the covers and paced into the bathroom. Anger flooded her body as she struggled to close the door quietly behind her. Hampton had always been persistent whenever she tried to break things off with him, but he had never threatened to tell Mark.

I don't know how I can meet with you now, Sarah Anne texted. *How could you say those things to me?*

Because I don't want to lose you.

That was the line that usually made her pathetically

sway back into his arms, but this time, she thought about how horrible it felt at dinner when her family almost found out about her affair. For the first time, she was really and truly afraid of Mark learning the truth. She'd gotten herself into this mess, so she'd have to fix it. And she knew she couldn't do that over the phone.

All right, we do need to talk about all of this. I'll meet with you after drop off tomorrow.

See you then.

She grimaced at the texts before deleting the whole conversation. She had this desperate urge to text Lauren and tell her all about it, but she held herself back. Lauren wouldn't be sympathetic. She made that perfectly clear at the park the other day. Sitting with her own thoughts was something she hated, and she did her best thinking out loud. To someone else.

With her phone turned off, she returned to bed. Mark was still sleeping hard—she could tell from his gentle snores. She looked at him as he slept, and she wanted to curl up next to him and take comfort from his arms. She knew she didn't deserve that, though. So instead, she popped a sleeping pill to calm her surging heart rate, rolled over, and tried to go to sleep.

The last thing she thought before falling asleep was, *How am I going to get myself out of this?*

33

MARIA

When James came home that night, Maria knew immediately that something was wrong. His broad shoulders were bowed, and when Ariana raced to hug him, he hugged her back, but without his usual enthusiasm. For once, Maria hadn't been the cause of his misery—at least, she didn't think so.

"You doing okay?" James said, because he'd been asking her that ever since she woke him up crying that she had ruined their new life here.

"I'm fine, but what about you?"

He just shook his head. "Later." He smiled down at Ariana. "Let Daddy change, and then we'll go play outside, okay?"

"Okay!" Ariana raced to get her shoes on.

Maria thought about following him into the bedroom to interrogate him, but there was also a part of her that didn't want to know. She didn't think she could handle another piece of bad news today. So she went back into the kitchen to check the lasagna she'd put into the oven half an hour ago.

After closing the oven door and going to the fridge for a soda, she glanced at the picture Ariana drew for her. It was her newest compulsion, one that made her wince every time.

Seeing the picture was a constant reminder of what had happened that night, but Maria would never take it down. She needed those memories to keep herself from going down that path again.

After James had woken up that night, Maria told him about losing her job and stealing small amounts again through ugly sobs. But he hadn't even cared. He was too disturbed by her packed bag.

"Were you trying to leave me?" he had asked, his expression stunned.

"I thought you and Ariana would be better off without me destroying your lives."

"Our lives would be nothing without you," he had said, pulling her into his chest. "There's nothing worse than the thought of you leaving us."

They'd talked about everything after that, and the next day, he'd returned everything in the living room to the furniture store. She wasn't sure how he'd done that, but it had brought tears of relief to her eyes. No more furniture payments. Their living room was empty, but it was a small price to pay. They just watched TV in their room now.

It gave her hope that they could get through this and that Maria wouldn't have to take her therapist's advice and pull Ariana out of preschool. She would honestly rather take out a title loan on her car than give up her place at the school. It would feel too much like defeat. Like admitting they could never truly fit in.

Even turning down Sarah Anne's invitation to the park the other day had been hard—she liked to seize every opportunity to be with the other moms—but she just couldn't do it. Spring break with no job and no distraction of taking Ariana to preschool had sucked all the energy she had. She knew she wouldn't be able to fake being normal this time.

And now James had more bad news for her. Had something happened at work? She watched him play with Ariana outside for a moment, her insides twisting nervously. She tried to push the question away, but it just kept circling in her head:

What if he lost his job?

———

Ariana had been unusually difficult to put to bed that night, and Maria knew it was because she could sense the tension. She clung to Maria and wanted her to stay with her while she fell asleep, but every time Maria thought she'd finally drifted off and she tried to leave, Ariana would pop back up. Where bedtime usually took twenty minutes, that night it had taken an hour. As soon as Ariana finally succumbed to sleep, Maria hurried to her own room to talk to James.

"What happened?" The words tumbled out of her barely a moment after walking into the room.

James rubbed his face, and Maria could see the stubble had already returned. He looked tired. "I didn't get the promotion."

There had to have been a mistake. Sarah Anne's husband had even said he'd put in a good word for him. "How can you be sure?" she demanded.

"Because another guy got the job."

"But we *need* that promotion!"

He snorted. "And you think those corporate bastards care? Way I heard it, it was a friend of J.D. who got the job."

Maria's heart sank. This was almost as bad as James losing his job. She felt the pressure for her to get another job settle on her shoulders. James didn't want her out looking—he said she needed some time to get her head right in therapy—but she couldn't wait that long.

"So J.D. is the one who made the final decision? Not Mark?"

James shrugged, but his jaw was tight. This had hurt him, too. "Could've been both of them. They're all the same."

"I should have gone to that play date with Sarah Anne. I could've done something...convinced her to talk to Mark."

James gave her a sharp look. "We talked about that after the Christmas party."

"This is a different situation, though. Talking to other moms is not the same as getting drunk and trying to convince your bosses to promote you."

"Didn't your therapist say you shouldn't make that your problem anymore?"

Maria groaned. "I never should have told you that."

"She has a point, though. Look what you're doing to your arms."

She glanced down at the scratch marks and dropped her hands to her sides. "I can't scratch an itch now?"

He shook his head. "Maybe we should talk about taking Ariana out of preschool."

"She only has two months left! What's the point?"

"The point is: we're school-poor instead of house-poor. We can't do anything this summer. We can't even afford to drive up and visit our families in New York." He rubbed his face. "I'm going to try and get some overtime so we can afford our car payments."

"I have to get another job, James. We can't afford for me not to be bringing anything in."

"We can't afford for you to get arrested for theft either," he said, so bluntly that she winced. "Do you really think you're ready to go back to work?"

"Working to help us would get rid of my anxiety faster than sitting around worrying would!"

He searched her face for so long she had to resist the urge to start scratching her arms again. Finally, he sighed and nodded. "I guess you're right. I'd go crazy if I was holed up at home every day without a job."

She wanted to say something flippant, like she was doing just fine at home with Ariana, but she knew it wasn't true. Ariana provided a pretty good distraction, but when she wasn't around, Maria did terrible things to try and get more money. Like online gambling. She'd already lost another hundred dollars they didn't have.

"Let's just watch a show so I don't have to think about any of this shit anymore," he said wearily. He laid back against the pillows of their bed, and she crawled in next to him.

"Fine with me," she said. "What do you want to watch?"

"Anything mindless."

So she put on a reality show that didn't require them to think in any way. But maybe that was a mistake because it left her mind too much room to worry. She opened up a job search app and tried to find another job she could do without a degree, resume, or references. She definitely wouldn't be able to list Diane as a former boss, even though she'd never pressed charges.

She found a few leads, but she knew the pay would be crap. She opened Facebook as an escape, and after several minutes of mindlessly scrolling, she saw a link Sarah Anne had shared from Sissy's page. Sissy was asking for help with someone to deep-clean her house. Maria's lip curled. She could just imagine Sissy, sitting up there in their giant house, her husband casually choosing his friend over James for a job they desperately needed.

Maria gripped her phone hard. That terrible thought she had was back: she should have stolen more than just some soap. She imagined going to Sissy's house again and taking something more valuable.

Possibilities ran through Maria's mind, of jewelry, artwork, and antiques, but what she kept coming back to was a bank statement. Identity theft was where the real money was. And someone like Sissy, with tons of money at her disposal, probably wouldn't even notice small amounts missing. Not if Maria was smart about it.

A plan formed in her head so fast that she sat there going over every angle of it for several minutes. What if she applied for the cleaning job but didn't tell Sissy who she was until she got there? If Sissy knew in advance, she would definitely tell Maria no. But if Maria showed up on her doorstep ready to clean…

All she'd have to trade for the chance to steal bank account information was her pride. Sissy would know then that Maria was a house cleaner, but Maria thought she could live with that. Sissy hated her anyway, and James had lost his chance at a promotion. The more she thought about it, the more she was convinced it was the best thing to do.

She'd need help getting that job, though.

Her first thought was Sarah Anne. She was gullible and kind, and she wouldn't ask too many questions.

Maria pulled up her messages and texted Sarah Anne about seeing the Facebook post.

I have the perfect person for the job. My cousin. She'll be staying with us for a while, and she cleans your house like it's her own. Sissy will love her.

It wasn't long before Sarah Anne texted back. *Are you serious? This is amazing! Sissy has had such a hard time finding someone, so I know she'll really appreciate it! What's your cousin's name?*

Sabrina, but she doesn't speak English very well, so you can text me and I'll get the message to her.

Hah! Even better. Sissy likes when her cleaners don't speak English because then they don't talk to her.

She added an eye-roll emoji, and Maria just shook her head.

She'll love Sabrina then!

Sarah Anne responded with a laughing emoji and then told Maria she'd pass it along to Sissy right away.

James started to snore as Maria jumped up to pace in the hallway. Eventually, she made her way downstairs to clean the kitchen while she waited for a response from Sarah Anne and Sissy.

It wasn't long before Sarah Anne texted back.

Sissy said your cousin has the job if she can be there tomorrow morning.

Maria waited a while to pretend to be relaying information to a cousin she didn't have. *Sabrina said she'll be there.*

Perfect! Do you remember how to get to Sissy's?

Maria remembered all too well. She'd spent an embarrassing amount of time on Google Maps looking at the house and imagining herself living in that neighborhood. But to Sarah Anne, she just said having the address would help. Once Sarah Anne sent it to her and wished her cousin good luck, Maria thought she'd feel a sense of relief. If anything, though, her anxiety ramped up another notch.

She cleaned her kitchen until it gleamed, but she was still wide awake. Her insides shook at what she had arranged. She was equal parts terrified and dying to know how Sissy would react to seeing her on the porch instead of "Sabrina." Would she refuse to let her in? Or would she be happy to have something like this to hold over Maria?

It was the hit to her pride that was the hardest. Her insides crawled at the idea of standing on Sissy's doorstep, offering to clean her house. At the same time, though, she knew she would do whatever it took.

She also knew she should feel guilty or ashamed at so complacently deciding to commit a crime like this, but she couldn't summon even the tiniest feeling of regret. Only determination.

It was at that moment, though, that she thought of her therapist. She could imagine the disappointment she'd have in Maria that she was going this far off the deep end.

They'd spent the past couple of weeks working on her anxiety and her klepto-tendencies. Her therapist had never been convinced that Maria had kleptomania because of an addiction, but rather, she became so anxious over her lack of money that she felt compelled to steal.

Well, Maria felt compelled to steal right now.

Still, she opened up the therapy app on her phone. The most recent message from her therapist said:

Remember, the best way to overcome compulsions is to let yourself feel that anxiety. You can't be afraid of feeling anxious. The more you let yourself feel it, the less control it will have over you. And if you do some of the techniques we talked about, you'll be able to manage your symptoms of anxiety in a healthy way.

Maria hadn't answered yet, and she didn't know if she would now. The techniques her therapist had talked about included journaling and breathing exercises to deal with the anxiety, but in the face of this new fear of not having any money, it made Maria want to laugh. Yeah, like taking deep breaths was going to turn their negative bank account positive again.

Her chest started to feel tight, and she was sweating heavily even though the AC was running. It was clear she wasn't going to sleep tonight without something to help take the edge off, so she made her way up to the bathroom. Poor James was still passed out with the TV on, but she didn't want to wake him and face all his questions. He'd take one look at her and know she was close to having a panic attack. He took everything more seriously ever since she'd almost given in to her compulsion to leave the house in the middle of the night.

She popped an Ativan, hating that she had to rely on a pill to help calm herself. Couldn't even children calm themselves? How had she gotten to this point—where she couldn't even slow her own breathing?

She went through the motions of brushing her teeth and getting ready for bed, hoping the routine would soothe her nerves. Well, that and the Ativan. At some point, James must have heard her, and he stumbled into the bathroom with her.

"I don't know when I fell asleep," he said groggily.

"Pretty much right away," Maria said, touching his arm as he put toothpaste on his toothbrush. "You must be stressed."

"Just tired. I'll be fine tomorrow." His gaze met hers in the mirror. "You okay?"

"I'm fine," she said, even as she closed her hands into fists so he wouldn't notice them shaking. The anxiety always caused this huge rush of adrenaline that made her shake like a junky.

She went to bed first, and he came after stripping down to his boxers. He was asleep again only a few minutes after his head hit the pillow, his arm across her middle. She could feel the Ativan going to work on her anxiety—slowing her racing thoughts and calming her breathing—but she still couldn't fall asleep.

She laid there, staring at the ceiling for a long time, wondering if she should take another pill, when her phone buzzed with a message. She didn't want to wake up James —not when he had to get up early for work—so she took her phone out into the hall.

When she saw the first picture, she immediately dropped her phone. Not this shit again.

It was her mugshot from years ago, the picture as hideously shameful as it had been the last time she'd received it in a text. Only this time, there were other pictures: one of an entrance to a rundown neighborhood with mobile homes in the background, one of Lauren's husband kissing some woman, and another of Sarah Anne and Hampton making out in a parking lot.

But what made the color drain from her face was when she saw who the message went out to. It was a group text to Sarah Anne, Lauren, Sissy, and Maria. So now the other three women would know Maria's secret.

An even worse thought occurred to Maria, and she nearly threw up: Sissy would know that Maria had been arrested before for theft.

Maria felt her blood pressure rise despite the pill she'd taken. There was no way in hell Sissy would let her into her house now!

This completely ruined her entire plan, and now they were right back to being screwed on money again.

Angrily, she texted the anonymous messenger, her fingers racing over her phone's screen.

I don't know who you are, but you better hope I never find out because I want to kill you for messing with us like this.

Her heart pounded so hard in her ears that her head started to hurt. She stared at her phone, willing the texter to respond so that she could take out all her frustration on them. But they never did.

Coward.

34

SISSY

Not long after the group text went out, Sissy woke in the middle of the night with that terrible feeling something wasn't right. The text message had been annoying, but it didn't make her afraid any of them would be able to put two and two together to realize the significance of the neighborhood sign. No, whatever had woken her up had nothing to do with the text messages. She laid in bed for several minutes, just listening. Was one of the kids sick? Sometimes she woke up because she heard one of them puking or crying over a fever—mom's intuition. But she didn't hear anything.

Still, she got up just to check on them. Mary Elizabeth's room was closest, and Sissy found her sleeping peacefully when she peeked in. A unicorn night light illuminated the room enough that she could see her little chest rising and falling rhythmically. Just down the hall was her son's room, and she could see him in his tangle of sheets. He still kept a night light on, though it was much smaller and plain. He was sound asleep, so Sissy knew it hadn't been him who woke her either.

But then she thought of her mama, and her stomach dropped. She hurried down the hall, barely knocking before opening the door in a rush. Her mother's bed was empty.

"Mama?" she called softly.

She found her on the other side of the bed, splayed out on the floor.

"Mama!" she cried as she grabbed hold of Loretta's shoulders. She struggled to turn her over, and even then, her breathing was so shallow, it was almost undetectable. Sissy tried for a few moments to wake her, but when she couldn't, she knew she'd have to call an ambulance.

She hated to leave her mama even for a moment to get her phone, but she didn't have a choice. She didn't think J.D. would wake up if she shouted for him from here, although thank God he hadn't been drinking.

When she grabbed her phone, she glanced at his peacefully sleeping form and thought about waking him for a second but decided against it. She didn't have time to explain everything right now. She'd wake him and tell him what was going on once the ambulance was on its way.

"911, what's your emergency?" the operator said, the words strangely familiar even though Sissy had never called 911 before.

"My mother has lung cancer, and I just found her passed out on the floor. She's not breathing very well, and I can't wake her up."

She listened for a moment to the operator's instructions before confirming her address and that the ambulance was on its way.

Then she went back to her room to wake J.D., her heart racing. She shook him—not very gently—and he rolled over to look at her with bleary eyes.

"Sissy? What's wrong?"

"It's Mama. I found her passed out on the floor, and I can't wake her. The ambulance is coming."

He looked fully awake now. "Damn. Okay, what do you want me to do?"

"I'm going to wait with her in her room. Can you let the paramedics in when they come?"

He nodded as he got out of bed and pulled on some pants. "I'll wait for them downstairs."

Sissy rushed out of the room before thinking of something else and turning back around. "I'm going with her to the hospital, and I don't know when I'll be back. Can you let Yvette know? She needs to come here to watch the kids."

Yvette was their part-time nanny who helped out three days a week, or any time Sissy had to do things for the board. Luckily, Sissy had warned her that with Loretta being so sick, they might have to call her in the middle of the night. Yvette had agreed happily. She loved taking care of the kids, but Sissy knew she also liked that huge night-time nannying bonus.

"I'll call her," J.D. said.

Sissy nodded and hurried back to her mama's room. She found her lying there in that disturbingly still way, but at least she was breathing.

"I'm here, Mama," she said from the floor next to her. "The ambulance is coming."

Sissy didn't have the best relationship with Loretta, but that didn't mean she was ready for her to die. Still, she was surprised by the flood of tears and the lump in her throat as she held Loretta's hand.

Please don't die, Mama.

———

M any hours later, in Loretta's dark hospital room, Sissy lay awake. She had never been able to go back to sleep—even after Loretta was breathing well on oxygen. It turned out her mother had been dangerously low on oxygen, which is what caused her to pass out. Sissy was convinced it was because Loretta was *still* smoking. Only her mama was tired of hearing Sissy nag her about it, so she snuck away to smoke when Sissy wasn't around. The doctor had recommended that Loretta have portable oxygen, which just made a new concern for Sissy. Next thing she knew, Loretta would light a cigarette and blow herself up. Sissy would have to search Loretta's room and throw away all her hidden cigarettes. She was kicking herself for not doing it already.

Her phone buzzed with a message, and she glanced down to see it was Sarah Anne.

Did you still want Maria's cousin to clean? Hopefully theft doesn't run in the family!

She'd added a grimacing emoji, and Sissy just scoffed. She'd forgotten all about it, actually, but it would be nice to come home to a clean house after all this mess.

My nanny is there, so I'll let her know. I do still need it deep-cleaned.

Okay, just text Maria. Also, did you get those texts last night?

Sissy started to form a response, but then she closed the message instead. That was the last thing she wanted to talk about, and she knew Sarah Anne was just trying to figure out what the neighborhood picture had to do with Sissy.

She texted Maria instead.

Just letting you know that my nanny will be there to let your cousin in. I had a family emergency, so I won't be home all day, but Yvette knows where everything is and can help get her set up. I'd like everything deep-cleaned, so baseboards and windows and blinds.

Maria responded right away.

She'll be there. Thank you for letting me know!

With that handled, Sissy leaned back in the chair and closed her eyes. Maybe she could finally sleep.

But then Loretta coughed, and Sissy's eyes popped open again. "Mama?"

Loretta's eyes opened, and she turned her head toward Sissy. Immediately, Sissy got up and went to her side. "What happened?" Loretta asked weakly.

"You passed out, and I had to call an ambulance. Apparently, you were dangerously low on oxygen. Let me call the nurse."

Sissy pressed the nurse call button, and it was only a few moments before a nurse named Mary came in to check on Loretta. She measured her oxygen level and the flow going into Loretta's nostrils.

"Your oxygen levels are still lower than we like to see," Mary said, "but the good news is I don't think you'll need a ventilator. Any pain or difficulty breathing?"

Loretta shook her head.

"I'm glad to hear it. Do either of you need anything? Water?"

"We're fine, thank you," Sissy said when Loretta didn't say anything.

"All right then. I'll update your doctor, and you just rest

for now," Mary said, briefly touching Loretta's shoulder before leaving the room.

"Do you have any idea why your oxygen levels might be low?" Sissy asked, looking at her mama pointedly.

Loretta gave her a withering stare. "You really want to do this here? While I'm lying in a hospital bed?"

"I think I do. You haven't taken any of this seriously since you were diagnosed. You just had surgery a couple of weeks ago!"

"So? I can't live my life now?"

Sissy let out a frustrated sigh. "Plenty of people live without smoking, and everyone else who gets diagnosed with lung cancer stays far away from cigarettes. I just can't understand why you don't."

"They cut out the bad part of my lung, so what's the harm?"

Sissy felt her blood pressure rise. "Are you being serious, or are you just trying to piss me off?"

"I'm still capable of making my own decisions."

Sissy shook her head. "It really doesn't seem like it. You're here in the hospital because your body is low on oxygen, and I can almost guarantee that the doctor is going to decide you need a portable tank. Then what are you going to do? Continue to light up when you've got a tank of highly flammable gas right beside you? You'll blow my house up!"

"Well, we wouldn't want that, would we?" Loretta said nastily.

Sissy's hands curled into fists at her sides. "Are you trying to imply I don't care about you? How can you say that? You're staying at my house to recuperate after surgery, and I'm here in the hospital with you now! If I didn't care, I would have just left as soon as you were stable."

"Yes, but that would have looked bad, wouldn't it? That's what you really care about."

Sissy could feel a vein pulsing in her neck, but she tried to hold herself back. Her mama was, after all, lying in a hospital bed. Though Lord knew Loretta deserved getting screamed at right now, even if it was in a medical facility.

"Because I care about you and don't want you to die, I'm going to make sure you don't have any packs of cigarettes. I know you probably have hidden packs around your room."

Loretta's eyes narrowed. "Then why don't I just go home?"

"How am I supposed to let you go home now? You can't even be trusted at my house when I'm around to watch you!"

"I bet you're just loving this," Loretta said with a wheezy breath. "You finally get the chance to get back at me."

Sissy watched her mother for a long moment. "What does that mean?"

"I think you already know."

Loretta closed her eyes like she was falling asleep again, and Sissy took a deep breath. "I'm going to go get some water," she said quickly, and walked out of the room before she said something she regretted.

It didn't take Sissy long to find a vending machine for a bottle of water, but after she got one, she didn't go back to her mama's room right away. Her blood was boiling. She couldn't believe Loretta brought that up, and in a hospital of all places. Although maybe that was why. The last time they'd talked about that night, Sissy had stopped seeing or communicating with her mama for years. It was only once her son was born that she had tried to forgive.

But she'd never forget.

All her life, Sissy's mama had brought in an unending string of loser boyfriends. Some of them were just trashy, but others were abusive. The older Sissy got, the more unwanted attention she received from Loretta's boyfriends, and with such a small living space, there was nowhere to escape. Sissy was an early-bloomer, with a curvaceous body and long, thick hair. At thirteen, she could easily pass for sixteen or older. Loretta noticed right away, but instead of having a normal motherly response of wanting to protect her daughter, she started scheming ways to take advantage of it.

Loretta had been a beautiful woman when she was young, but the years had been hard, especially when she allowed cigarette smoke and sun to ravage her skin. Her face turned leathery before its time, and she knew she wouldn't be able to compete with her younger, prettier daughter. The fact that she thought she should compete with her showcased just how disturbed their relationship was.

It wasn't long before Loretta realized she could use Sissy as a lure to catch men with much deeper pockets than the ones she could pick up at a bar. So as soon as Sissy was legally old enough to work, she helped her get a job at a golf club.

If anyone has money, it's men on a golf course, her mama reasoned.

Sissy readily agreed to work there because it beat working fast food, and she had plans to save up her money to get far away from the house she grew up in as fast as she could. If that meant she had to go along with her mama's schemes to do it, then she was willing to suck it up.

It wasn't long before men—much, much older men—started propositioning her. She flirted with them all, but she never let it go further than that. This enraged Loretta.

You'll never catch a man like that. They'll get tired of your little games. You afraid because you ain't never had sex? I know a guy who can fix you right up. I'm just trying to help you, Sissy.

Sissy knew the guy her mama was talking about was her current boyfriend. That night, Sissy installed a deadbolt on her bedroom door.

Not long after that, Sissy started seeing one of the younger men who had shown interest in her at the golf club. Younger being a relative term, as he was in his thirties and she was fifteen. Every nice thing he bought her got turned over to Loretta to pawn. That kept her off Sissy's back and prevented her from making any more abhorrent propositions. She strung the man along for a few months until he lost interest in her, and then Loretta was right back on her case.

If you wanna get out of this town, then you gotta marry a rich man. You're not ever gonna have a good enough education to get anywhere, and you were born pretty. Pretty only lasts so long, though. You gotta use your assets while you got them.

I'm sixteen, Mama.

Yeah, and that means you have a couple years to bag a rich man as soon as you're legal.

It became Sissy's goal, too. She figured she could marry young, save up money, and divorce if she was unhappy. And chances were—from everything she'd seen about relationships—she was guaranteed to be unhappy.

She met J.D. at the golf club when she was a few days short of turning eighteen. When she first spotted him, so handsome and charming, and only seven years older than her, she pursued him as relentlessly as a bloodhound. He came from a rich family, had his business degree, and he was already working at Mercedes. But best of all, he wasn't an old married man. Up until then, that was the only type of man Sissy seemed to attract—other than the caddies who were her age and equally useless.

And maybe it was because he wasn't an old married man, but Sissy had to use every wile she'd developed over the years working there. He flirted back, but when it never went further than that, she knew she'd have to try a different tack. He was a playboy, with a different girl every time he visited the club. To attract him, she knew she'd have to become unattainable.

So she enlisted the help of every caddy and friend she had at the golf club. She got them to talk about her when J.D. was around—how difficult she was to date, how she preferred much older men, how only rich married men appealed to her. From the outside, it even looked true. She was cold and dismissive when J.D. spoke to her, to the point of ignoring him outright. At home, she studied books on etiquette and watched movies of rich women until she felt like she could sit down with the Queen of England if she had to.

Her machinations paid off after only a month, and that was because Sissy kept it up that long. J.D. seemed fascinated after only a week, and after the fifth time begging her to go out with him, she finally agreed.

To keep him from losing that thrill of the chase, she

imposed rules on their relationship. They couldn't have sex, and he could never meet her mother.

But even though they hadn't met, Loretta knew all about him.

He didn't shower Sissy in gifts like the married men did, and it was mostly because of this that Loretta despised him. Every day she told Sissy she was making a mistake.

He'll use you, then spit you out, and you'll be ruined. Every man around will see that you're still pining over him, and no one wants to deal with an emotional woman.

Loretta had told Sissy from the beginning that she wanted her to find a rich man and get out of town, but Sissy began to suspect that Loretta started to like the pawnable gifts too much.

Despite the way Sissy had manipulated J.D. into dating her, they genuinely liked each other. They both had the same ambitions: have a family and have a lot of money. In the conservative circles J.D. traveled in, he realized at a young age that a successful marriage—at least successful on the outside —was the key to moving up in the world. Everyone did couples activities and got their kids together. No one wanted to invite a playboy bachelor to their family-friendly parties, and those parties were where the job promotions happened.

They had a strong relationship, but the event that got a ring on her finger was when Sissy went with J.D. to one of those fancy parties. All those etiquette books had paid off, and Sissy had traded her hick accent for a genteel Southern one—thanks to watching Gone with the Wind about one hundred times. She was beautiful enough, polite enough, and aloof enough to capture the attention of everyone there. And as if she was interviewing for the position of a

Southern society wife, J.D. quickly realized she was perfect for him.

He proposed the very next day with an enormous diamond ring set in platinum.

"Marry me, and we'll get rich together," he said with a teasing gleam in his eye.

But when she told Loretta that her dreams were finally coming true, Loretta was furious.

You're selling yourself short! You can do better. You said yourself he's a playboy. He'll leave you at the altar.

No matter how much Sissy argued, Loretta wouldn't listen. It became clear that all she ever cared about was using Sissy for money. She didn't care about Sissy's goals or happiness, and she sure as hell didn't want her golden goose to leave town.

But Sissy was eighteen and didn't need her mama's permission to get married. She and J.D. would move in together, and then Loretta wouldn't be able to stop her.

Loretta knew it, too.

So she did the one thing that could threaten Sissy's marriage to a man who wanted the perfect society wife: she got drunk, dressed up like a whore, and showed up at their engagement party.

All the color had drained out of Sissy's face when she saw her, and for one horrible moment, she thought she'd be sick. But Sissy was a fighter, and she could think quick on her feet. She told all of them that this was her poor aunt who had suffered a head trauma and had never been right after that.

It ruined the party, and she had to leave immediately to take her "aunt" home. For one horrible week, he broke off their engagement and she nearly lost her chance to escape Loretta and the trailer park.

She got him back though—in spite of everything. Still, Sissy had to constantly prove herself after that to J.D. and his parents.

Through blood, sweat, and tears, Sissy had won, and Loretta had failed despite her best efforts.

And it was five years before she talked to her mama again. Another year after that when she told J.D. the truth about who she was.

Because for better or worse, Loretta made Sissy into the resilient fighter she was today. She hadn't meant to in the end, but she got Sissy out of that town, just like she said she would.

Trapped in her memories, Sissy only distantly registered a Code Blue being announced overhead. Not long after, a nurse came running in the hallway to find her.

"It's your mama, honey," she said. "She's lost consciousness again and her heart is failing."

After reliving those horrible memories, Sissy's first thought was, *Isn't it what she deserves?*

But then she came to her senses and hurried after the nurse to her mama's room.

Don't die, Mama.

I'm not ready.

THE PRESENT

The others wait for another hour, their voices hushed as though we're in church, but then they slowly start to leave. I stay. I don't even know what I'm waiting for. Who knows if her parents will leave the hospital room? I sit on one of the uncomfortable waiting room chairs, far from the other people here, and stare at the floor. I can't even look at my phone. My stomach is still churning, and I worry I'll have to run for the bathroom again if I move too much.

My thoughts torture me. I think of when I first saw her swimming with the others, wearing her bright pink floaties. I sneered then at the way her mother didn't pay her any attention—how she even had her back turned to the pool! But even though I remember thinking, *She could drown and her mother wouldn't even know!* It had just been in that vague worst-case scenario way. I never thought it would actually happen. And then when it came down to it—to saving her —I'd been slow to react at all.

The rest of the moments after I saw her in the pool blur together until they're just a rush of terrible images and feelings. Until I'm standing on that circular driveway, watching the ambulance load her small body into the back.

There are moments in time where I so desperately want the power to turn back the clock, but I've never felt it like I have today. Where it's just this horrible, gut-wrenching sense of wrongness. If I could go back to just a couple of hours ago, I wouldn't just sneer and think mean thoughts. I would go to her mother and tell her that she needs to watch her little girl while she's in the pool. That just because there are other adults around doesn't mean any of us are watching. Hell, most of them were drunk by then!

But when I search deep within myself, I know I didn't say anything to warn her mother because I was too busy watching the chaos I orchestrated. I don't think there is a time I've hated myself more.

Thinking these things makes my mouth go dry, and I stand to find a vending machine to get a bottle of water. I can't even bring myself to talk to the nurses at their station, so I just wander around until I find a lonely machine with cokes and bottles of water. I fish around in my bag for a dollar. As I pay, someone comes behind me.

When I turn with my bottle of water, I recognize her immediately. There are dark circles under her eyes, and her face is drawn, and she looks at me completely without the hatred I deserve.

"Maria," I say in surprise.

She shocks me speechless by stepping toward me and hugging me.

"Thank you for saving my baby," she says with tears in her voice. "I didn't even know...she was just drowning in

front of all of us, and I didn't even notice. She was probably absolutely terrified. I'll never forgive myself."

I don't understand how Maria isn't blaming me for this,
so I'm slow to react. "How is she?"

"She's stable. She seemed to respond to our touch and
our voices, and now she's sleeping. I just…I had this terrible
feeling inside me and I had to get out for a second."

"I can't imagine. I'm so sorry——"

"Have you been waiting to talk to me?" Maria asks, as
though suddenly realizing I'm here. At the hospital.

"Well, yes. I wanted to see how you were doing, and——"

"You can come see her. She's stable now, so I think they
would allow you to come in, too."

"Oh, I wouldn't want to impose like that," I say, even
though this is exactly what I need to do. I need to own up
to the horrible mistake I made. But when it comes down to
it, I'm a coward. This has been my problem all along: I'm a
coward who lashes out at people secretly rather than tell
them how I really feel. Of course, this is just the tip of the
iceberg of problems I have.

"It's not at all. James wants to thank you, for one thing,
and maybe it would even help her to hear you. You're the
one who pulled her out, after all."

I shudder. I did, but that was after…

Maria is insistent, though, and I don't have the strength
to tell her no again.

"All right, I'll come with you."

We're quiet as we walk through the hallways, and I try
not to look in any of the rooms. I don't want to see children
in ICU. My heart can't take it.

The room is dark when we enter, and the glow from all
the different medical equipment is eerie. James sits beside

Ariana's bed with his head in his hands. He's the picture of misery, and my heart twists.

My gaze is drawn reluctantly to the hospital bed, where a tiny form lies unmoving. Horribly, she is intubated and connected to a ventilator.

"When they saw that she was waking up but still struggling to breathe, they gave her medicine to put her back to sleep and hooked her up to all of this," she said with a nod at all the medical equipment. "They said her lungs needed some extra help for a while."

"Have they said how she'll be when she wakes up?"

"The doctor said he's hopeful that she'll be just fine. Apparently, brain damage can occur if they don't get out of the water in five minutes or less, and you acted right away."

And here it is. The moment where I confess the truth. Maria and James weren't watching, so they don't know when the drowning happened. They don't know how long it took me. The precious seconds lost.

I take a deep breath, and my voice wavers. "I need to tell you something."

SARAH ANNE

S arah Anne had a Pavlovian response to the coffee shop as soon as she smelled the rich scent of coffee. It made her abdomen flutter low, echoes of lustful desire for Hampton from all the times they'd flirted and come outside to make out like teenagers.

She saw him right away, sitting at their usual table in the darkest corner of the shop. He took a sip of coffee as he looked down at his phone, and it was hard to believe that this handsome, professional-looking man sent her endless, obsessive text messages even though she'd asked him repeatedly to stop.

With a deep, bracing breath, she walked over to their table.

As soon as Hampton saw her, his face lit up, the corner of his eyes crinkling handsomely. He hugged her before she could stop him, and she kept her spine stiff.

"I got you your overly sweet coffee of choice," he said, pushing the latte toward her.

"Thank you," she said, but she didn't take a drink.

"I'm glad you finally agreed to meet me here." When she didn't say anything, he bravely forged ahead. "I was watching that show we love last night—the haunted house one," he said, and Sarah Anne just smiled. She actually hated that show. It scared the bejeezus out of her. "But I couldn't even enjoy it. I missed your little shrieks."

"Those were genuine screams of fear." When he looked surprised, she nudged him with her elbow. "I told you about a hundred times I can't stand ghost shows. They freak me out."

"Seriously? I thought you loved that one though."

"Well, you just don't listen. Like when I say you've got to stop texting me for instance."

"I thought you liked my persistence," he said with a teasing grin, but when she didn't smile back, he sighed. "I'm not going to lie, Sarah Anne, it's been hell for me being separated from you. I don't know how I'm going to make it through the summer not seeing you at the preschool every day."

"I'm sad about it, too, Hampton, but it's for the best. I told you before that I'm not willing to hurt my family over this, and we narrowly avoided disaster with poor Ava nearly walking in on us."

"She didn't even notice!"

Sarah Anne gave him a look. "She noticed enough to tell her friends at school—you know that. And I'm lucky Erica didn't say anything to Mark. She certainly threatened to."

"Erica wouldn't do that," Hampton said, waving her off.

"I'm pretty sure Erica is behind those incriminating texts, so I wouldn't put it past her, which is why I'm just calling the whole thing off."

"She's all talk—that's why she's a lawyer."

Sarah Anne shook her head. "I don't care. I don't want to risk it."

"If Mark found out, then there wouldn't be anything to risk anymore."

Sarah Anne looked at him sharply. "That's a completely illogical way to look at it. If he found out, I don't even know what would happen, but it wouldn't be good. It has the potential to destroy my family. I would never want my kids to find out."

"I just don't know what I'll say to him when we play golf," he said in an unsettling tone. "He'll probably ask about my girlfriend—you're the one who told him I have one."

Sarah Anne glared daggers at him over her untouched cup of coffee. "Who said you have to keep hanging out with him, Hampton?"

"If he calls to go golfing, what am I supposed to say? I can't tell him no."

"You're a doctor! Everyone knows you're busy as hell! And anyway, you can tell him the truth now: you broke up with her."

She shot down his ridiculous excuses, so then he switched tactics. "How am I supposed to see you every day and not want to kiss you…or touch you?" He'd reached out and touched her hand, but she didn't waver.

All she had to do was think of Mark's question in the

dark, and the horrible feeling of betraying him. "Well, the school year is almost over. I think you'll recover fine come summer."

His warm hazel eyes looked pained. "This is it then? I guess there's nothing I can do to change your mind...?"

"No, there isn't."

He nodded and leaned back in his chair like he was finally accepting the inevitable. "I guess I'll see you at Sissy's party."

"Sure," Sarah Anne said with a smile as she stood and grabbed her bag.

When she walked out of the coffee shop, she took a deep breath, and it was like she could finally breathe again. She should have done this a long time ago, and she was annoyed at herself for putting it off for so long. Especially since all she felt now was an incredible sense of relief.

Sarah Anne didn't trust Hampton for a second, though, so the first thing she did when she got in her car was what she should have done a long time ago: she pulled up his number in her contacts and blocked him.

THE PARTY

MARIA

Maria didn't expect an invitation to Sissy's party, but it came anyway. It was printed on stationary so beautiful it could have been for a wedding. Holding the creamy paper in her hand, a gnawing desire grew in Maria's heart. All the invitations must have cost hundreds of dollars. What was it like to blow that kind of money on pieces of paper?

Hell, I'm more careful with Sissy's money than she is, Maria thought to herself darkly.

This invitation was just another sign that Maria's luck was changing. She couldn't believe it two weeks ago when Sissy texted her and said she wouldn't be there to let "Sabrina" in. When Maria had first seen Sissy's name pop up on her phone, she'd been almost too afraid to open up the message. She didn't want to see Sissy's reaction to the news that Maria had been arrested before, and she was convinced Sissy would say not even a family member could come clean her house. But she didn't say that at all. Clearly Sissy just wanted her house cleaned.

Maria had arrived without fear and was let in by a harried-looking older woman who said she was the nanny. She showed Maria where the cleaning supplies were, but after that, she was busy helping the kids get ready for school. That worked out just fine for Maria since she wanted to avoid the kids seeing her—she knew they'd recognize her and possibly mention it to Sissy. It was almost too easy. Maria went into every room on the first floor as though she was deciding which was the best one to clean first, but really she was looking for the office. She knew a man like J.D. would have a home office as well, and it was in a tucked-away part of the house, off the laundry room.

Everything about it indicated wealth and status. There were huge antique maps on the wall, bookshelves holding matching leather-bound books, and a custom-made mahogany desk that jutted out from the wall. The wide windows gave a sweeping view of the backyard, and the computer was sleek and high-tech. Maria knew almost nothing about computers, so she didn't even bother with that, but she did know from being a house cleaner that people still tended to keep at least a few paper copies of important documents. Ones that made it too easy to find their credit card information.

In a mahogany filing cabinet—metal wasn't good enough apparently—was a locked drawer that Maria knew would contain everything she wanted. She pulled two paper clips from her pocket and had the drawer open in about twenty seconds, which was about ten more than it would have taken her before. She'd gotten rusty.

The contents were labeled with folders that identified each section. It took less than thirty seconds to find the "credit card" folder. Inside was a copy of each of their credit cards, including a black American Express with a sky-high limit. It looked like it was one they used often, so Maria pulled out her phone and took a picture.

She closed the drawer, locked it back up with her paper clip, and went back to scrubbing baseboards. Her heart beat furiously in her chest, but she knew from experience that her facial expression was unchanged. She had perfected her poker face in juvie.

With every beat of her frantic heart, as she moved from room to room cleaning, she knew she'd crossed a line. This was more than taking the soap, or even pocketing a little extra money from her house cleaning. Even though it had been ridiculously easy to do, the risks of what she planned to do were higher than anything she'd ever pulled before.

But Maria knew how rich people were. They didn't obsessively check their credit card statements, not like the poor schmucks living paycheck to paycheck. They may set alerts for limits—like if some idiot stole their credit card and tried to buy something over $1,000, but Maria knew how to get around it. Small exchanges were the way to go. They'd never even miss the money.

Maria spent the rest of the time cleaning Sissy's house until it was immaculate. It was a fair trade since she was positive Sissy would underpay her for deep cleaning this massive house. As she scrubbed, dusted, and vacuumed, she thought of what she could use the credit card for. Anything, as long as she could order it online.

She waited for the heavy feeling of guilt to fall on her like a boulder, but all she felt was a sense of relief. It was like being thrown a lifeline.

And now, just a few days after cleaning Sissy's house, as she held this beautiful invitation in her hand, she thought of those credit card numbers. She didn't have a dress to wear, and they definitely couldn't afford one ordinarily.

Maria couldn't think of a better thing to use the credit card for than this. She pulled up her favorite online dress shop and scrolled through possibilities, her mood lighter than it had been in a long time. Maybe since moving here.

She could tell that Lauren and the others had thought her dress at the Christmas party was too low-cut, but Maria was drawn to every dress in that style. After a moment of struggling with herself, she finally thought, *Screw them. I'll get the dress I want to wear.*

She chose a bright, tropical print with a halter top. The dress looked like it would be snug but flattering to her curves. It cost a hundred dollars, and Maria even applied an online coupon to save on shipping.

See? I'm taking better care of your credit card than you do, Sissy.

As soon as she submitted the order, a message popped up on her therapy app from her therapist, and Maria jumped guiltily. It was like the woman was keeping tabs on her.

Reluctantly, Maria opened the message.

Maria, it's been a while since we last talked, and I just wanted to check in on you. Have you been using the breathing techniques we talked about? Have you found another job?

Maria's first instinct was to ignore her, and she almost closed up the app. But something stopped her.

She didn't want her therapist to repeatedly message her

or think she did something horrible like commit suicide, so she typed out a quick response.

The techniques have been working well. I'm still looking for a new job, but at least Ariana is almost finished with preschool.

There. Plenty of positivity. Or at least enough that her therapist wouldn't feel the need to call the cops to make sure she was still alive. Maria hurriedly closed the app before she could respond.

She was about to put her phone away when she thought, *I could use some new shoes to go with that dress.*

It felt so good to be spending someone else's money.

———

The day of the party, all three of them were wearing brand new outfits thanks to Sissy's credit card. Maria just told James she got everything massively on-sale, and he accepted that excuse because Ariana was lit up like a ray of sunlight. She was obsessed with mermaids right now, and her bathing suit looked like rainbow mermaid scales. Her coverup matched, and she wore rainbow flip-flops. Her little face glowed with happiness.

But as they arrived at Sissy's party, Maria's stomach tied itself into one massive knot. She was afraid of so many things. The nanny might be there and would recognize her. Sissy would somehow know about her credit card info being stolen and accuse Maria in front of everyone. The crowd would overwhelm Maria's fragile nerves and render her a panicky, anxious mess.

Even her knees felt weak as she got out of the car and started the long walk to Sissy's house. There were so many cars that they all had to park in a grassy area to the right of the circular driveway.

James whistled when he got a look at the house. "This is some place. Must be nice being the big boss."

Maria let out some sort of weak response, and he glanced down at her with concern in his dark eyes.

"You okay, babe?" he asked.

"Fine," she said with a quick nod.

He wrapped his strong arms around her comfortingly. "You look gorgeous. Way hotter than all these uptight bitches in here."

She snorted a laugh. "Thanks. I think."

"Mommy! The pool! I hear splashing!"

Ariana was practically quivering with excitement. She hadn't been swimming since last summer, and that had been at a public pool. Swimming with all her friends from class was something new and exciting.

"I know, baby. So exciting! But remember, you can't get in until we put on your floaties, okay?"

"Okay!"

Maria touched her arm and made her stop skipping for a moment. "Look at Mommy. I'm serious, okay? You've only had swimming lessons once, and that was a long time ago. You have to keep your floaties on every second you're in the pool."

"She's got it...she's got it," James said with a dismissive little laugh. "The pool will be surrounded by grown-ups. She's not in any danger."

Maria let out a huge sigh. "You're right. It's going to be so much fun," she added with a bright smile for Ariana.

"Yeah! Hurry, Mommy. Everyone is having fun without me."

Maria shared a smile with James. This reminded her so much of the first day of school, when Ariana was happy and excited, but Maria had just wanted to hide under a rock.

At least this time she had James with her. His presence beside her felt warm and solid, and it gave her one person she could talk to without feeling awkward. That was the worst part about parties—when you had to go up to a group of people and try and join their conversation. Most of the time, Maria just chose to hover on the outskirts of groups who were talking. Well, unless she got drunk.

They rang the bell, and the door was immediately opened by an older woman in a uniform. "Come on in," the lady said. "Everyone is out back by the pool." She held her hand out to indicate the back door that you could see from the doorway.

"Thank you," Maria said, trying not to laugh as James turned to give Maria a slow glance with one eyebrow raised.

"The pool!" Ariana shouted, and then Maria had to hurry to keep up with her.

"Wait for us," Maria said.

"This place is unreal. This is like some Downton Abbey shit," James said with a jab of his chin toward the...door woman? Maid? Maria wasn't even sure.

"Not so loud," Maria said in a laughing whisper.

But if the inside of the house was as formal as Downton Abbey, the backyard was like a tropical oasis. The pool was enormous, with a waterfall, swim-up bar, and water slide. Wrought iron tables were laden with food: chips and dip, incredible fruit displays, a fajita station, and a full bar.

There were so many lounge chairs and table sets that it looked like a resort.

"Man, this landscaping is incredible," James said.

There were palm trees and tropical flowers, a riot of color and lush greenery. The people there were dressed just as colorfully in paisley pastel dresses and seersucker suits.

Sissy was off on her own by the pool, looking down on the rest of them like a queen surveying her subjects.

All of this had to be taken in at a glance, though, because Ariana was already making a beeline for the pool.

"Hey, hey, you know the drill," Maria said as Ariana jumped from foot to foot eagerly. "Sunscreen and floaties first."

"Okay, okay," Ariana said in a long-suffering voice that gave a good indication of what she'd be like as a teenager.

As Ariana stripped out of her coverup, Sophie came over, dripping wet and smiling widely. She was wearing her floaties, too. "Come on, Ariana!"

"Okay, just a minute. I need my sunscreen and floaties."

Maria nodded with approval. "We're almost done, okay? Then Ariana can swim with you."

Putting sunscreen on Ariana was like trying to put it on a wet cat, but somehow, Maria succeeded. She fastened the buckle on her pink floaties, which also had a mermaid on the front.

"All right, you're good to go," Maria said. "Let's go to the steps."

She walked Ariana to the wide steps and helped her into the pool. It hadn't been warm outside long, even though it was in the eighties today, so Maria expected Ariana to complain immediately that the water was too cold. But Maria was surprised to feel that it was warm. It must have been a heated pool.

The other little girls flocked to Ariana as soon as they saw her on the steps.

"I like your mermaid swimsuit," Emily said with a shy smile.

And then they were all happily comparing swimsuits and floaties. It made Maria smile.

"Stay in the shallow end, okay?"

"Okay!"

When she returned to James, Mark and Sarah Anne were there with colorful drinks in hand.

"There you are!" Sarah Anne said with a bright smile. She threw one arm around Maria for an enthusiastic hug. She smelled like coconut and rum, and her turquoise-colored dress showed off her tan. She looked like a Barbie. "You've got to get you one of these drinks. They're amazing."

"It smells good," Maria said. "What's in it?"

"No idea, but it's coconutty perfection. Matches my dress, too," she added with a laugh.

Maria had missed whatever greeting Mark and James had given each other, but she could see by James's stiff shoulders that he was uncomfortable. Did he blame Mark for not giving him that promotion? Maria felt a stab of annoyance on her husband's behalf.

"Sophie is so excited that Ariana's here," Sarah Anne continued, her gaze on the girls swimming in the pool. "We'll have to continue getting them together over the summer."

"Ariana would love that."

James touched her arm. "I'm going to go get a beer. Did you want something?"

"I'll have what Sarah Anne has," Maria said, promising herself she'd just have one.

"You can order the signature drink," Sarah Anne added.

"I can't believe she has a full bar," Maria said when James walked away. "This must have cost a fortune."

Sarah Anne laughed. "It does, but they don't even blink an eye."

"Must be nice," Maria muttered. "And who was that answering the door? Did they hire a doorman?"

"I don't think Sissy took it that far. I'm pretty sure that was one of the caterers. It must have been part of the package to save Sissy from having to stand by the front door all day. I wish I'd thought of it, actually."

They watched their girls playing happily in the pool for a minute, and even Mary Elizabeth seemed to be behaving. She had passed out mermaid Barbies to all who wanted one, and Ariana's face was a picture of pure joy.

James returned with her drink, and Maria took a sip from the vibrantly blue concoction. Immediately, she could feel the alcohol hit her blood stream. It was fully loaded, for sure.

"Good, right?" Sarah Anne asked with a knowing smile.

It tasted like coconut and pineapple, and Maria knew that she'd be drunk after only a few, so she resigned herself to only enjoying one.

"It's fantastic," she said.

Out of the corner of her eye, she saw that James went

and sat at a table by himself. When he took out his phone, Maria frowned. Not a good sign.

"Lauren, I love your dress," Sarah Anne said from beside her. Maria turned to see Lauren coming toward them, wearing a bright pink dress with golden pineapples. She had on matching golden sandals.

"Thanks. Yours is gorgeous, too," Lauren said, giving Sarah Anne and Maria a quick hug. She and Maria exchanged compliments that Maria was never sure were actually genuine or not.

The talk changed to observations of what the kids were doing, and then Sarah Anne shook her empty cup. "I'm going to get a refill. Y'all need anything?"

Maria and Lauren shook their heads. "No thanks," Lauren said, and Maria noticed all she had was a glass of sweet tea. Maybe Lauren was trying to avoid a repeat of the Christmas party, too.

"James is looking miserable," Lauren said with a concerned look toward Maria's husband.

Maria sighed. "I don't know why he's being so unso-ciable—that's usually what I do at parties. Well," she glanced down at her drink with a sheepish look, "unless I've had too much to drink. But anyway, he talked to Mark when we first got here, but then he apparently decided his beer and phone were better company."

"I hope he's not upset with Mark over the promotion," Lauren said, and Maria glanced at her in surprise.

"How did you know about it? Did Sarah Anne tell you?" Maria asked.

"No, it was Wesley. He said that Mark had James lined up for the job, but he got shot down from someone higher up." She nodded her head toward J.D., who was lounging with one arm on the back of an outdoor sofa, watching a baseball game with some other men.

Maria took a huge gulp of her drink, trying unsuccessfully to suppress the anger rising in her abdomen. "I shouldn't be surprised."

"What surprised me is that y'all actually came to the party—I mean, I'm so glad you're here. It would have been so sad if Ariana had missed it. But I thought you'd be furious with Sissy, especially."

Maria stilled. "What do you mean?"

Lauren looked like she regretted saying so much. "You know those horrible anonymous text messages we all got?" Maria closed her eyes and nodded. She knew where this was going. "Sissy showed the one about you to J.D. and used it as some insane excuse to pass up your husband for one of their friends."

Maria felt like she'd been punched in the stomach. Nausea hit her hard, and she had that terribly desperate feeling that she wished she could disappear.

"What I did when I was younger was terrible, but what does that have to do with James?"

"It doesn't make sense, but she convinced J.D. that if James was in a higher position, and you got arrested again, it would make the whole company look bad."

"That's fucking ridiculous!" Maria snapped, and several women standing nearby gave her matching sharp looks. Maria just glared at them until they turned around again.

"I know. I'm so sorry...I shouldn't have told you any of this," Lauren said, looking miserable. "Wesley said he thought James knew, so I thought he would have told you... I thought you came here to make a statement, you know? Or maybe because you didn't want Ariana to miss out..."

Lauren kept trying to explain why she'd dropped a bomb like that on Maria, but Maria stopped listening. She watched Sissy instead. Sissy stood across the pool from them, designer sunglasses shielding her eyes as she laughed at something one of the preschool board member moms said to her. Maria doubted Sissy even knew Maria and her family were here.

Sissy had seemed to hate Maria from the moment she met her, and Maria had done nothing but continue to try and be her friend. No matter what Maria did, though, Sissy acted like a cold-hearted bitch.

Maria had never tried to confront Sissy, but this time Sissy was messing with Maria's husband.

And she wasn't going to let Sissy get away with it.

38

___

SARAH ANNE

When Sarah Anne refilled her drink and returned to Lauren and Maria, the atmosphere had totally changed. "You look like someone kicked your puppy," Sarah Anne said to Maria, whose face was as dark as a storm cloud.

"I'm fine," Maria said as she drained the last of her drink. "I think I just need a refill."

She stalked off, and Sarah Anne glanced at Lauren for an explanation.

"We were just talking about Sissy," Lauren said.

"Oh Lord. What did she do now?"

"Remember what we talked about with the text messages?" When Sarah Anne nodded, she leaned closer. "Sissy used that as an excuse to get J.D. to hire someone else for a promotion instead of James."

Sarah Anne's eyes widened. "Are you serious? He probably thinks it was Mark's fault! I practically promised them both that Mark would help him out."

"Don't worry. She knows who to blame now."

"What does Sissy care about promotions at Mercedes anyway?"

"I think she just hates Maria and wants to screw her over to be honest with you," Lauren said with a frown.

"That's messed up. These are their *lives* we're talking about." Sarah Anne heard the slight slur of her words and glanced down at her drink. Lord, she should slow down a bit on the free booze if she was already slurring. But then her gaze landed on Mark and she saw that he hadn't even finished his first beer. He would make sure they got home in one piece, so what was the harm?

Lauren didn't seem to notice, or at least, decided not to comment on Sarah Anne's state of inebriation. "You know how she is, though. She can be cold-hearted. I wouldn't be surprised if that trailer park picture was from where she used to live or something. She's always seemed as mean as a junkyard dog to me."

Sarah Anne looked at Lauren with her mouth open, both because of that pretty nasty insult and because her own thoughts on that picture had been totally different. "I thought it might have been someone she was having an affair with, though I couldn't picture her with some Billy Bob in a mobile home."

"As far as I know, the only thing Sissy cares about is the preschool. Judging from how often her husband has affairs, she doesn't care about whether or not she has sex either."

Sarah Anne nearly spat out her drink. "J.D. has affairs?" She glanced over at where he was lounging on the outdoor couch, watching a ball game. "I guess I can see that, actually. But wouldn't that throw her into the arms of another man even faster? Or maybe she isn't interested in men at all," she added, lowering her voice.

Lauren shrugged. "Could be, but being a secret lesbian doesn't excuse her from acting the way she does."

Sarah Anne laughed. "That's true enough."

"So, speaking of affairs," Lauren said, and Sarah Anne stiffened.

"Girl, what a segue," she said with a laugh.

"Hampton asked me to tell you he wants to talk to you in the house, and I debated not passing that along, but he seemed resigned. So then I figured you must have finally called it quits."

They'd been broken up a week, and just as Sarah Anne had predicted, Hampton hadn't really given up. He couldn't text or call her anymore, but he still emailed. And he didn't hesitate to talk to her any time they were at the preschool at the same time, which was every day.

She was embarrassed to admit she still thought about him, especially at night. It was like her body was addicted to him or something. She had cravings. So far, though, she'd managed to avoid giving in.

Only now Lauren was unwittingly tempting her with the news that he wanted to talk to her here. There was always that part of Sarah Anne that craved attention from a man, and she'd barely gotten a brief once-over glance from Mark today when she knew she was looking tan and busty and incredibly hot. Hampton would skim his hands along her slim waist and drink her in with his eyes, wearing that crooked smile of his.

"Yeah, we did finally agree to call it off," she finally said to Lauren, even as her body was starting to hum. Admittedly, that may have been the booze, but Sarah Anne felt like a drug addict being offered a hit.

"Well, he's in there waiting for you. Last I saw him was in the kitchen."

Sarah Anne glanced down at her drink and realized she'd somehow sucked it down in the course of their conversation. "I'll go see what he wants then."

Her thoughts were swimming in her head, but she did have the presence of mind to check where Mark was again. He'd taken his beer over to where J.D. was and seemed totally engrossed in the game. If it was anything like it was at home, he wouldn't get up again until the ninth inning. She was about to walk off when she remembered she hadn't checked on Sophie. Mom guilt hit her hard.

Sophie was still in the shallow end of the pool with the other girls, playing mermaids on the steps. Jackson and William were playing with a floating basketball hoop. Neither were in any danger, but Sarah Anne still felt a little sick that she almost hadn't made sure.

"Will you keep an eye on Sophie and Jackson for me?" she asked Lauren. "I don't trust their daddy to turn around regularly to check on them."

Never mind that Sarah Anne had almost run off without checking either.

Lauren smiled, but there was something in her expression that made Sarah Anne pause. "Sure," Lauren said.

Sarah Anne quickly forgot what it was that bothered her and patted Lauren's arm absently. "Thanks, honey. I'll be back in just a minute."

Her heels struck out on the flagstones as she made her way through the clusters of people drinking and talking. She caught snippets of conversation as she went.

I don't care how ugly Sissy can be as long as she keeps having parties like this, one flush-faced preschool mom said with a laugh.

Do you want to order some exercise gear from me? I just started selling it, and it's incredible stuff. Sarah Anne didn't even have to look to know it was one of the gym rat moms. Even at a party, they could only talk about one thing.

Does Sissy seem colder than usual to you? This is a party, but she looks like someone spit in her drink.

Lots of not-so-nice comments about Sissy, which made Sarah Anne's heart twist. Here they all were, eating up her food and drinking her alcohol, but no one could scrounge up something nice to say? Not even Sarah Anne and Lauren, her so-called friends, had been complimentary. How awful. Did Sissy have any real friends?

Her train of thought slipped out of her head the moment she stepped into the kitchen. There were quite a few people—the caterers, she guessed—who were in various states of food prep and cleanup. She didn't see Hampton, so she continued out into the hall between the kitchen and living room.

"I didn't think you'd come," Hampton said from an alcove near the powder room.

Sarah Anne tried not to notice the way her body instantly came alive at the sound of his deep voice.

"Lauren said you were waiting for me in the kitchen," Sarah Anne said because it was all she could think of. Her mouth had suddenly gone dry. Talking in the busy kitchen was one thing, but here, in this secluded hallway made her heart beat too fast.

"The caterers kept giving me funny looks—I think they thought I wanted to steal something," he added with a grin, "so I came in here. But now that I see you dressed like that, I'm regretting it."

"Why?" she asked, even as heat crept up her neck.

"Because you look incredibly sexy."

She knew he would make that comment—had been counting on it, actually—but it still brought an embarrassing level of desire flooding into her body.

I'm pathetic, she thought, but only briefly. The alcohol helpfully pushed such unpleasant thoughts quickly out of her mind.

"I know you didn't want me to come talk to you just to say that, so what do you want?"

He took a step closer to her, his warmth filling the small space. "Well, right now, I want you."

She reached out and put a staying hand on his chest. "Sweet talk aside…be serious. Didn't we go through this already?"

"I've felt terrible since our last conversation. I can't tell you how relieved that you agreed to come talk to me here."

"That's against my better judgement, honestly." She knew he was baiting her, but she couldn't help herself. "Why have you felt terrible? Because you kept threatening me?"

He winced. "I didn't mean to come across like that, baby. I was just desperate to keep our relationship going. But what I wanted to tell you is that I did what you told me to. Mark invited me to go golfing, but I told him we were completely slammed at work."

Sarah Anne just huffed and raised her eyebrows.

"I'm sorry, okay? I'm sorry I made you worry that I would tell Mark anything. Of course I would never do that to you." When she still didn't say anything, he reached out and took her hand. "Forgive me?"

She made the mistake of meeting his gaze. With his hand still holding hers, the electric connection they had leaped between the two of them. There was a moment where she thought, *He's going to kiss me,* and then he leaned toward her. Like lighting a match, that was all it took. Every honorable thing she'd thought went out the window, hurried by her slightly booze-addled brain.

They kissed like they were starved for each other. He pushed her against the wall, and she moaned so loud, she was afraid the caterers would hear. "We can't do this here," she said breathlessly as he kissed her neck.

That was when he guided her to the nearby powder room, kissing her senseless the entire way. They closed the door, but when Hampton fumbled for the lock, it wouldn't stay.

He shrugged and kept kissing her, hiking up her dress to skim his hand up her thigh.

One last time won't hurt anything, she thought. *One more time and then I'll never do this again.*

39

SISSY

The end-of-the-year party was usually Sissy's favorite day of the year. She liked it better than Christmas. The weather that was warm but not blazing hot, the kids screaming happily in the pool, the catered food, and to be perfectly honest, the naked admiration and jealousy from all her guests.

But this year, she couldn't stop thinking about her mama. It was hard to be in a party mood when Loretta was in the hospital dying. Sissy went to see her earlier that morning, and she couldn't believe how fast her condition had deteriorated. She was barely conscious and struggling to breathe because of the pneumonia that had taken root in her lungs. What happened to the cancer being treatable? What happened to the surgery being successful?

Sissy knew the answers to those questions, though. Loretta had continued to smoke, that was why. She couldn't give up her ridiculous, stupid, dangerous habit to save her life. But that was her mama in a nutshell. Even though she was undeniably worried about Loretta, at the same time, she couldn't believe her mama had reminded her of that horrible night that nearly destroyed their relationship. Sissy wasn't sure she'd even be talking to her now if she wasn't dying—not after bringing that shit up again. But Sissy would never do that to her children. She'd never deny them a grandparent, especially when they really only had one good one. J.D.'s parents were older and spent almost all of their time either on the golf course or at the club. Their grandchildren were viewed as a novel entertainment suitable only for major holidays.

Loretta would die, and Sissy's children would be left with grandparents who never went to any of their activities and really only wanted to see them at Christmas. Sometimes Easter.

A lump formed in Sissy's throat, and she took a sip of her drink to force the emotion down. The last thing she needed was to start crying in front of all the preschool parents. They were like circling sharks. They already sensed that something was wrong with her—she could tell by all the frequent glances her way. Right now, they were probably remarking on how unsociable she was being, which was true. She was pretending to watch the kids swim and oversee the catering, but really she was trying to talk herself into joining the party. She knew having a breakdown in front of all of them would make their day—not that they were sadistic, but there was nothing people loved more than having something really juicy to talk about.

She hadn't even said hi to Sarah Anne or Lauren yet, but she saw them both talking with Maria. She wasn't sure she could stomach any more of Maria's pathetic attempts to network and get her husband a promotion, so she was avoiding going over there. Even facing Lauren right now made her feel an overwhelming sense of weariness. She didn't want to deal with thoughts of her sleeping with J.D., even though he swore it was already over. Lauren was fully engaged in a conversation with Sarah Anne anyway, so it gave Sissy an excuse not to go interrupt.

She watched all the kids playing happily in the pool, though she knew it was only a matter of time before Mary Elizabeth got hungry and started taking it out on Ariana. Sissy was hoping she'd hold it together for another hour or so before Sissy was forced to go into full-on mom-servant mode when she'd have to bring Mary Elizabeth endless snacks and drinks.

Across the pool, Maria had gone off somewhere, and Sarah Anne was making slightly unsteady progress through the clusters of parents talking. She seemed to be headed toward the main house, even though there was a pool house with a bathroom. Her drunk ass clearly forgot though. Sissy saw how hard she was sucking down those drinks, and ordinarily she'd try to intervene, but it might actually be a good thing. If parents had a wildly drunk Sarah Anne to gossip about, then they might ignore Sissy's obvious unhappiness.

With no one left to talk to, Lauren made her way over to Sissy, and Sissy tried to school her features so she wasn't giving Lauren a nasty look. It was hard, though, considering Sissy's expressions were rarely warm and welcoming.

"This is a great party as always, Sissy," Lauren said.

"Thank you. I hope you got something to drink."

Lauren smiled in an odd sort of way. "I'm not drinking. Besides, I think everyone else is drinking enough for me."

"Well, it is a party. I couldn't help but notice Wesley didn't come with you."

"He's on his last hunting and fishing trip of the season, and then he'll be home all summer."

Sissy gave her a knowing look. "Is he actually hunting this time?"

"He's not sleeping with Tiffany this weekend if that's what you mean. Even she goes on the back burner when it comes to his last chance to shoot a big buck."

"And what about you? I understand your affair is already over." She tried not to make it a question. J.D. was many things, but he wasn't a liar. That was part of their understanding.

"I got what I wanted out of it," Lauren said with a tight smile.

"Wesley came to his senses about his affair?"

"He won't be seeing her anymore."

"Well, then I'm glad J.D. could do that for you at least. It's more than he usually gets out of his one-night stands." She couldn't help that last little dig—putting Lauren in the same category as cheap women J.D. picked up and discarded the next day. She didn't like Lauren's attitude just now, like she deigned to talk to Sissy at all. It should be the other way around! And Sissy was quick to put her in her place.

To her credit, Lauren didn't flinch. "Two times with J.D. was more than enough, honestly."

Sissy had to keep from glancing at Lauren in unpleasant surprise. She was under the impression that it had been only once. "Then you and Wesley have resolved things?"

"You could say that."

It didn't exactly answer Sissy's question, but she

shrugged it off. It was a strange feeling for Sissy, but she found herself desperate to talk to someone about what was going on with her mama. If Lauren had opened up the least bit about Wesley, Sissy probably would have. *My mama is dying,* was on the tip of her tongue. She didn't say it, though. The way Lauren was acting, she wasn't even sure she'd care.

"I've found that there are more marriages that have... certain agreements...than you'd think. I guess people just don't always talk about them. It's not something you'd regularly post about on Facebook."

Lauren smiled. "You're right about that."

From across the pool, Sissy's gaze was drawn to Maria, who was glaring at her with drink in hand. "Hey, any idea what Maria's problem is? I'm not sure what about a party that I spent a small fortune on is making her glare at me like that."

Lauren glanced in Maria's direction before turning back to Sissy. "I have no idea, but James has been looking pretty broody, too, ever since they got here. Maybe they're arguing, but it just looks like she's glaring at you."

"Hm, ordinarily I would accept that explanation, only she's headed this way and still glaring at me."

Maria was wearing high heels, but she managed to keep her balance as she marched over toward them determinedly. She wore a dress with a cleavage-bearing bodice similar to the one she'd worn to the Christmas party, only it seemed slightly more appropriate here in the warm weather by the pool.

"Sissy, can I talk to you for a minute?" Maria asked in a rush, like she had to screw up her courage to even say that.

Lauren took a step away from them. "I'm going to go sample some of the food."

When she left, Sissy turned back to Maria. "You clearly have something on your mind, so yes, we can talk."

"I just really want to know what your problem is," Maria said, her eyes flashing angrily. Her entire body was stiff. "You've been nasty to me since the very first time we met."

"I don't know where this is coming from, Maria. I invited you to my party, and I haven't even spoken to you today until now, so I'm a little confused."

"So you're saying you don't hate me?" she demanded.

Sissy shrugged. "You're not my favorite person, to be honest, but no, I don't hate you."

Maria let out her breath in a scoff. "That right there. That's why everyone is here enjoying the free food and drink, but no one is fighting to come over to talk to you. No one even wants to be around you. I'm only here to yell at you, and Lauren was probably only talking to you because she's a decent person. If you don't hate me, then why have you always acted the way you have toward me?"

"Like what? Made honest comments to you? I'm sorry you took them so badly, but I don't like to put on a fake act for anyone. And if you must know, your palpable desperation to force your husband to crawl his way from the bottom to corporate at Mercedes is hard to watch."

Maria leaned back like she'd been struck but then nodded. "Okay, so if you want to go there, then I won't hold back. It's one thing to be bitchy to me, but why did you mess with my husband's chances at getting a promotion?" Her voice had risen to the point that others noticed there was some sort of argument going on, and Sissy could tell they were straining to hear.

Sissy tilted her chin up just a bit. "And how did I do that?"

"You know what you did! You have no idea how much we needed that money, and you just swooped in and ruined his chances for no reason. What kind of evil bitch does that?"

Maria stepped closer to Sissy until she was practically shouting in her face. It was obviously an intimidation technique, but she hadn't factored in Sissy being raised in the country. Sissy put her hand out as a forced buffer zone between her and Maria. She didn't physically touch her, but it was enough to make Maria take a step back.

"Who told you this?"

"Lauren," Maria said, her eyebrows raised and her tone clearly saying, *So you're screwed.*

Sissy turned to look for Lauren and spotted her talking to Mark and J.D. Mark looked upset by whatever she was saying, and Sissy frowned. "What did she say?"

40

LAUREN

L auren glanced down at her phone at the most recent message.

We'll be in the downstairs bathroom, it said.

She knew he wouldn't answer, so she didn't bother to text him back. She'd asked him earlier if he was sure he wanted to do this. Once they crossed the line, they couldn't go back.

I'm desperate. She'll leave me if I don't do something extreme. It didn't even work before when the kids were talking about her being at my house. This is my last chance.

There was a time when Lauren would never have entertained doing something like this, and even though he thought she was doing it to help him, the truth was the opposite. Lauren knew what it was like to be the one cheated on in a marriage. She also knew that Sarah Anne would never stop—not unless she was forced to. Lauren was only being a good friend.

Lauren could see J.D.'s expression turn wary the moment she walked up to where he and some other dads were all watching the baseball game.

Relax, this isn't about you, she thought with a roll of her eyes. *I already got what I wanted from you.*

"Hey, Mark," Lauren said, pointedly ignoring J.D. as Mark turned to her with a politely curious expression. She'd always liked Mark. He was a great guy who treated his wife like a queen and was always there for his kids. He didn't deserve what was happening to him, but he was also the only one who could stop it. "Sarah Anne sent me to find you."

"She did?" he asked, glancing around for Sarah Anne, but of course she wasn't out here anymore. "What's going on?"

Lauren lowered her voice. "She had a little too much to drink, and now she's really sick. She's in the bathroom right off the kitchen."

His expression immediately turned to one of concern, and he stood and moved away from the other men. It almost made Lauren feel bad for what she was doing. Almost. "Oh man, are you serious? Is she throwing up?"

Lauren twisted her face into a regretful one and nodded. "Could be food poisoning or something, too."

"I hope not," he said. "I didn't see her drink that much, but those fruity drinks were strong."

"That's what everyone has said. I'm glad I didn't have any."

As they walked toward the house, Lauren saw Maria get in Sissy's face. She'd have to hurry back to see how that panned out. Would Maria finally be pissed enough to tell Sissy how she felt? Or would she react the way she always did, like a beaten dog that keeps coming back to an abusive master?

The caterers were still hard at work when they entered the kitchen, and Mark glanced at Lauren. "Which way is the bathroom?"

"It's right through here," Lauren said, leading him to the hallway. The kitchen had been loud, so the hallway seemed even quieter by comparison once the door shut behind them.

Because of the quiet, they could hear a moan coming from the powder room.

Mark made a face. "She sounds miserable."

Lauren had to suppress a laugh and force her face into a sympathetic one. Yeah, she was really miserable in there.

Mark knocked on the door softly, but there was no response except for loud thumps. "Sarah Anne?"

She didn't answer, so he tried the door. It was unlocked, as Lauren knew it would be. That door never locked properly, and Sissy had never fixed it because the kids used to lock themselves inside.

Mark pushed open the door, calling his wife's name again, but was cut short when he saw what was happening inside the bathroom. From Lauren's vantage point, she could only see their reflection in the mirror: Hampton had Sarah Anne up against the wall.

Mark stood there like he'd been shot for one terrible moment until Sarah Anne screamed.

This brought Mark to his senses. "Sarah Anne, what the f—"

Lauren walked away before she could get caught up in the aftermath. She didn't want to leave Emily alone in the pool for long, even though Emily had learned how to save herself from drowning as an infant and took lessons every year. Besides, Lauren had another dramatic scene to play witness to.

———

W hen Lauren went back outside, Maria had stepped so close to Sissy that she was practically shouting in her face. Many people had stopped to watch the argument unfolding, but when Lauren looked around for James, she didn't see him anywhere.

Unbelievable. Then who's making sure Ariana is still safe?

Sarah Anne had at least asked Lauren to keep an eye on Sophie for her before running off to have sex with Hampton. Emily, Sophie, and Ariana were fine at the moment— still playing on the pool steps in the shallow end—but still. Maria certainly wasn't checking on her. She was too busy telling Sissy off.

Lauren moved closer to where Maria and Sissy were arguing so she could hear. This put her across from the middle of the pool, facing the waterfall.

"Yeah, I really want to know what your problem with me is," Maria was saying, her New York accent stronger than ever.

"Since you've cornered me at my own party and demanded to know, then I won't hold back. I wasn't a bit surprised to see that mug shot of you. You seemed desperate and grasping from the first time I met you, and I find it repulsive how obsessed you are with your husband's position at work. Don't you have your own goals?"

Lauren had to agree, although she found it a little ridiculous coming from Sissy. Wasn't Sissy the one who clawed her way out of the country by latching onto the first rich man she could? Sarah Anne stupidly thought the picture of the mobile home neighborhood was because Sissy was having some sordid affair, but it was obvious that wasn't true. Sissy was *from* that trailer park, and her mama still lived there. With chickens.

"You've never had to work for anything in your life," Maria said with a sneer as she waved her hand toward Sissy's elaborate backyard. "You have no idea what it's like to not have enough money to pay your bills. So yeah, I was doing everything I could to help James out because that's what a good wife does. I don't have a fancy degree or the luxury of just being on some preschool board without working, so that was the only thing I could do."

"Well, you did it in the most pathetic and obnoxious way," Sissy said, with her characteristic coldness. She sounded like she was making a casual observation, while Maria had turned red in the face with obvious anger.

"And you decided to ruin my life by making sure James couldn't get a promotion?"

"Look, all I did was tell J.D. about the text messages. I can't help that you have a history of being arrested."

"But that has nothing to do with James! He isn't the one with the record!"

Sissy shrugged. "I just told the truth."

"Yeah, but the point is, you didn't have to tell him that. You *wanted* to. Because you're just a mean bitch who likes to step on other people to feel better about herself. And how's that working out for you, Sissy? I don't see anyone over here kissing your ass today. No one wants to come talk to you because no one actually likes *you*. They like your pool and your house and your free drinks. But everyone hates talking

331

to you because you never care about anything anyone else says. It's like talking to a brick wall."

Maria's face was thunderous as she accentuated each thing she shouted with violent hand motions. Everyone was entranced by the showdown between the two of them, and no one was watching the kids in the pool.

Emily and Mary Elizabeth had taken off their floaties and were taking turns diving for mermaid Barbies off the pool steps. Lauren had seen them do it, but she hadn't been concerned. Both girls were better swimmers than she was and had been swimming together since infancy.

So when Ariana stood on the top step and unclipped her floaties, she wasn't immediately alarmed. "Mommy, I'm gonna try swimming!" she said.

Maria was too wrapped up in arguing with Sissy to hear her, and Lauren shook her head. Did Maria ever pay attention to her daughter?

Ariana jumped off the top step and did a little doggy paddle before returning to the steps.

"Try diving for it, Ariana!" Mary Elizabeth commanded.

"This is why everyone hates you!" Maria screeched at Sissy, drawing Lauren's attention back to the fight.

When she looked back at the girls, one was missing. Heart in her throat, she scanned the pool for Emily and let out her breath when she spotted her turquoise swimsuit. She was swimming to the side in the shallow end.

Mary Elizabeth emerged from under the water, grinning and holding a Barbie. Sophie still wore her floaties and was lazily treading water.

Dark hair floated under the water, and she realized

Ariana was down at the bottom. Was she trying to get the Barbie? But then she saw her arms flailing uselessly.

Lauren's gaze darted to Maria. Surely she would sense something was wrong with her daughter! But no, she was shouting at Sissy like a crazy person. Horribly, Lauren had a fleeting thought of: *This serves her right for being such a terrible mother.* She stood there for what felt like a full minute, just watching.

But then Lauren realized this was a child's life, and not part of her plan to get back at the others.

Ariana still hadn't surfaced, and her movements slowed. Lauren couldn't wait for Maria to suddenly realize her daughter was drowning. So she jumped in, fully-clothed.

She quickly grabbed hold of Ariana and hauled her out of the pool. The girl wasn't moving. Or breathing.

The other girls noticed what had happened and swam over to the steps.

Other moms and dads closest to the pool slowly realized what was happening—they had been watching the argument—and started shouting.

Lauren had learned CPR when Emily was just a baby. She wanted to be prepared for any emergency situation, and now she was glad for that training.

"Someone call 911!" she yelled to the nearest mom, who stood watching the scene open-mouthed. This brought her to her senses, and she pulled out her phone.

Lauren started compressions and breaths, taking care not to press too hard on Ariana's delicate sternum. She didn't want to break any bones, but she was desperate to get her breathing again.

At the same time, Maria finally realized it was her

daughter who lay lifeless at the side of the pool, and she let out a terrible scream before running to Ariana.

She fell to her knees beside her, and started sobbing and babbling to the point that Lauren wanted to slap her. It was only the rhythm of the compressions and breaths that kept her from doing just that.

"Isn't Dr. Hampton here?" Sissy shouted.

"I think he's inside," a mom answered before hurrying in that direction.

An ominous silence fell over the whole backyard that was broken only by Maria's incoherent sobbing and pleading as Lauren continued to give Ariana CPR. Lauren's arms burned, but she kept up the pace, her heart pounding. *Why hadn't it worked yet? Where was the ambulance? What if I'm doing it wrong?*

So many frightening thoughts, and CPR that seemed to be going on far too long.

At last, they heard the wail of sirens in the distance. Sissy and J.D. hurried out the side gate to bring the paramedics in, and James returned from wherever the hell he'd disappeared to, but Lauren stayed focused. She wouldn't stop until the paramedics came.

It seemed to take an eternity, but it couldn't have been more than a minute before a man with a low, soothing voice was asking what had happened and how long she'd been doing compressions.

"Since the 911 call," Lauren said, tears sliding down her face. It hadn't worked.

And then Ariana coughed.

The paramedics rolled her gently to her side and a torrent of water came out. She started breathing, but she still wasn't conscious.

In rapid movements, the paramedics got her on a stretcher and carried her to the ambulance, Maria on their heels.

Others followed them out the side gate, and after ensuring that all the kids were out of the pool and being watched over, Lauren did the same.

As the paramedics loaded her lifeless body into the ambulance, a terrible thought rose in Lauren's mind like a dark drum beat:

This is all my fault.

41

THE PRESENT

MARIA

Lauren looks so upset that Maria starts to tear up as they stand around Ariana's hospital bed. It's been a horrible day, and Maria knows it hasn't just affected her little family. "What is it?" she asks gently.

"I saw Ariana take her floaties off, but I didn't do anything about it right away. I could tell you weren't paying attention, and I knew James wasn't around."

Bile burns Maria's throat at the thought of what she had been doing instead of watching her baby. She wants a hole to open and swallow her up when she thinks of how she was screaming at Sissy like a lunatic and drawing everyone's attention away from the pool.

"That was our fault, Lauren," James says. "I was out in the car, so I wasn't even there."

"And you saw how I was acting," Maria adds.

Lauren doesn't look relieved by their words. "I should have acted faster. It's just that our girls have taken swim lessons for so long that I stupidly thought Ariana was okay, but of course I didn't know that. And then I looked away for a second, and..." she trails off, looking sick.

Maria glances over at Ariana, unconscious and intubated. Flashes of what happened go through her mind:

Ariana lying on the cement, not breathing.

Had she been scared when she slipped under?

Was she calling for Maria?

"You saved her," James says. "You got her to cough up that water. Got her to breathe again."

James's jaw tightens, and Maria knows he's holding back tears of his own. She swallows hard.

"Please don't blame yourself," Maria says. "We're her parents, and we failed her. To us, you're her savior."

Lauren lets out a ragged breath. "Yes, but you don't understand. It's all my fault that you were distracted. I told you about Sissy and the job promotion because I knew it would start a fight between the two of you."

Ordinarily, Maria would react badly to that—she hates shit-stirrers—but not after what happened to Ariana. Nothing else seems as important now. "It's something I needed to know, though. I feel bad about yelling at her like I did, but that doesn't mean I shouldn't have confronted her about everything."

"I did it for the wrong reasons, though. I wanted to screw up her party. She's said some things that have eaten away at me, and I wanted to embarrass her."

Maria definitely can't fault Lauren for wanting to take revenge on Sissy. Honestly, who doesn't?

Lauren turns to watch Ariana for a moment. "I wanted to teach you a lesson, too," she confesses quietly.

Maria glances at James in confusion. "Me? Why?"

"Because I wanted you to know that there are more important things than money and getting a better job." She looks at Ariana again, and the message is clear.

Maria blinks like she's been slapped.

"The truth is," Lauren continues, "there's something wrong with me. There's been something wrong with me since I lost all those babies. It's like I'm broken inside, and I just want everyone else to be as broken as I am. So I do horrible things and create all this drama to teach all of you a lesson, but then it went too far." Tears stream down her cheeks. "I didn't mean for Ariana to get hurt because of it. I thought the text messages would be enough to help all of you realize what you should really care about."

"Those were from *you?*" Maria demands. "Those horrible anonymous texts? I nearly had a nervous breakdown because of that!"

"I'm so sorry," Lauren says, shoulders bowed.

Maria isn't sure what to say. She stares at Lauren, completely floored that she would do something so unhinged. "And you just, what? Went around taking pictures to blackmail us with? Or, I guess in my case, you somehow figured out my maiden name and Googled me."

"You sent those messages?" James asks, looking from Maria to Lauren in obvious confusion.

"You told me your maiden name once. On the playground," Lauren admits.

Maria can't believe the lengths she's gone to. "Look, I have my own problems, okay? I've talked to a therapist off and on for years. Believe me when I say, I think you need to go talk to someone. As soon as possible. None of this is normal. We were your friends, and this is what you did to us? Do Sarah Anne and Sissy know?"

Lauren shakes her head.

"Well, I think you need to tell them, too. And find a therapist—I know you've been through a lot, but..." Maria trails off, unsure how to continue. She wants to choke Lauren for all the trouble she's caused, but at the same time, it's because of Lauren that Ariana is alive. Even if Lauren stirred things up between Maria and Sissy, she didn't make them fight. She didn't make James wander off to his car. That's on Maria and James.

Maria suddenly thinks of that day at the park. "But, you got a text, too! It was of your husband and his secretary."

Lauren can't meet her eyes. "Someone else sent it to me."

Maria's stomach drops. "Wait, so someone else knows about all of this? Someone else was helping you?" She shares a horrified look with James. The last thing she needs is for another person to know about her past.

"Yes."

"Who? Not Sarah Anne...or Sissy, right?" Maria doesn't think she can handle a shock like that. It's bad enough that Lauren has revealed herself to be totally unhinged. What if they were all in on it?

"No, it wasn't them. I'd just rather not say who it was, but I can promise you that none of those texts will ever be sent out again."

"How am I supposed to believe that now, though, Lauren?"

"Because none of this was about you. I'm so sorry,

Maria. You were always just collateral damage—just to make it hard to figure out who the real targets were."

Maria feels unpleasantly like she's a side character in a movie she doesn't understand. Exhaustion and stress hit her hard, and she suddenly very desperately wants Lauren to leave. She may have saved Ariana's life, but the last thing Maria needs is more insanity in her own life. Thankfully, she manages to convey all of these feelings into one pleading glance at James.

"We appreciate what you did for Ariana," James says, "but I think you should go."

Lauren just nods like she was expecting to have been kicked out long ago. "I understand." She walks toward the door but turns back to look at them. "Will you let me know how she is? When she wakes up?"

"I can do that," Maria says.

"Thank you," Lauren says, and ducks quickly out of the room.

Before they can react to the train wreck that is Lauren's confession, the doctor comes in.

"I want to take your daughter off the ventilator and see how she does with oxygen going into her nose with a nasal cannula. It's not good to keep her intubated too long, and I like how well she's responded so far."

They agree because they're desperate to see Ariana wake up. It's terrifying to see her lying in the bed, sedated and with tubes down her throat. But at the same time, Maria is terrified there will be brain damage.

She reaches out for James's hand, and he pulls her against his side. They watch in wordless fear as a team of nurses come to remove all the equipment and give Ariana new medication to wake her up.

"It could be a while before she's conscious again," the nurse warns. "But she's looking good so far. See how her little chest isn't struggling to breathe? When kids are having trouble breathing, then you'll see their ribs poking out with each breath."

"Oh thank God," Maria says, her words catching in her throat as her eyes fill with tears again. "Can I touch her now? Is that okay?"

"Of course, mama," the nurse says with an encouraging smile. "That'll help her to hear your voice."

Maria strokes Ariana's hair as James rubs her arm. "Mommy and Daddy are here with you, baby. You're safe now. You just need to wake up so we can see how you're doing, okay?"

Every minute that passes feels like an eternity, but after an hour, Ariana's eyes flicker beneath her eyelids.

"Ariana? Baby? Can you hear me? It's Mommy and Daddy," Maria says.

"We're here," James says, rubbing Ariana's arm.

Her beautiful brown eyes open, and she croaks out, "Mommy?"

Maria smiles through her tears and nods. "Yes, baby, it's me."

Ariana turns her head toward James, who's openly crying now. "Daddy?"

"I'm here," he says, his voice gruff.

He lays his head down on Ariana's chest and hugs her gently. Slowly, she moves her little hand until she's patting his head comfortingly.

Maria chokes up before finally calling the nurse to tell her the good news.

As she searches Ariana's face, hope soars unchecked

within Maria's chest. Surely a brain-damaged child wouldn't think to comfort her father. Surely, they'll have their little girl safe and sound again.

———

L ater, when Ariana is again sleeping peacefully but without the looming threat of never waking up, Maria pulls out her phone to update the other moms. She creates a group message and hesitates on Lauren's number. Reluctantly, she adds it to the group.

After watching her baby's chest rise and fall comfortingly for a few minutes, Maria turns to James. He pulls her close, and she lets herself be held. "What Lauren did was insane without question, but I think it's a sign of how I've lost sight of what's really important. All I cared about this year was money. Not even you getting a promotion, but the end result: more money. I knew we couldn't afford that preschool, and I sent her anyway."

"You're not the only one who screwed up, Maria," James says in a deep rumble beneath her ear. "I did, too. I didn't pay attention to our finances, and I just let you shoulder all that pressure—even when I knew you were breaking under it."

"I don't care about any of it now," Maria says. "I just want our baby to get better."

"She will. She's a fighter."

Maria thinks of her dreams of living in a house like Sissy's, and it all seems so inconsequential—even childish—now. All that matters is that her family is healthy and whole.

"We need to sell the house," Maria says with increasing

decisiveness. "Move into something smaller and pay off some debt."

James pulls back a bit to look at her with surprise. "Are you sure? You love that house."

"It's just a house," Maria says with a shrug, and she finds she means this, deeply. "I don't want Ariana to return to the preschool either. She could go there for kindergarten, but I honestly don't want to see any of those women again."

James snorts. "I don't either. They're all fucked up beyond belief."

A weight lifts off Maria's chest, and it's like for the first time, she can take a deep breath. She doesn't have to try and be something she's not anymore. Remembering one last thing, she takes out her phone and opens her photo app while James is busy stroking Ariana's hair. She presses delete on a picture of a black American Express credit card number. Her phone tells her it will permanently delete the picture across all devices, and for one terrible moment, she hesitates.

But then for once in her life, she does the right thing.

Lauren said Sissy and Sarah Anne had nothing to do with any of the manipulations, but it doesn't matter to Maria. In her mind, the three women are linked. Part of something that Maria once desperately wanted to belong to, but now she sees that she's much better off without them.

Maria doesn't know what's wrong with Lauren, but it honestly sounds as though she has even bigger problems than Maria.

And that's saying something.

SISSY

Sissy is in another hospital when her phone chimes with a group text. She glances at her mama, who is still struggling to breathe before reaching for her phone. With a prayer that this isn't more bad news, she opens the message.

Ariana woke up and said Mama! Dr said this is a really good sign

Sissy lets out a breath in relief. She knows she played a big part in Maria not paying attention to the pool just by allowing that ridiculous argument to continue. She also should have hired a lifeguard. She would never make that mistake again.

She can't go back in time and stop the argument, but there's still something she can do. She pulls up Maria's number and sends her a message.

I'm so relieved to hear that about Ariana! Would it be okay if I came to visit? I have something I want to say.

Sissy can tell that Maria doesn't know what to say because of the long silence, although that might also be because she's busy. Still, Sissy is sure Maria is wary of talking to her again.

Finally, a text says, *Yes, we're in room 12A.*

I'll be there soon.

Sissy touches Loretta's hand. "I'll be back, Mama."

Maria said before that Sissy was cold and selfish, and honestly, she's right. It's time to do something about it.

———

The medicinal smell of the hospital combined with low lighting and the beeping of unfamiliar machines is completely jarring when it's the backdrop to a child's hospital bed. Even though Sissy just came from another hospital, her heart twists at the sight of Ariana lying there so helplessly.

Maria and James have shadows under their eyes and watch her warily as she comes into the room. Sissy tries not to take it personally, but it galls her that they think she's come to instigate something in their daughter's hospital room.

"Has she said anything else since you texted?" Sissy asks, knowing it's the best icebreaker as parents love nothing more than to talk about their kids.

Maria looks relieved. "Yes, she said, 'Daddy,' too, and she smiled at us. The doctor asked what her name was, and she was able to answer. But then she started getting sleepy again, which the doctor said is normal, too."

"Kids are so resilient. I know she'll be fine, but I'm so sorry it happened at my pool."

"We should have been watching her better," Maria says, reaching out to touch Ariana's cheek.

"I'm not here to rehash what happened at the party, other than to apologize," Sissy says, keeping her hands clasped in front of herself. She's never been comfortable with sincere apologies. "But because it happened there, and I feel responsible, I want you to know J.D. and I will pay for all of the medical bills."

"Doesn't your homeowners policy cover that?" James asks, arms folded as he watches her.

Sissy straightens her spine. So it's going to be like that. All right, fine. She deserves it.

"Yes, so I spoke to J.D. on the way here, and he said there's another opening at work that's yours if you want it. It's a manager position that pays significantly more than you're making now."

She knows she's said the right thing when James relaxes his arms. "I don't know what to say." He glances at Maria uncertainly. "I don't want a job out of pity, though."

"That's what I never got to say to you at the party," Sissy says. "I did tell J.D. about those text messages—it's true. But he didn't care. He said Maria's past had nothing to do with your job performance, and there would be a better job coming open anyway. I'm just sorry J.D. didn't tell you that when you were turned down for the first job, James. He can be...he just doesn't think sometimes."

Maria's eyebrows shoot into her hairline, and she sits down heavily on one of the chairs. She looks at James, who is wearing a matching stunned expression.

"I think I owe you an apology too then, Sissy," Maria says. "I shouldn't have talked to you like that. I just had a lot of things on my chest that had built up over time."

"Well, no hard feelings between us then." Sissy walks over to Ariana's side and touches her arm. "I hope she gets better quickly. And please let me know if you need anything."

Maria stands and hesitantly approaches Sissy. Awkwardly, Maria reaches out and gives her a hug. "Thank you."

James thanks her, too, and then Sissy leaves, feeling immeasurably better than when she walked in. Maybe she should think about doing nice things more often.

Before the elevator doors close, a sloppily-dressed man tries to make it on with her, but Sissy quickly presses the button before he can get on.

Well, she can't be nice all the time.

———

Loretta's pneumonia ends up killing her faster than the cancer, and she doesn't live many weeks past the party. The letter arrives for Sissy the day after Loretta died. Sissy isn't sure if she planned it that way or if it's just good timing, but either way, she's thankful to have one last chance at hearing from her mama. The end had been hard, full of tubes and gasping breaths, and Loretta had never been able to say much more than goodbye.

Sissy sits on the bed that was Loretta's while she stayed at her house, still smelling faintly of cigarettes and hairspray. With her throat thick from tears, Sissy opens the letter and begins to read.

Dear Sissy,

If you're reading this, then I guess I'm dead or dying. Even if I didn't have cancer, it's always been my fate to die early. I never did like to live healthy, and we got bad genes. My mama died when she was only fifty. Daddy died young, too. I may be dying young, but I lived a hard life. That was mostly my fault. But let me pass on some wisdom to you.

Men and money ain't everything. I know I made it seem like they were. That was before I met my grandbabies. Living with you like I got to do these past few weeks, I see they ain't your priority. Sure, I know you're a stay at home mama, but you're happiest when you're planning a fancy party.

I'm not judging you. Hell, I was you. You weren't my priority either. And that was the biggest mistake of my life. Might even pay for it in hell.

All your life, you watched me put men before your happiness. You watched them treat me bad and treat you bad. Some of them did terrible things to you. And then when you grew up so pretty, I took advantage of your good looks to get us rich men who would give us shiny things I could pawn. I understand why you got out of there as fast as you could, and I even understand why you stopped talking to me for so long. I would have done the same.

But listen to me now, Sissy. You think those grandbabies of mine don't see how their daddy gets drunk and treats you bad. You think you keep it hidden that you only stay with him for that fancy house and all that money, but they see. They know. Just like you did. And look what it taught you. You ended up just like me.

No, you don't live in a trailer. No, you don't have bruises anybody can see. Your relationship looks perfect from the outside, but I've been on the inside with you. You're being abused, too. It's just happening behind closed doors.

Stop it now, Sissy. Stop it before Mary Elizabeth winds up just like you—with some man who pretends to love her but sleeps around with everyone but her and gets rough when he drinks.

Think of William learning to treat women like that. Marrying *some sweet girl that he hollers at and maybe even beats when he gets to drinking.*

Because I was wrong about you, Sissy. I always have been. You're clever as a damn fox, resilient and strong. You need to tap into those mama instincts before it's too late. I wish I had. But maybe this letter will help you break the cycle.

I love you, Sissy. I wish I had loved you better when you needed me, but I know one thing: you're a smarter and better woman than I ever was.

Now act like it.

That night, when the kids are asleep, Sissy turns to J.D. with her mama's words echoing in her mind.

"We need to talk about your drinking."

SARAH ANNE

S arah Anne and Mark sit on opposite ends of the couch from each other at Lauren's house. She sits across from them, looking like a total stranger. Gone is the sweet smile, or even a look of regret. Her face seems devoid of any emotion at all.

"I just feel like I owe an explanation to you, and I don't think you're going to get a straight answer from Hampton."

Mark flinches at the mention of Hampton, and Sarah Anne swallows hard. She can't believe she agreed to rehash that horrible day. Mark walking in on them having sex was the worst moment of her life. It was one of those traumatizing times where every single thing that happened seemed to burn an image on her mind. She sees Mark's face change rapidly like a kaleidoscope: concern, confusion, realization, horror. She didn't think he could look more painfully stunned than if she had stabbed him with a knife. He had grabbed Hampton by the throat and shoved him against the wall, and it was only her grabbing his arm that stopped him from punching him in the face. She knew he deserved it, but she was terrified Hampton would press charges for assault.

"You are dead to me," Mark had growled at Hampton.

He'd shoved him again before stalking away, Sarah Anne at his heels. But then they'd gone outside to find out a tragedy had occurred that was much worse than an affair. And for one horrible moment, Sarah Anne had been afraid it was Sophie.

The relief she felt when she saw dark hair instead of blonde lying on the ground still brought the flush of shame to her cheeks.

That night, when the kids were safely tucked in bed, Mark's behavior was almost worse than his initial discovery. He quietly packed his things and left their room. Anger and shouting would have been easier to deal with. She begged him to talk to her, to give her a chance to explain, but he ignored her, went into the guest room, and locked the door.

Now, a few days after the party, Sarah Anne jumped at the chance to talk it out with Mark, even if it is with Lauren. She doesn't understand Lauren's level of involvement in all of this, but she knows she at least lied to Mark about Sarah Anne feeling sick. Clearly, she wanted Sarah Anne to be caught. Though Sarah Anne can't blame Lauren entirely—she wasn't the one banging Hampton in the powder room, after all.

"I think Hampton has liked you for a long time, Sarah Anne," Lauren says, "but he wasn't able to act on it because he knew you'd never go for a married man."

Mark snorts beside her, and Sarah Anne stiffens. She knows what he's thinking: *But her own marriage wasn't a problem.*

"When his divorce went through, it finally gave him the chance to hit on you. I'm sure I don't have to tell you what happened after that," she says, and Sarah Anne avoids looking at Mark. "But he was always afraid it would be a short-lived relationship. He said you're fickle and would likely lose interest fast."

"How do you know all this? Why did he tell you?" Sarah Anne asks. It's the question she's been asking herself since the party.

Lauren bristles. "I've told you before, but you don't listen. You've never really cared about anything I say, so I suppose I shouldn't be surprised. Hampton and I grew up together. He was my neighbor, and we were really close as kids." Sarah Anne glances at Mark for his reaction. She doesn't remember Lauren ever saying anything like this before. "We drifted apart as we got older, but we never stopped talking entirely. When we had kids going to the same preschool, we started texting again regularly."

"You and Hampton text regularly?" Sarah Anne repeats, unable to even picture that.

Lauren gives her a look. "That's what I said. Anyway, he wanted me to take a picture of the two of you together so that we could text you anonymously. Then he had an insurance policy if you tried to break up with him. He swore he would never actually send it to Mark, but you didn't have to know that."

"What the hell is wrong with you?" Mark demanded. "It's not enough that Hampton was sleeping with my wife, but he roped her supposed friend into blackmailing her, too?"

"We never actually blackmailed anyone. We just sent the texts."

Sarah Anne feels like her mind can't properly absorb what Lauren is saying. "Then why did you send them to Maria and Sissy? And you! There was a text with Wesley and his secretary."

"I wanted to get back at Sissy for all the nasty things she's said to me, and when Hampton suggested this anonymous texting idea, it gave me the chance to dig around and get some dirt on her. I knew there had to be something. No one is perfect."

It's like Lauren has been replaced by this other, horrible person that Sarah Anne doesn't know at all. "And Maria?"

"That was just to make it seem like the texts were coming from Sissy."

"Then at what point did you decide to have Mark walk in on us like that?"

Lauren lowers her gaze to her lap. "That was Hampton's idea, too, but I did it to help you."

Sarah Anne lets out her breath in a rush. "Help me? Honey, how the hell does it help me? It was the worst day of my life." The tears fill her eyes again, and she tries not to let them fall. It just seems manipulative at this point.

"I knew you were addicted to the thrill of the affair, and that only Mark walking in on you and forcing you to stop would end it for you. I know what it's like to be the one whose partner is sleeping around, and I didn't want Mark to continue to live like that. He didn't even know!"

"Don't act like you did me any favors," Mark says, his

whole body tense. He's furious—Sarah Anne can tell. And who wouldn't be? No one likes being manipulated. "All you've done is shown us how fucked up Hampton is and how you're no friend of Sarah Anne's." He turns to Sarah Anne. "I think we should go. We've heard enough. Hampton was my friend, and you both betrayed me. Lauren was yours, and she threw you under the bus just to get back at Sissy and to teach you some kind of sick lesson."

He stands, and Sarah Anne does, too. Honestly, she's just relieved he's talking to her.

"All right, I understand," Lauren says as they move toward the door to leave. "But remember: if it weren't for me doing what I did, you'd probably still be sneaking around on Mark, Sarah Anne. Y'all will thank me for this one day."

Mark looks furious, and Sarah Anne puts her hand on his arm. "Lauren," she says, "a real friend would have let me make my own decision about my marriage. Not forced the outcome she decided was the right one."

As they walk out Lauren's door, Sarah Anne knows this is the last time she'll see her, and she can't help but feel a twist of grief over the loss of her friend.

But she can't have someone that batshit crazy running amok in her life.

———

Later that night, Mark surprises her by coming back to their bed. "This doesn't mean I forgive you," he says. "It just means that I understand you were caught up in some sick, manipulative shit."

Sarah Anne is so relieved she breaks down crying. Mark

sits beside her, but he doesn't move to comfort her. She knows she deserves that. She knows he has more of a right to cry than she does.

"I'm going to see a therapist on Tuesday," she says when the tears have stopped enough for her to speak again. "Not for us both—but just for me. There was never anything wrong with our relationship. It's always been something inside me—just this *need* for attention, even if it's bad for me. We don't need couples counseling, though. This was my fault, and I'm going to fix it."

Mark watches her quietly, and when she finishes speaking, he sighs. "Sarah Anne, if we need to go to couples counseling, then I'll do it." She reaches for him to hug him, but he pushes her away. "I'm not going to let this destroy our marriage, but I also need some time, okay? I can't just unsee what happened at the party—no matter how desperately I want to."

"But…you'll stay in our bed with me?"

"Well, yeah. This is the most comfortable bed in the house," he says with a ghost of a grin. "But I also don't want to upset the kids. We're going to pretend like everything is normal while we fix things."

Sarah Anne feels the tears slip down her cheeks again. "I love you," she says, voice breaking.

Mark shakes his head. "God help me, I love you, too."

LAUREN

I walk up the shaded pathway, breathing in the sweet smell of summer from the freshly-mowed lawn, blooming magnolia trees, and the Confederate jasmine that crawls over the front porch. I ring the doorbell of the cozy brick house downtown. Susan, my therapist for the past month, opens the door, smiling welcomingly. She's extremely short—just barely five feet tall, older, with mousey-gray hair, and though she has always been non-judgmental and kind, I've struggled to open up with her.

Because the truth is, I know Susan won't like what I have to say.

"Come on in, Lauren," Susan says.

We begin as we always do: with small talk that I know is designed to make me feel secure and comfortable. As we waste time discussing the warm weather, Emily's swim lessons, and the beauty of the flowers outside, I decide I'm finally going to give Susan what she thinks she wants.

"Do you think you can tell me how you feel about everything that happened?" Susan asks, just like she does every time.

I look at Susan's open face. This is where I usually start talking about something inconsequential, like my job. Instead, I say, "Yes."

To her credit, Susan doesn't even blink in surprise. "That's great, Lauren. I'm glad you feel comfortable enough to do so today."

I nod. I had already told Susan the facts of what I'd done—the text messages and the events of the party—but I haven't opened up about how I feel.

"When I wasn't sure what would happen to Ariana, I blamed myself for creating so much chaos that Maria didn't notice she had taken off her floaties until it was too late. And when I thought she might die or be permanently damaged, I felt physically sick. I actually threw up at the hospital waiting to see her. I wanted a giant black hole to swallow me up. But then when she got better and better, and fully recovered..." I trail off, unwilling to continue.

Susan waits for a moment, but when I don't continue, she prompts, "And now how do you feel about it?"

I gently rest my hand on my abdomen where a small baby bump protrudes. "Now I'm focused on the future. I'm finally giving my baby girl the sibling she deserves. Now she won't ever have to be alone like I was." It wasn't hard to convince Wesley the baby was his. Men always want to believe in their own virility.

Susan shifts in her seat and leans forward slightly. "Focusing on the future is good. But it's also important you examine your actions in the past. So when you think back over this year, where you followed your friends and took pictures of them to use against them, and destroyed things your husband loves, like his baseball card collection, or when you made sure your friend's husband would catch her in the act of having an affair, or when you started an argument between two of your friends that resulted in the drowning and near-death of a little girl, how do you feel?"

I meet Susan's gaze unflinchingly. "I feel like they got what they deserved."

I cradle my arms around my growing abdomen. "And I got what I wanted."

ACKNOWLEDGMENTS

Thank you to God and to my family, especially my husband, who is thankfully nothing like any of the husbands in this story. To my five beautiful children, who are always a source of inspiration for me: thank you for letting Mama write!

I always have to thank my parents and in-laws for their support, especially for my mom who reads everything I write. Thank you, also, to my cousin Kelsey, who is always willing to read and give me the best feedback—even if she just had a baby!

Thank you to David and Inked Entertainment for making sure this book got out there and was heard—in record timing! I'm so happy to be working with you.

I also want to remember all the sweet teachers and staff at SMMCP. Thank you for all the years teaching my sweet babies!

Never Miss A Release!

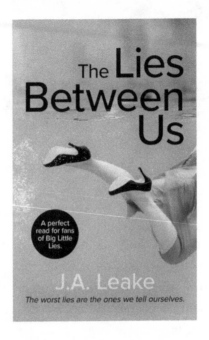

Thank you so much for reading **The Lies Between Us**. I hope you enjoyed it!

I have so much more coming your way. Never miss a release by joining my free newsletter where I'll be sure to keep you updated on upcoming books!

To sign up, simply visit
http://jessicaleake.com/

Thank you for reading THE LIES BETWEEN US! If you enjoyed the book, I would greatly appreciate it if you could consider adding a review on your online bookstore of choice.

Reviews make a huge difference to the success or failure of a book, especially for newer writers like myself. The more reviews a book has, the more people are likely to take a shot on picking it up. The review need only be a line or two, and it really would make the world of difference for me if you could spare the three minutes it takes to leave one.

With all my thanks,

J.A. Leake

CPSIA information can be obtained
at www.ICGtesting.com
Printed in the USA
BVHW030948210721
612519BV00014B/448/J